Standing In My Shadow

Standing In My Shadow

C.S. ARNOLD

ReadersMagnet, LLC

Standing In My Shadow
Copyright © 2021 by C.S. Arnold

Published in the United States of America
ISBN Paperback: 978-1-953616-38-8
ISBN Hardback: 978-1-953616-39-5
ISBN eBook: 978-1-953616-40-1

This book is written to provide information and motivation to readers. Its purpose is not to render any type of psychological, legal, or professional advice of any kind. The content is the sole opinion and expression of the author, and not necessarily that of the publisher.

All rights reserved. No part of this publication may be reproduced, stored in a retrieval system or transmitted in any way by any means, electronic, mechanical, photocopy, recording or otherwise without the prior permission of the author except as provided by USA copyright law.

ReadersMagnet, LLC
10620 Treena Street, Suite 230 | San Diego, California, 92131 USA
1.619.354.2643 | www.readersmagnet.com

Book design copyright © 2021 by ReadersMagnet, LLC. All rights reserved.
Cover design by Ericka Obando
Interior design by Shemaryl Tampus

Also, by the author:

A novel

Dangerous Legacy, the Second Son–Given an Editor's Choice award by the publisher, iUniverse. Rated 4 of 4 by OnLineBookClub.org

Children's Books:

The Patchwork Princess, Adventures of Ra-me, a Traveling Troubadour – Book 1

Won the Pinnacle Book Achievement Award for December 2019

Blaze the Dragon, Adventures of Ra-me, a Traveling Troubadour–Book 2

Won the Pinnacle Book Achievement Award for December 2019

Mudcat the Pirate, Adventures Ra-me, a Traveling Troubadour–Book 3

Won the Pinnacle Book Achievement Award for December 2019

Miscellaneous

Short, short stories in various faith-based papers
Other short stories

Dedication

To my husband, my best friend, who has supported me all the way through my writing efforts.

PART 1

Prologue

He had literally kidnapped the doctor, and the return ride had been a hard one. But now they were back—if it weren't too late.

The sweat-drenched girl on the bed struggled against the pains that ripped through her body. Every few minutes, a scream would escape her lips.

"You shouldn't have involved the doctor. We can handle this. You know he will never be able to return."

"She'll die. And then where will your plans be?"

The young man beside the girl on the bed held her hand, but he listened to the two whispering in the shadows. He and the girl had planned to escape before the birth of their child, but labor came upon her suddenly before they could get away.

"Doctor, do something for the girl." It was the woman who issued the command. "We will return." The two left, leaving the girl and the young man with the doctor.

The girl was whispering to him, and he leaned closely against her cheek. "You must get away. Take our child. I cannot live. I feel my life slipping away."

"No, don't say that." He held her against his chest.

"You know it's true."

A deep moan issued from the girl, and a tiny infant came into the world. The mother stopped breathing.

"Go quickly," the doctor said. "Wrap up the child and go. You can't stay here."

The young father grabbed the pack waiting by the door, took his tiny daughter and stumbled out the back way and disappeared into the night.

The other two came back into the room. "Doctor, what has happened? My daughter?"

"My patient couldn't survive the birth, but there is a child." He lifted the second infant to the woman. "She is very weak and may not live."

"Oh, she'll live. I'll make her live!"

"And what of the young man?" It was the man at her side who asked.

"He panicked at her death. He ran," the doctor lied.

She took the child from the physician and wrapped it quickly.

"Doctor, we'll take care of the burial of my daughter."

As the doctor turned to get his bag, he felt the knife go deep into his back. He knew his life, too, was over.

A shadow passed over the man's face as he turned to the woman. "What shall we do about her husband? We'll never find him tonight."

"Oh, we'll never find him at all. He won't make it out of the valley. He was just some unfortunate who discovered us when he stumbled in here blindly, and he will never be able to find his way out. The animals will take care of him for us."

The young man held the babe close in his shirt for warmth, and he ran. He knew that he must put as much distance between himself and his dead wife as he could. The evil wanted this tiny babe—his daughter. But did he have a chance?

Driven by his need to escape, he stumbled through rocks and the brambles that tore at his body. He could feel blood running down his face, and now, his breath was coming in gasps. The adrenaline that had fueled the movement of his body forward was waning. His foot caught on a vine and he fell, hitting his head against a rock. Just before losing consciousness he tucked himself around the baby. He never heard the rustle of the man and burro as they came to where he had fallen.

Chapter 1

Linda Grainger gripped the ebony handle of the umbrella, her fingers clenched white in contrast. With her free hand she pulled the lapels of her trench coat closer about her neck. It had rained the night before and all morning, until the smooth, manicured grounds of the cemetery could absorb no more, and she could feel water soaking through the suede of her slippers as it ran over the stone footpaths that wound around the graves and flower gardens at Cresthaven Memorial Cemetery.

Two short rows of wooden folding chairs sat on the artificial grass blanket huddled beneath the tent shelter. The rain-soaked canvas looked black. Although rainwater was beginning to seep through the seams, the temporary canopy offered cover for the approaching mourners. The rectangular grave, just inside the protection of the canvas, was in front of the wooden chairs, and its proportions couldn't be completely disguised by the grass-green drapery. An old caretaker, shrouded in a wet, gray slicker, leaned against a long-handled shovel under the cover of a tall, bushy-limbed pine. He wasn't trying to hide his purpose. Banks of flowers surrounded the grave, but the rainwater had beaded on the blossoms, looking like swollen tears ready to overflow.

Pathetic fallacy. The words came into her mind in response to the occasion. Nature's supposed weeping in sympathy with man's sorrow.

Well, if it were true that Nature groaned with the sorrows of man, Linda thought dispassionately, sympathy for her was sympathy misplaced. Or, perhaps, just late in coming. She had lost her father long ago.

"Ashes to ashes, dust to dust... we commend the spirit of our dear departed..." The preacher's voice couldn't command her attention as he read from the prayer book in his hands.

Her father had made a life for himself at the university where he had taught archeology for the past eighteen years. He was a well-respected figure in his field and had written a textbook ten years ago that was still used in the major schools.

Weekends and summers found him mountain climbing or checking school-sponsored archaeological digs. He was on his way to deliver a series of lectures at a neighboring university when he was killed in an automobile accident. He had lived in a man's world. No doubt almost any man alone would find a young daughter a hindrance.

It hadn't always been that way, she mused. From the deep recesses of childhood memory, she had recalled, or had it been a dream, that she sat on his knee and felt loved. He had stroked her short, blue-black hair and called her his little blackbird. She had liked the feeling of his big hand against her hair. She felt safe. But she didn't want to be called a blackbird.

> Sing a song of sixpence
> A pocketful of rye
> Four and twenty blackbirds
> Baked in a pie

There was a picture in her Mother Goose book of blackbirds struggling to escape a huge steaming pastry shell. No, she hadn't wanted to be called *blackbird*. They were caught, but they wanted to be free.

Perhaps it had been a portent of things to come. She would be sent away, imprisoned in exclusive schools, given a good education. She must learn to be a lady, he had said, to curb her wild imaginings. Tame her spirit. She struggled. Oh, how she had struggled. Her spirit was bruised into submission, but they couldn't break her.

When she was ten, Linda gave her father a make-believe funeral and pronounced herself an orphan. This horrified the teachers at her boarding school. But it helped her cope with her feelings of rejection. If she had no parents, they couldn't reject her. She was told that her mother died at her birth, so she only needed to deny that she still had a father.

She could remember the day clearly in her mind when her father began to push her away. The scene forever burned just behind her eyes. It was the summer before she started school. She was playing in her room. Her dolls were organized in tiny chairs around a white painted table. There were little blue cornflowers painted on the chairs, and her plastic tea set was blue and white. Her curtains and bed coverlet were pink and ruffled. The warm, evening breeze coming in at the window billowed the curtains gently into the room.

"Now, Sally, you sit up straight in your chair," she had told her doll as she pushed it closer to the table. There were two more dolls in one chair, and she sat in the one at the head of the table. She pulled the other empty chair close by her side.

"My little blackbird, are you having a tea party?" Her father came into the room.

As he kissed her cheek, his face felt smooth, and he smelled of clean soap.

"Yes, Daddy. Want some tea?"

"No, thank you, I can see that this is a party just for girls." His blue eyes twinkled at her.

She giggled at him. "Let me introduce you to them all." She pointed her tiny finger. "This is Sally, Mary, Jane."

She slipped her arm around the back of the empty chair at her side, "and this is my friend."

"Oh, so you have a make-believe friend, too?" he said.

She was suddenly serious, her round black eyes grave. "Oh, no, Daddy, my friend is real. She lives here."

"Here with us?" he enquired.

"Yes." She shook her head slowly. "She stays in our house."

"Oh, I see." He smiled. "Does she have a name?"

"Oh, I just call her my friend," she answered.

"And what does she call you?"

"She calls me *mi amiga.*" Her tone was innocent.

"What?" The color was draining from his face.

"Where did you hear that?" he asked. His voice was soft, and he sank to his knees before her.

"Daddy, my friend calls me *mi amiga*. She is a very, nice little girl. She will play any game that I want." She was struggling in his grasp. She wanted him to smile again and not look at her so hard.

He let loose of her arm and looked at the empty chair beside his tiny daughter. "Tell me, Linda, is your friend still here?" he whispered.

"No, Daddy, you frightened her. She gets scared, and I tell her not to be afraid. She cries, and I talk to her." If only he would understand.

"Linda, what does your friend look like?"

"She looks just like me. Daddy, I can't always see her real plain, but I can feel when she's here." She twisted uneasily in her chair. When she saw the lines in his face relax, her chatter continued. "But her hair is long; it hangs way down." She put her little hand behind her back at her waist to indicate the length of her imaginary friend's hair.

A look of understanding dawned on Mr. Grainger's face. "Would you like to let your hair grow long, Linda?"

She looked at him strangely. "No, Daddy, but I'd like to have a dress like my friend."

"What kind of dress? A party dress for drinking tea?" He was trying to regain the tone of their earlier conversation.

"Oh, no. It's just white all over with black pictures along the bottom. There are funny pictures of sheep and turkeys." She was tired of this conversation and started pouring more tea into the cups for her dolls. Sally had flopped over again into her saucer. She scolded her and set her primly back into place.

"Good night, Linda. Martha will tuck you in tonight." Mr. Grainger left the room. Martha was their housekeeper.

He was shaken. There was a perfectly natural explanation for her choosing an imaginary friend that would look exactly like herself. An only child would need a playmate. But where had she heard the Spanish word for 'my friend'? There was a new family in the neighborhood, and it was possible that they were Spanish-speaking people. The most inexplicable thing was her description of the dress. He had seen a dress like that years ago, but Linda had no way of knowing about it. It was before she was born.

Linda remembered that incident as the beginning of the end. The next night her 'Uncle' Max came to dinner. He was a colleague of her father's at the university. He was a psychiatrist with a private practice along with his teaching. Martha had fixed all her favorite foods, and 'Uncle' Max brought her a present. They laughed, and the three of them had a party. Max asked questions, and she talked freely about 'her friend'.

She went to bed with a feeling of happiness.

Forgetting to kiss her father goodnight, she tip-toed back to the study door where they were talking about her. She listened.

"Well, Max, what do you think?" Her father's voice was serious.

"Linda is a charming and spirited little girl," Max consoled. "Perhaps she does have an unusually vivid imagination for such a young child, but she can't be termed mentally ill."

"Oh, I never said she was mentally ill." Adam was abrupt, angry.

"Minds are complex things," Max continued. "She has given her imaginary playmate all the characteristics that she thinks you would like to see in her."

"That's silly. I don't criticize the child." His denial was quick and adamant.

"She is hypersensitive. Any feelings of displeasure that she picks up from you are taken and twisted in her young mind. In her mind she is saying, 'Daddy doesn't like me this way'. If she can't, or won't, change, she invents the perfect child."

Adam frowned deeply. "It sounds too far afield."

"Just remember, tonight when she cited every one of the imaginary playmate's good qualities, she added 'not like me'." Max rubbed his hands together as he stressed his point.

"Well, yes," Adam agreed. "She can be a wild little thing at times. Martha and I are always trying to quiet her. The tantrums that she can throw leave the entire house in shambles. The only time she is really quiet is when she is giving tea to her dolls."

"I have a theory about that, too."

"Yes, Doctor?" Adam's tone was a bit on edge.

"It's a way to bring 'her friend' into her real life. The tea party is a vehicle, bringing her dolls and her imaginary playmate together. She can watch them act out the normal little girl play without compromising her identity."

"Oh, help us, Max! You've gone over the edge! I don't understand a word of that. If little girls are that complicated, no wonder we can't understand women!" Adam was ready to laugh the whole thing away.

"No, Adam, not all little girls are like this. She has created another 'Linda', another identity, that she can crawl into. A place to hide. It isn't good; but a few sessions, and it should begin to straighten itself out." Max was confident.

"Max, what about *mi amiga*? What about the Spanish words for 'my friend'?" Adam urged.

"She has simply heard it somewhere. She is a very bright child and could have picked it up around campus here. We have at least one Spanish-speaking professor that I know of."

Adam shook his head slowly, "I wish I could believe that."

"What do you want to believe, Adam? That the child is hearing voices from her dead mother?" Max was being hard on Adam.

"What do you know about her mother?" Adam demanded.

"Nothing," his voice was cajoling. "You mentioned one time that your wife was Spanish."

"Oh." The relief on Adam's face puzzled Max. "And the dress? What about the dress she described?"

"Well, Adam, I have no explanation except that anyone in your house could pick up one of your archaeology books and find pictures of animals that were once used to decorate the clothing and pottery of ancient people. Your daughter is a highly creative child."

"Maybe," Adam agreed. "She must be made to suppress her imagination. She must deny this fantasy."

"Yes, I agree. This could develop into a deep split in her personality. She might, in time, vacillate between her real self and the personality she calls 'my friend'. Naturally, 'my friend' must be," he groped for a strong word, "destroyed."

Linda couldn't understand most of the words and when their voices were low, she couldn't even hear. She had caught 'my friend' must be destroyed and ran, terrified, back to her room.

She knew what destroyed meant. It meant to be taken away and never come back. Missy had been her best friend, a warm, soft puppy that was her own. Missy slept with her and followed her everywhere. Then Missy got sick, and Daddy said she must be destroyed. Her puppy never came back.

It had taken about two days before she had realized that the dog was gone forever. When the truth hit, she reacted with fits of anger and tantrums. The hurt tore through her little body and hurled itself at those around her. A doctor had been called. A little later her 'friend', that called her *mi amiga,* had come and helped take the hurt away. She didn't want another puppy.

The frightened child squeezed her eyes tight and clenched her fists. 'Her friend' wouldn't be taken away. If Daddy couldn't see 'her friend', then he wouldn't be able to carry her away. She would protect her—stand in front of her with her own body. They were the same size; and if she stood in front, she would hide 'her friend' just in case 'Uncle' Max might be able to find her. With this childish answer to her problem, Linda had gone to sleep, exhausted with emotion.

She was comforted by the presence in the room with her. The essence of the other child was so strong that Linda could see her image in the darkness. Another child with her face, but whose hair, unlike her own blue-black cap, hung in long, shining locks to her waist.

The next morning 'Uncle' Max had come for brunch. It was Sunday, and he said he could spend the whole day. But now Linda was on guard. After eating, the three of them sat on the flagstone terrace at the back of the Grainger house. Later, they strolled on the walk winding through the wooded park on the university campus. As they went from place to place, Adam grew quieter as Max gently asked questions.

"Linda, do you come to play in the woods?" He was studying an oak leaf that had fallen from the overhead tree and tangled in the few wisps of brown fuzzy hair on his balding head.

Linda giggled as she watched him pull the leaf from his hair. "I can come to the woods as long as I stay where I can see our house."

"Sometimes Martha brings you, too, doesn't she?" her father asked. "You go to the lake and feed the ducks?"

"Yes, but mostly I play on the terrace or in my room." She was happy now. She walked between her father and 'Uncle' Max, hand-in-hand with them. As they came to a break in the rough, pebble-textured concrete, she would pull up her feet, and they would swing her lightly over the cracks.

"That's good that you play so close to home. It keeps your Daddy and Martha from worrying about you," Max suggested.

"I guess. But 'my friend' won't go anywhere with me." Linda quickly skipped, adjusting her stride so she wouldn't step on a crack.

"Your friend that calls you *mi amiga*?" Max kept his voice casual.

Adam's face had grown sad. His beautiful, little daughter looked so carefree at this moment. Could Max be wrong? Surely it couldn't be true that Linda was on the verge of developing a schizoid personality.

"Yes. 'My friend' won't go further than our back terrace. She's afraid. If I play in the woods, it's with Billy. 'My friend' stays in our yard."

"Who is Billy? Your boyfriend?" he teased.

"Uncle Max," she answered primly, "he just lives next door.

"Billy is the son of Foster Blevins, the new economics professor who joined the university last year. His son is already in school, a couple years older than Linda," Adam filled in for Max.

"Does Billy bring a friend with him?" Max probed. "Does he know your 'friend'?"

"Billy doesn't know 'my friend'. He really doesn't like girls too much. He only plays with me because I don't scare Herman," she confided.

"Herman?' Is that his little brother? His friend?"

Linda's laughter was pure delight. "Herman is Billy's frog!" She put one hand over her mouth as her laughter ended in a giggle.

Adam's booming laughter was tinged with relief. At least when she was with other children, she behaved normally. He swung her to his shoulders where she rested her face on his sun-warmed hair.

The walkway through the woods led to a band shelter. The Sunday afternoon concert had started. The band members were volunteer faculty and local townspeople.

Adam and Max found an empty bench away from the main body of listeners. They could talk under cover of the music of the band, but they were far enough away to neither be overheard nor interrupted.

Adam settled Linda in his lap and adjusted the sleeping child's head against his chest. He rested his hand lightly for a moment on her thick, short hair. The sunlight picked up glints of blue in its blackness, reminding him of a raven's wing. He thought of someone else he'd held close long ago, in another world really. Her hair had been the same color, but it was long and free. That time could have been a dream or a fantasy, except for the reality of their child.

In the peaceful atmosphere of this Sunday afternoon open-air concert, Adam relaxed. He was certain his friend, Max, could help Linda with a couple professional sessions.

"Adam," Max's voice broke into his thoughts abruptly. "It isn't going to be as easy as I'd anticipated. It's further advanced than I suspected. She's becoming a prisoner of her other identity."

"How do you figure that." He kept his voice low.

"Linda is setting bounds for herself. She says, 'her friend' won't leave the house, so she plays either in the house or within sight of the house."

Adam nodded. "She stays in her room a great deal."

"Adam, why haven't you enrolled Linda in the Education Department's kindergarten here at the university? The faculty say it's great."

"Linda wanted to go. I tried." He didn't want to say more.

"And?"

"It seems my child has a temper. Her tantrums frightened the whole staff. Mrs. Lowe, the director, called me and said Linda wasn't ready emotionally for kindergarten."

"I see. And what happened when you brought Linda home?"

"Well, by the time I got to the school she was exhausted. I carried her home in my arms, and she was as limp as a rag doll. Hardly even conscious of where we were going."

"How long did it take her to recover?" Max was making mental notes.

"I brought her home and put her to bed. I had a class to teach, and when I got home for lunch, she was up. Martha said she'd slept nearly three hours. As we ate, she seemed fine. I'd say she completely recovered in the three hours."

"Or we could say coming back to the house acted like a tranquilizer. Adam, this wasn't the first such occurrence, was it?"

"No, Max. I finally asked for your help because the last incident at the kindergarten was worse. But of even more concern to me is this 'friend' whom she says calls her *mi amiga*."

"You can't separate the two problems—they're one."

"What is your opinion. Your answer?"

"A hard one, Adam. The only consolation is that it will only have to be temporary."

"And that is? Send her away? An institution?"

"No, man, she doesn't need that!" Max was adamant.

"Then what do you mean?"

"She needs to go to a private school where she will be completely cut off from familiar things—this house, her room, and even you."

"That's hard, Max."

"It's for her health, her future."

Max watched Adam's face as he continued. "Linda is a delightful child. You say she learned to read with what little help Martha gave her. She is an exceptional child, really. But, Adam, something in her life, here and now, is threatening to split her very being."

Adam nodded.

"Adam, I have a school in mind. It's a Catholic school. Do you mind?" Max knew Adam attended a small, local Protestant church. His life was dedicated to his faith in Christ, and he took Linda with him every Sunday. She had told Max that she loved the Sunday School with the exciting stories of the bible heroes.

"Linda's mother was Catholic." It was a flat statement and an agreement.

"I know the doctor at the school, and we can trust him. If the stress gets too great and her tantrums occur, we can rely on him to prescribe the correct medications."

"I'll consent, Max." He touched the little hand that lay curled against his arm.

That evening at supper, Adam brought up the idea of school. Sundays Martha was gone, and it was just the two of them.

Adam showed her pictures of the school that Max had left for her. The lawns were wide and spacious for the playing children. There were stables for the horses that the students were taught to ride. The rooms the girls shared were light and gaily decorated. Important to Adam, students enrolling from a protestant faith were exempt from their catechism classes. They were bussed weekly to local protestant churches for Sunday School.

Linda studied the pictures closely, and the friendly scenes caught her interest.

"Daddy, it looks like fun," she smiled, tremulously. "But I don't want to leave you, and Martha and our house."

"Or your 'friend'?" he asked gently.

She nodded slowly, her short black hair against her smooth cheek. "'My friend' couldn't go." It was a statement.

"No, Linda."

She thought, if she could get her 'friend' to leave, then Daddy and 'Uncle' Max couldn't destroy her. She still remembered the conversation she'd overheard. If her 'friend' would leave, then she would go to the school. But she could never go off and leave her 'friend' alone in the house. Her 'friend' was shy and would be frightened.

"Daddy, may I talk to my 'friend' about it?"

Adam nodded his assent. He watched her leave and go into her room. Quietly, he followed her and listened. There was no sound for several minutes, then he heard her soft, childish voice.

"I'm being sent away."

Adam's heart twisted in pain. Linda wasn't fooled. She grasped the situation with an understanding beyond her years.

"No, my 'friend', you mustn't be scared. You must go home—back where you came from. Now, don't cry. I'll be back someday, and then you can come back. When I return, I'll come to this room and wait for you."

There was a long silence.

"It will be all right." Then Linda was silent.

Adam went quietly back to the study to wait for Linda.

"Ok, Daddy, I'll go to school. She was a different person, older somehow. "My 'friend' will go home."

"Where does she live, Linda?"

"Far away, Daddy. She says there are mountains."

Linda's face was very white, but she was calm.

Adam had overheard Linda promise to meet her imaginary friend when she returned. He knew she would try. He knew now sending Linda away could turn into a permanent thing, at least for all the years she was in school. They would have to meet away from the house; she couldn't be allowed home even for vacations.

Linda went to school, thinking it was for a short time. If she worked hard and did well, she could come home sooner. But the very steps she took, thinking they led home, carried her in the opposite direction. She was forging her own prison chains at the school with her excellence.

But time performed the task Adam had hoped for. Linda never again mentioned her 'friend'.

Linda had settled the matter with her 'friend'. What came to be the harmful reality in her life was the loss of her father.

Chapter 2

The wind blew a shower of water from the dripping edge of the tent shelter into Linda's face. A thin, cold rivulet trickled down her neck to the warmth of her breast beneath the trench coat that covered her black, wool dress. The sudden chill brought her from the past.

She now saw the end of what had happened when she was a child of five. Her father began to die in her eyes then. The two incidents, being sent off to school and his funeral, weren't so unlike really. He had died in her mind when he sent her away, except he was painfully resurrected on uncomfortable meetings away from their home on holidays. As she got older, she made more and more excuses for not seeing him at vacation time. There were always school mates with invitations for her to their homes.

Linda was known as the most brilliant and beautiful student in the school, and everyone was anxious to show off such a friend to their family. A paragon. She didn't know at first why there were so many invitations; but even when she figured it out, they were still gratefully accepted. Linda was friendly and outgoing as though she were afraid to stop and look inward or be alone. She feared what would be waiting. Loneliness, she was sure; but there was something else. There was someone she couldn't remember, but neither could she quite forget.

"Linda, dear, are you ready to leave?"

Linda looked up into the face of Mrs. Smith. There was distant sympathy in the older lady's face. She nodded and followed them to their car.

The Smiths were the mainstay at the university. Dr Smith had been the president for many years, and his wife had her hand on the pulse of university life at all times. They had met her at the airport and had arranged for her bags to be taken on to Adam Grainger's house while they escorted her to the funeral home. The plane had been late. Mrs. Smith was fulfilling her obligation; and when they delivered her to the house, it would be over.

The trip from Cresthaven Cemetery to the Grainger house wasn't a long one. When the car approached the street that wound through campus to her father's house that sat with its back to the wooded park, Linda felt a tightness in her chest. She was coming home after being exiled for fifteen years.

The house wasn't as large as she remembered, but the front door was exactly the same. Its dark wood surrounded the blues, yellows, greens, and reds of the patterned stained glass. The picture was of the Good Shepherd protecting one little lamb.

She opened the front door and stepped into the small modest foyer. The walls still held pictures of the ancient American Indians. Pieces of pottery and other artifacts were displayed on the library table against the wall of the narrow hall. Wall shelves were full to overflowing. Linda let the atmosphere settle on her.

The door to her father's study stood open, and she could see a fire in the fireplace. The desk stood cluttered with papers and a lamp shed a pool of light on the contents.

Whoever had brought her bags must have started the fire. The aroma of chili was spicy and tempting. Someone had been thoughtful. She hadn't eaten since yesterday. Her father must have found a new housekeeper since Martha died.

Slowly, she slipped out of her trench coat and hung it on the golden oak hall tree. She ran her hand through her damp hair.

Pausing slightly, she started up the shadowy staircase to her old room. The study looked inviting, but first she wanted to change clothes. The trip had been long, the afternoon grueling.

Linda found her bags in her old room. As she flipped the switch, the pleasant childhood memories came flooding back with the light. She experienced a slight shock. Her father had made little change in the room. The pink and white spread on the bed was now nearly white. The curtains had been replaced, but they were still pink. The dolls still sat around the small table having their tea party.

It was unexpected. She felt no sympathy for her father, though. He could have had her back at any time. She had waited for him to bring her home.

She unpacked a velour lounging robe and put it on a hanger. It was white with bold black geometric patterns in wide bands around the hem and sleeves. It would be warm. She thought longingly of sitting in front of the fire downstairs with a bowl of the chili she had smelled.

She had her bath, used the blow dryer on her hair and put on the robe and black, leather bedroom slippers. The warm bath had added relaxation to her weariness, and she started slowly down the stairs, trailing her hand along the banister.

Light from the study still came out into the dim hall, but now there was the sound of music. A full-string orchestra was softly playing an accompaniment to a melody that was hauntingly familiar.

Linda pushed the door open and looked into the room. The man sat cross-legged on the floor with his back to her. He was so engrossed in what he was doing that he didn't hear her. Before him on the floor stood a black trunk. Its lid was open, and he rested his elbow on the edge of the trunk as he read from the book he held in his other hand.

He looked at home in the room. His suit coat had been thrown aside and his shirt sleeves rolled up above his wrists. His hair was the color of autumn—russet or cinnamon. Maybe with the light on it, it would be the color of flame.

"I'm starving. May I have some chili, too?" She saw his bowl sitting on a table, its steam rising thinly in the air.

He turned around as he stood up. He was very tall. "I didn't expect you so soon." His eyes didn't leave her face.

"Then, I can't have any chili?" she asked.

"I made it for you, but it was for later." He still stared at her.

"But you're eating it."

"I was hungry."

"So am I." She looked away from his searching gray eyes to the slow cooker plugged into a metal utility table in the corner.

He walked over to her, taking in every feature of her face. With one fingertip he traced the bone structure, pressing gently against her high cheekbones.

Linda knew she should feel outrage, but his touch was completely impersonal. She could almost hear his mind click as he made mental calculations.

"Same bone structure, alabaster skin, blue-black hair, except it should be long." He still held his hand against the side of her face.

"She walks, talks, sleeps, and even eats if given the chance." She walked away from him suddenly.

"I'd have known that you belonged to Dr. Grainger even if I'd met you outside this house. I didn't see you up close at the funeral." He had come to some conclusion.

"My father? Try again, whoever you are. I don't look a thing like my father!"

She took the food he held out to her. "Thank you. I really am famished." She smiled, revealing beautiful, even teeth.

"You are flawless, perfect!" His tone held awe.

"So, I've been told, many times," she retorted mockingly. "The line is old. Who are you?" Her eastern accent was very slight.

"Touché. I deserved that. But you have my meaning wrong. I'm typically good enough with words, but you caught me by surprise."

"Bowled you over with my beauty?" She raised one shapely dark brow expressively. Her tone was condescending.

"Oh, there's no doubt you are beautiful," he shrugged that off nonchalantly. He turned his back on her as he refilled his own soup mug. "Maybe I can explain."

"Don't be modest. You think amazingly fast on your feet."

"What a wicked tongue you have!"

"I've been told that, too. But I'd especially like to hear about my resemblance to my brown-haired, blue-eyed father," she mocked him.

"I didn't say you looked like Dr. Grainger. I said *you belonged* to Adam."

"*Adam* now, is it?" she said mostly to herself.

He ignored her and went on. "Your father was a respected authority on the ancient Indian tribes in the Southwest. I'm sure you've read some of his books."

"No."

He looked at her strangely but continued. "Well, you could have stepped from a page of the one that I've been looking at this afternoon. You are a perfect flawless example. A walking artifact."

"Today I do feel very old." Her black, almond-shaped eyes held glints of amusement.

He waved away her light remark. "Look for yourself." He held the manuscript out to her.

"Has this been published?" she asked as she accepted it.

"No."

The manuscript was bound in a thick cardboard folder. The pages were obviously old.

"Why are you looking at this? And who are you? I'm not so entirely bewildered as to realize that you haven't yet introduced yourself."

"I'm Brett McAlister, ma'am, from New Mexico." His western drawl was well-pronounced. "I was fortunate enough to have been accepted to come here three years ago to finish my graduate work under your father. I finished last year, but I decided to stay one more year when I was offered the position as his assistant."

"It's beginning to get clearer. Please, continue." She held the manuscript in her hands loosely.

"He left me an envelope to be opened in case of his death. I guess that sounds a little theatrical. It was a request to come and destroy the contents of this trunk. The trunk always sat over there under the double windows, but it was never mentioned. I thought I'd have plenty of time before you arrived."

"I didn't want to go eat with the Smiths. I make no apology." He nodded.

"Did my father say you could also examine, minutely, the contents of the trunk?" He could still sense her unbelief.

"Here's the letter. Read it." He pulled the envelope from his suit jacket pocket and handed it to her.

She stood before the fire and read:

Brett,

Please destroy the contents of the black trunk in the study in case of my death. The papers and articles are very personal and could fall into the wrong hands. They are of no concern to anyone at the university. These things were collected in the days before I came here...Thank you

Adam

That was all. She turned the paper over, but there was nothing more. She stooped down and put it on the flame.

"Now, Brett McAlister, or whatever your name is. Don't talk of destroying any of my father's papers. It's only your word against mine."

"Miss Grainger take your time looking them over. But be assured, I'll carry out Adam's request. He only said that they were of no concern to the faculty." His soft gray eyes hardened.

"That's fair, I suppose," she agreed. Sitting down on the sofa, she opened the manuscript.

The color photographs were fading, but the coloring was still there. Close-ups of people showed another race.

"These people don't look like any Indians I have ever seen."

"No, they don't." He sat down awfully close to her. She was disturbed a little by his nearness, but he seemed interested only in the book in her lap.

"You're right. Look at this picture closely. These people have light skin. And their features are delicate—no broad foreheads, wide noses, or recognizable Indian features. You can imagine my surprise when you walked in looking like one of Adam's artifacts, complete with that black-and-white thing you're wearing." He pointed to another picture. "This group of people is different, definitely Indian, but still not exactly like any tribe that I know."

"Yes, I see." He watched as she walked over to refill her soup mug.

She was classically beautiful, and there was no question of that. But there was an aura about her—haunting, illusive. There was an arresting grace in her movements. She was a work of art sparked with vitality and life. But whatever deity that had brought this lovely statue to life had yet to change her heart of stone to flesh.

Brett knew he loved this daughter of his late boss and mentor, Adam Grainger. It was inevitable. He had been pre-conditioned through his study and love of archaeology and ancient peoples. When Linda walked into the room, it was as though she had sprung from the page of the book he was reading and took control of his heart and mind.

He felt safe that she seemed totally unimpressed, yet he was hopelessly gone. But he knew, instinctively, that she would be irretrievably lost to him if she guessed his new emotion.

It was a new feeling. Adam had introduced him to many of the young people from his church. He had dated some of the girls, but there had never been a woman that could hold his attention very long. They disappeared when his work claimed so much of his time and he neglected them. Looking at Linda, it was as though God tapped his shoulder and said, "she's the one." He would be only too happy to comply.

"Tell me, Mr. McAlister…"

"Brett, please." His voice shrugged aside the formality, brusquely.

"Brett, then," she conceded and continued, "If my 'archaeological' father was so blessed as to have a child that is a walking artifact," she raised her head high in a small attempt at humor, offering him a queenly profile, "how could he bear to part with her?" With her hand, she alluded to the vast collection of treasure just in this room.

Now that Brett actually saw Adam's daughter in person, he had wondered the same thing. Her profile was clean, pure, her neck finely molded, disappearing into graceful lines beneath the black-and-white caftan melting with the high, firm rise of her breasts.

"Every child has to go to school." He knew it sounded hollow. This wasn't a playful question. He had found the chink in her armor. He also knew that this was the first time she had given voice to this question.

"My college professor father sends his child away to another school, another state even, because the facilities are better perhaps?" Her tone was cynical. "Not much faith in the local talent, would you say?"

"Linda, he talked about you with great pride. He loved you." If only he could offer her some consolation. But he had none.

"Brett, do you know how old I was when my father sent me away to school?" She didn't wait for an answer. Her manner wasn't agitated or emotional but detached as though she were speaking of someone else. "Only five years old."

"I didn't know you were so young. I know that in the past three years your father made several trips to visit you. I taught his classes while he was gone. He made a trip just three months ago."

"Yes, I remember well. Do you know why he made that unscheduled visit?"

"No, he didn't say."

"To reprimand the school for allowing my picture to appear on a magazine cover!"

"I don't understand."

"I don't either, really. But when I was enrolled in school, one stipulation, that has been enforced all these years, was that my picture was never to be in any publication—not in the school yearbooks or any newspaper."

"Did you know why?"

"I still don't know why." She shrugged it off. "But our school is exclusive, and the faculty is adept at handling eccentricities. Some of the requests probably could be labeled stranger than my father's." She shrugged it off again as unimportant. "Anyway, last spring our school competed in the St. Augustine Dressage Riding Competition. In the East we are rather into all types of equine competitions."

"Yes, ma'am," his drawl was as lopsided as his smile," where I'm from, we're rather fond of horses, too."

"Oh, I am sorry. I didn't mean to sound so condescending. We live in such a tight community at our school, that it's hard to imagine an outside world." Her smile was small, but its warmth appeared in her eyes for the first time. "And, don't call me 'ma'am'."

"Sure, enough. Duly noted." He tipped an imaginary hat.

Brett still sat in the floor beside the open trunk, but now he rested his arm on the edge, its contents forgotten. The warmth he'd seen in her eyes was another facet of her personality and was gone nearly as soon as it appeared. She might never hurt someone knowingly, but one felt stung from her cold withdrawal.

She carefully set her soup mug on the end table beside the sofa. Her smooth, shapely hands were folded calmly in her lap. On her white hand was a ring set with a small ruby, her birthstone, a gift from her father on her sixteenth birthday.

"*Women Equestrian Champions* contacted the school for permission to use candid shots of our competing students taken at the show for its magazine. We had a new public relations director who approved the pictures hurriedly, I suppose. There were a few small black and whites in the magazine, but I was on the cover in brilliant color. My father was livid. But it was done."

"Did he explain?"

"No. He didn't even congratulate me for winning the competition." If there had been a hurt, it was healed. "That, Brett, was the last time I saw my father. I did receive a couple of letters, and one vaguely apologized. Then I got the news of his accident."

"It was a shock to all of us. He was admired so much, a truly brilliant man in his field."

"Every great man has his point of embarrassment. I must've been his. As a child, I used to think perhaps if I'd been a boy, he would have wanted me at home with him. When I was about twelve, I thought probably I was an illegitimate baby that some woman had left on his doorstep. Of course, very soon I learned men are free of such responsibilities." There was self-incrimination in her tone.

"Linda, I don't pretend to know any answers to Adam's personal behavior. But I do know that he loved you and even saved every letter from you."

"Unopened?" she asked with a tight smile.

"Of course not," he said gently. Her cold demeanor was only a façade. It was threatening to crack. "He never read any of your letters to me, but when he got quarterly school reports, he would brag like any proud parent." He couldn't tell by the expression on her face if his words had made any impression.

"Brett McAlister, this has been a puzzling day. At my father's funeral I had my thoughts straight. Adam Grainger removed me from his life because I was a nuisance. Now you talk of feelings that I never attributed to him. It sounds like two different men. Maybe we neither one knew him."

"Linda, I knew Adam well, but I didn't know you. Whatever he did was for your welfare with careful concern for you. He wasn't thinking of himself."

Linda's eyes searched his face for any hint of insincerity. She found open honesty. Even if Brett were wrong, he believed what he said.

"Did you know this is the first time I've been allowed back into this house since I was five years old?"

"Allowed back. What do you mean?"

"Father never brought me home again; he always arranged our meetings and vacations close to the school." She looked to him with questioning in her face.

"Linda, I don't know why. He must've had his own reasons."

"You're very loyal. This has been a strange eulogy for your friend and teacher and my father, Adam Grainger. But I'm home again, and it feels good. It's comfortable, like the house has been waiting for me. My room was friendly. I suppose that sounds odd, but I don't know how else to express it."

"Being sentimental is nothing to be ashamed of."

The remark seemed incongruous with this rugged individual seated on the floor before her.

"No, I have no sentimental feeling. It's like coming into a warm room from the cold. The experience is physical more than emotional."

Brett wondered if Linda would be able to define a genuine emotion. Her classical beauty was ageless, but her real emotions lay young and untried.

There were the beginnings of smudges beneath her eyes; it had been an extremely hard day for this composed girl before him. Although the two hadn't been close, it was straining to lose one's father, especially if he were her last known relative.

She was truly alone. He longed to protect her. It was hard for him to realize that until a couple of hours ago she'd been only a name and picture to him, the ever-absent daughter whom Adam had loved to talk about.

"Linda, I know this has been a hard day for you. Maybe you should rest." He suddenly remembered something. "Dr. Tyler asked me to tell you that he will come over tomorrow evening to extend his sympathy."

"'Uncle' Max?" she said the name tentatively.

"Uncle?" Brett echoed.

"Oh, no, not really. He was a close friend of my father."

"Are you sure?" Brett looked puzzled. "I don't ever remember him being at the house or even seeing them together."

Linda looked at him sharply, a frown creasing her brow. "I don't remember much of the time I had here before I was sent to school. But I do remember Max. Father knew him well enough to discuss me with him, and he was here the weekend father told me he was sending me to school. I've always felt he'd influenced father to send me away."

Brett watched her. She was talking to him, but more than that, she was using him for a sounding board. He said nothing.

"I'll call him and invite him for dinner tomorrow, but I don't want to see him alone. Will you come, too?" She was surprised at herself for asking this man, who was so nearly a stranger, for support. A flash of insecurity washed over her at the look on his face.

"Of course, Linda, I'll be here. I live here. Didn't your father tell you? I have rented a room in this house ever since I moved here from New Mexico."

Her face was smooth again, inscrutable. "It seems you were another small item father neglected to mention. I wouldn't have needed to humble myself to beg for your help," she smiled slightly.

"You wouldn't have been saved the humiliation. Only an invitation from a special person could convince me to have dinner with Max Tyler." His smile was warm, genuine. He continued in a teasing tone, "you are a special person, Linda. Why else would your father go to such trouble to protect you—private schools from age five through college. And not tell you about his handsome assistant."

"I want to find out why." There was no levity in her tones. "I'm going to start by questioning Max. And," she paused looking at the trunk where Brett sat, his arm over the edge in protection, "there may be some clues in that trunk. Please wait for me to go through it with you."

She swayed slightly and Brett sprang lightly to his feet and put his hand at her elbow.

"Are you all right?"

"Tired. Extremely tired. I can't recall ever being so worn out."

"You have every reason to be wrung out—your flight, Adam's funeral, and all the unanswered questions haunting you. Can you make it to your room?"

"Yes, thank you." She pushed his hand away unsteadily. She didn't know his angle, but he was too protective, too kind. She'd been betrayed too many times—her father, Max, teachers at school withholding so much information. The girls were the worst; her supposed friends only wanted her to attract the boys. Boys to beauty, bees to honey…

Willing herself erect, she climbed the stairs, gracefully lifting the folds of the long skirt of her black-and-white caftan. Her head high and regal, a queen ascending to her chambers.

As soon as she lay on her bed, she slept and dreamed. She stood on the entrance of a valley, the pines thick and protective; the meadows were lush, green, divided by a sparkling stream that had forced itself through the rocks and now flowed free and pure. The sky was blue, the flight path of a soaring hawk invisible on its surface.

The dream was only a place, no people. She had never seen it before, but it was not unfamiliar.

Chapter 3

When Linda awoke, she had a single purpose. She must examine the things in that trunk. She had always been able to detach herself from her past, but with the death of her father came an almost desperate need for knowledge. And with the source of that knowledge now beyond her reach, it would be a difficult search. As long as Adam was alive, Linda hadn't allowed her curiosity to surface. It was fear, fear that Adam would realize how very much she did care.

She needed roots—a home, people of her own. It was a struggle not to accept Brett. She wanted his help, wanted to depend on him. What a laugh! She had been known as the epitome of today's modern young woman.

Gorgeous, but cold—like viewing the sun from a deep freeze. But she is the sun—no one can touch her. I'd take her out any chance I get just to be seen with her, she'd overheard one man say.

It was a game at first. Her aloofness and beauty fascinated them. It became part of her, a built-in safety feature. Never get involved, never get hurt. None of the men she'd ever known could be trusted.

Brett seemed different. And he wanted nothing from her, at least so far as she could tell.

In the morning Linda felt light weariness still clinging to her. She didn't know what time it was, but the house was quiet. The emotions of yesterday had left her sluggish.

Deliberately, she flung back the cover and got up. The hardwood floor was cold on her bare feet. She went to the bathroom and turned on the shower until the small room was steamy. The mirror was fogged up, and she reached to clear a spot on it.

As her hand was about to touch the glass, a place cleared and she saw her reflection. Her face looked flushed, her eyes bright with unshed tears. Her hair hung in a thick wide plait over her left shoulder.

Linda closed her eyes tightly and gripped the sink.

It was her own face in the mirror, but it was different. There was a wildness in the expression, the hair was long. She could feel beads of perspiration on her face, a chill played on the back of her neck.

I'm going to open my eyes, she thought, and the distortion will be gone. It's a trick of the steam. The mirror is lined.

She lifted the towel that she held tightly in her hand and rubbed vigorously on the mirror. Then, she opened her eyes.

The face looking back at her was a little pale but totally her own. Her thick black hair was short, only a little mussed from her night's sleep. The steam began to cover the mirror again, but the reflection, though dim, was still her own.

"I'm more tired than I know," she spoke shakily to the girl in the mirror.

Linda showered more hurriedly than she had planned.

The suitcase was open, but her clothes were still packed. Later she would hang them up and hope the wrinkles would fall out of the dress she would wear for dinner tonight. Now she pulled on a soft, white long-sleeved turtleneck top under her jogging suit. Her room was cold, and she was also still shivering from fright at the distorted image in the mirror. Her emotions were as affected as her body.

She put everything out of her mind except the trunk. It held a fascination for her. Without knowing why, she sensed it held a key to many of the questions that possessed her mind.

It was as though while her father was alive, her energies were spent hating him for sending her away. Now those energies were loosed into a driving need for discovering why Adam had hidden her away from his world, nearly keeping her a secret.

As she came down the stairs, the folded white paper on the library table caught her attention. It was from Brett. His handwriting was bold and easy to read.

> Linda, hope you slept well. I teach this morning, and I'm filling in for Adam's classes, too. I'll be home in time to help with dinner. There's food in the 'frig.

A sigh of relief escaped her. There would be plenty of time to examine the contents of the trunk alone. Linda glanced across the hall through the open door of the study. The trunk still sat before the now-cold fireplace. Brett hadn't pushed it back to its original place in front of the double windows.

It looked inviting, but she was hungry. The chili she'd had with Brett yesterday afternoon was all she'd eaten in the last thirty-six hours.

An old-fashioned parlor was directly across the hall from the study. A huge walk-in closet separated the parlor from the kitchen. Across the hall from the kitchen was the master bedroom and the only downstairs bath. The floor plan of the house was quite simple.

"The kitchen can't remain untouched for fifteen years," Linda told herself crossly.

It was a pleasant room. The stainless-steel appliances were arranged economically with the dark wooden cabinets, leaving floor space for a waist-high chopping block that could double as a workspace. A bold yellow, orange, and brown striped textured roman shade was at the double French doors behind the round wooden table. There were orange placemats on the table. The centerpiece was the inevitable piece of pottery: an irregular-shaped bowl with stick men and horses made long ago by some ancient hand. It should have held a bright bouquet of flowers. But, instead, there were a couple small note pads and an assortment of stubby pencils and a few pens.

It was a man's kitchen, she supposed. Even the sun that splashed through the windows onto the beige tile floor and up the base of the dark wooden cabinets stayed in the rectangular pattern from the windows. There were no frills in this room, but she liked it.

Linda turned the burner on under the copper teakettle. In the refrigerator she found English muffins. She popped one into the toaster.

Lavishly, she spread butter and honey on the hot muffin and made a scalding cup of tea. She ate slowly. It was only ten o'clock. There was plenty of time to explore the trunk before shopping for food for dinner. She didn't have much experience in cooking, but there had to be a recipe book somewhere in the house. Surely, she could fix spaghetti, and she'd have a tossed green salad and rolls. For dessert she'd buy a frozen cream pie. Maybe that would be good enough to put Max into a talking mood. She intended to drain his mind of all that he remembered of her.

Linda jumped at a sound at the French doors.

"Oh, I didn't know nobody wuz here." The woman that came through the door was as startled as Linda.

"May I help you?" Linda began to stand up.

"Uh, I'm Miz Baskins. I clean house on Fridays. I figgered Mr. McAlister would want me to come even with Professor Grainger..." She stood silent as though she'd run out of words.

"I'm sure it is ok. Do whatever you usually do."

The woman was a little uncertain. She loosened the knot in her headscarf from under her double chin and uncovered her hair. It was thin and white with an ill-fitting hairpiece arranged to cover the top that was probably altogether bald. Without the hairpiece, she would look like a female Alfred Hitchcock.

"Mrs. Baskins, really it is ok. I'm Linda Grainger, Dr. Grainger's daughter and…"

"Didn't know he had no daughter." This had done nothing to reassure her. She had interrupted so quickly that Linda knew she was suspicious. "I don't know if I should be here." She glanced around nervously. "I'm sorry about your father…"

Then Linda knew. Mrs. Baskins was afraid. She was completely unnerved at coming back to a dead man's house. Perhaps because Adam Grainger had died so suddenly, Mrs. Baskins hadn't been able to grasp it yet. She expected him to appear.

"Thank you, Mrs. Baskins," Linda nodded slightly. "I'm glad you're here, because I need some help." This was the right approach.

Mrs. Baskins visibly relaxed. She slipped off her gray tweed coat. Underneath she wore a large red and blue cover-up apron over a neat gray work dress. "What kin I do, Miz Grainger?"

"Dr. Tyler was a friend of my father's. And when he asked to come over to extend his sympathy, I invited him to dinner. I'm afraid, Mrs. Baskins, that I'm badly in need of a cookbook. Do you know if there's one around here?"

"You can't cook?" It came out with more sympathy than she had expressed at the professor's death. Mrs. Baskins' round figure was testimony to her love of food.

"I've been away at school with no place to practice." Linda's simple confession drew a deep sigh from the housekeeper. "I thought I'd fix spaghetti if I could find a recipe for the sauce. I can make a salad and buy some frozen rolls."

"I'll help you." Mrs. Baskins tightened her apron strings in preparation.

Linda searched her mind frantically. By the time the woman cleaned the house and helped with dinner, Brett might be home. She'd have no time to look in the trunk.

"We'll make a bargain. Today you only do the downstairs and Mr. McAlister's room. I'll do the rest of the upstairs tomorrow in exchange for your help in the kitchen today."

"If you're sure?" Mrs. Baskins hesitated, but she was plainly tempted.

"Sure." Linda pulled pad and pencil from the clay bowl. "Tell me what to get from the store."

The kitchen was well-stocked, so the list was not long. Mrs. Baskins was up to her elbows in pastry dough before Linda could get ready to leave. She insisted only homemade rolls would do for spaghetti, and dessert would be her special lemon meringue pie.

As Linda walked past the study to the front door, she looked at the trunk longingly. Well, it couldn't be helped. First, she had to get rid of the housekeeper. At least she could work off some of her impatience on the walk to the store.

The next few hours passed quickly. Even if Mrs. Baskins' cleaning wouldn't bear close scrutiny, her cooking made up for it. The luscious-looking pie sat cooling on the counter. The yeast dough had been rolled and formed into crescents, which were beginning to rise. The spaghetti sauce was gently bubbling. All seemed in perfect order.

Mrs. Baskins wouldn't leave until the tablecloth and napkins had been found and the table set. Linda was beginning to wish she hadn't asked for her help. It was after three in the afternoon when Mrs. Baskins finally left. They had taken time to fix BLT sandwiches for lunch. It was welcome, but it had taken an extra half an hour.

Now she was alone. Linda could hear the clock above the refrigerator ticking. It seemed almost in rhythm with her own heartbeat. There was no reason to wait longer.

Deliberately, she walked around the trunk to the cold fireplace. Someone, Brett probably, had laid the kindling and logs, so all she had to do was touch a match to it. The flame licked hungrily at the wood.

A shiver of anticipation coursed over her. There was an icy sensation in her stomach. She lowered herself and sat cross-legged before the trunk and pulled at the oversized brass latch.

Nothing budged! She pulled hard. It was locked! Brett had locked it. How dare he?

She lay over and rested her head on the trunk and pounded the lid with her fist in angry frustration. Hot tears stung her eyes and burned narrow paths down her cheeks.

She hadn't cried since that first night away from home, a tiny frightened child not quite six. Now she couldn't control the sobs that racked her. A dam had broken within, and there was no stopping the flood of emotions that rushed forth.

Before Brett left the house that morning, he had written the note to Linda. She'd been so tired the night before that he was careful not to make any noise upstairs. He'd taken his clothes and showered downstairs.

As he walked toward the front door, he'd seen the trunk sitting in the study as they had left it. He walked to the desk and took out a large key. The brass latch caught with a distinct click, and he turned the key in the lock. They'd go through the contents of this trunk together. Just like they'd said.

The morning dragged for Brett. His classes didn't keep his attention. The subject had gone flat for him. He kept seeing

Linda. It was nearly three when Brett dismissed his last class and left for home. He'd promised to help with dinner.

He heard her sobs as soon as he came into the foyer. Their intensity shook him. With long strides he came to where she was leaning over the trunk. He knelt beside her and put his arm around her shoulders. The face she turned to him was white and stamped with pain, her eyes rimmed red from weeping.

"You!" Her fury blazed. "You locked it. You have no right to keep his secrets from me." She pounded his chest and cried uncontrollably.

Brett pulled her to her feet and held her tightly. She struggled fiercely, but he kept her arms pinned between them. Abruptly, she stopped fighting.

When Brett loosened his hold a little, she slipped her arms around his waist and clung to him, her face buried against his chest. He held her to him with one arm and with his free hand he gently stroked her hair.

Her anger was spent, leaving only grief. She felt the loss of her father. Never near her, he had continued to fill her life. Now he was gone.

"Forgive me?" Brett's voice surprised her. She nodded her head against him. She didn't have enough strength to move, and it was comforting where she stood.

"I lied," she confessed.

"Oh? About what?"

"I have read my father's books. I loved him, Brett. Why did he push me away?"

He could feel her tears through the front of his sweater. He tightened his arm about her.

"He was all I had."

"Linda, you have me." It came naturally. He gently pushed her back, so he could look into her face. "I want to take care of you, protect you."

"A chauvinistic idea." Her protest was feeble.

"True." He grinned at her. "I have five sisters, and each have accused me of having old-fashioned ideas."

She looked incredulous. "Five sisters?"

He rolled his eyes toward the ceiling. "I offer you a lifetime of guardianship, and you're only impressed by the fact that I have five sisters!"

"Any brothers?"

"No, much to my father's sorrow."

"So much family." She was awed.

"I'll gladly share them with you," he offered seriously.

"Yes, you'd introduce me as a living artifact dug up from Dr. Grainger's past. You could use me for 'show and tell' in your seminars. I can see it all now," bitterness edged her voice. "I've been exploited before." She tried to pull loose, but he held her.

"I'm afraid any resemblance to antiquity you had last night is gone in the light of day." His eyes took in her jeans and tee shirt. "I'm going to tell you once…" He slipped his hand over her mouth as she started her retort.

He started again. "I'm afraid that I've fallen in love with you," he ignored the expression in her eyes, "despite your ravaged beauty right now, and I'll probably not get over it. I fell in love with the girl that Adam was always talking about. Now, it's for real." He looked into those deep brown eyes where tears still glistened. "I know it's way too soon, and you're suffering from loss and confusion. I'm asking for absolutely nothing. I just want to offer you comfort in that the fact that someone here loves you. May I do this?"

She shook her head slowly, speechless. So much was happening. She, who had always prided herself on steel control, was totally confused.

He cupped both hands around her tear-stained face and laid his lips softly on hers.

Linda felt the gentle pressure from his mouth against hers and closed her eyes as she felt the warmth of his kiss surrounding her. The loving tenderness in his touch caused her to tremble. She had never experienced love before. But she recognized her feelings as the fragile beginnings of a never-ending enchantment.

She backed away but kept her hand against his shirtfront to steady herself.

"It's alright, Linda." His voice was steady and calm, but his heart throbbed heavily where her hand lay against his chest. His smile was reassuring. "I know you've been through enough emotional upheaval without anymore. I just want you to know that I love you."

He put his hand into his pocket and drew out the key to the trunk. He stooped down and unlocked it. The hinges squeaked as he lifted the lid.

"From what I can tell, there are two groups of people in these pictures."

"I do strongly resemble one group," Linda admitted. "But the other group looks like an ancient Indian tribe."

"Pueblo, I'd say."

"But isn't *pueblo* a general term for tribes like the Hopi and Navajo?"

"You have read your father's books." He smiled at her "You are right, of course, but I can't identify these. The pictures are good, but Adam hasn't put enough information in his writings. This particular book is more like…" he paused for a few moments, "like a family scrapbook. Pictures and names."

"Maybe the rest of the stuff in the trunk will tell us more."

There was a lay-in tray that set in the trunk. It had held the book of pictures. There were several bulging envelopes, too.

"I hope so." Brett ran a hand through his auburn hair and stood up. "Tyler will be here at six. We won't have any more time now."

Their eyes met in disappointment.

Brett held out his hand to her and pulled her lightly to her feet. "To the kitchen, then, I promised to help."

"You don't think I can cook?" She met his teasing tone.

"No." He was blunt. "You look too good."

Linda ignored his comment. "As a matter of fact, I can't cook, but Mrs. Baskins helped. Things are nearly ready."

"Baskins!" He put his palm to his forehead. "I forgot about her coming today. If she can't cook any better than she cleans, we may still be in trouble." He spooned a sample of the meat-and-tomato sauce and blew on it gently.

"It smells good," defended Linda.

Brett tasted the sauce and gave a non-committal shrug. "I'll *create* a salad." He began juggling a head of lettuce, a green pepper, and a tomato.

"You're crazy, you know," she countered.

"Sure, any clown can do this trick." He deftly caught the vegetables and bowed, flourishing a make-believe hat.

He had succeeded in putting her completely at east after her breakdown in the study. She'd never met anyone like him before. His kiss hadn't been demanding, and yet she believed him when he said that he loved her. Maybe because she wanted to believe him. She needed someone to love her, comfort her and stand between her and loneliness. It was an unfamiliar need, difficult and foreign to her nature.

But there was no explanation for her reaction to his kiss. She had seemed suspended in space, a warm delicious dizziness washing over her.

Linda had just finished brushing her hair when she heard the doorbell ring downstairs. There were the sounds of muffled male voices and the closing of the door.

Max was here. She clasped her hands tightly to try to still their trembling. What had happened to the self-confident, slightly cynical, young woman that she had been when she arrived for her father's funeral. Only yesterday? The bombardment of emotions since she had returned to her father's house had torn down the wall she had spent her short lifetime building.

"Max?"

The two men were still standing in the foyer when she came down the stairs. Dr. Tyler smiled and took the hand she offered him.

"It's been so long. What can I say? You're beautiful!"

Brett watched Linda smile at Tyler. He could understand she must have heard these same words every day of her life. *You're beautiful.*

But she *was* beautiful. There were no traces of this afternoon's stormy tears, and she no longer reminded him of an ancient princess. The dusty rose-colored dress of a lightweight, slinging suede met the top of soft leather boots. A heavy rose-colored rope belted the dress. A scarf in shades of red to rose was arranged becomingly with three strands of gold chain around her neck. Her earrings were slender gold circles, her perfume tantalizing and illusive. She was the picture of poise and self-control. Her stage was set.

Linda acknowledged Max's words of sympathy for her father's death. Brett followed them into the dining area off of the kitchen. He was a silent observer through dinner. He noticed that Linda ate little but concentrated on the conversation. Brett watched this professor of psychology and practicing psychoanalyst being totally set at ease by the power of a beautiful woman not even half his age. Tyler was blissfully off-guard.

"I don't remember too many people from when I lived here," Linda's voice was thoughtful, "but I do remember you, Max. You had lunch with us the very day before I went off to school."

"Yes, yes, I did." Max couldn't hide his pleasure. He rubbed the thin hair on top of his balding head. It was a nervous gesture Brett had noticed often. It was as though Dr. Tyler needed reassurance that he still actually had some hair.

"I wasn't quite six," Linda added. She fingered her coffee cup handle, delicately.

"You cannot imagine, my dear, how I felt when I had to urge your father to send you away to school. I remember my relief when the school started sending back such excellent reports on your behavior and academic achievement."

"You were responsible for my father sending me away to school?" Linda's voice was muffled as she rose to get the coffee to refill their cups.

"Don't tell me in her five short years she caused enough chaos that Adam called you in." Scorn underscored Brett's words. He succeeded in drawing Tyler's attention long enough for Linda to regain her slipping composure.

"Don't judge, Dr. McAlister, you weren't there!" The older man rubbed his head furiously.

"I remember nothing of what happened, so I must have recovered," soothed Linda.

"Of course, you've recovered!" Max nearly bellowed. Brett McAlister always irritated him. "I'm sorry, my dear, I didn't mean to storm at you."

He relaxed as she waved away the outburst and smiled.

"Many only children develop an imaginary friend."

"Is that why I was sent away?" The question had hammered at her for so long that it was incredible that the answer seemed so empty. Linda toyed with the chain around her neck.

"With five sisters, I never felt compelled to invent another child at our house, but it doesn't really sound serious." Brett winked at Linda in a conspiratorial manner.

"Of course, there was more." Max was sorry the minute that he said it. But he still wasn't aware of the trap.

"Tell me, 'Uncle' Max, what were the complications?" Linda looked at him innocently over the rim of her coffee cup.

"Well," he hesitated, "your friend was very real to you, and there were early signs of the possibility of a potential double personality. The imaginary playmate was holding you to this house, which, of course, was retarding your normal childhood development."

"I see." Linda felt like something was trying to come alive in her own memory. A shadow was emerging.

"And, your friend spoke to you in Spanish."

"Where did I learn Spanish?"

"That's really what concerned Dr. Grainger. Your mother was Spanish…"

"Don't tell me you convinced Adam that Linda's dead mother was trying to communicate with her." Brett expected his brusque interruption to rouse Tyler's anger again.

"No." Tyler crossed his hands across his slight stomach paunch and sighed. "No, nor did Adam suggest that to me. Of course, I told him there was a reasonable explanation. We had a new Spanish professor moving in about that time…"

"Sure, you can pick up almost any language around the university from time to time," agreed Brett. The two men agreed on this at least.

"*Mi amiga…*" Linda spoke, suddenly.

"Yes, that's it." Max nodded. "That's what you said your playmate called you. Do you remember anything else?"

"I don't think so." Linda shook her head, slowly.

"Good. Don't try. It was a childhood fantasy best left alone." Tyler relaxed in his chair.

"But you said my mother was Spanish."

"It was about the only fact that ever slipped out about Adam's past personal life." He straightened in his chair, then stood. "I only know that your mother's name was Inez and that she was Spanish. I am sorry…"

Linda and Brett walked with Max to the foyer. Dr. Tyler turned and took both of Linda's hands in his.

"Again, I want to say how sorry I am over Adam's death, my dear," Max hesitated, then added, "and, you cannot imagine how delighted I am that you have grown into such a wonderful young woman. It makes up for losing Adam's friendship. After you left, he became withdrawn for several years."

"He never forgave you for urging him to send Linda away?" Brett's remark cut through to the point.

Max looked at him like he'd forgotten he was there. "Yes, quite so. But I was right. Just look at her."

"You take credit for quite a lot!" Brett wasn't going to help this man salve his conscience.

"It was a hard decision," Max shrugged into his coat. "If you need me, Linda, don't hesitate to call."

"Thank you, Max." It was all she could say. She rested her hand briefly on his coat sleeve.

The cold air that came in as Max opened the door to go out chilled even her hopes. She had learned so little from Max that would give her a clue to her past. She had learned that her mother was Spanish. Period.

"Inez is a beautiful name," Brett read her thoughts.

"I never even knew her name. But all I've really learned is that I was a neurotic child shipped off on the suggestion of a part-time shrink." Her anger kept her from breaking.

"What now, Linda?" Brett held up the key to the trunk. "Shall we look further?"

"Not now, Brett." Her anger drained, leaving her no support. "I'm going to take a sleeping pill and get some rest."

Brett watched her go up the stairs. He wished he could hold her and offer her his strength. That would only complicate her life further.

Methodically, Linda hung up her clothes as she undressed. She had taken half of the sleeping pill as soon as she got to her room and was waiting for its relaxing affect. She slipped on a long nightgown of a brushed fabric with a smocked yoke held together by three tiny buttons. The sleeves ended in ruffles at her wrists.

She finally felt drowsy enough to get into bed.

Linda wasn't aware of when the warm comfort of her darkened room began to change. The scene of the night before had slipped before her eyes—the lush green valley was her idea of peace. The hawk again sailed with the clouds in the blue sky and a few white sheep dotted the grassy pasture beside the stream.

In her state of semi-sleep, she murmured the words that came to her mind. She'd memorized them as a child when she attended Sunday School with her father.

The Lord is my shepherd, I shall not want. He maketh me to lie down in green pastures, he restoreth my soul, he leadeth me beside still waters.

It was the ultimate comfort. But then a change came over the scene. The peaceful feeling was gone. The hawk dived, and she could see his razor-sharp talons. She heard the death scream of a rabbit as the hawk flew away with its prey.

A girl was running toward her as though in flight. Linda felt the girl's fear as though it were her own. The girl glanced back over her shoulder as she ran. She was young, barefooted, and her long black hair mingled with the wind as she fled. She was running toward Linda. Something was threatening her. They were both in danger.

The unknown figure was getting close enough for Linda to see her face. As she neared, she looked straight at Linda.

Time stood still. The face Linda saw was her own in another time, another place. But there was no shock on the girl's face when she looked at Linda. She seemed to be seeking her. But the fear intensified. Her mouth moved soundlessly.

The girl began to wave her arms frantically, motioning for Linda to go away. Darkness began to cloud the dream, so that Linda couldn't distinguish the features of the threatening figure closing in on the girl. She couldn't even tell if it were a man or a woman.

Linda was one with the girl as the waves of terror washed over them together. They were one, yet they were separate.

Suddenly, the girl stopped and faced her adversary. She was standing in the gap between Linda and the evil threatening them both.

The laughter that came from the pursuing figure echoed throughout the valley and rang in Linda's head. She put her hands over her ears to shut it out. When she saw the girl being carried away, Linda screamed. She would be next. The evil would be back after her.

She screamed again, fought the blankets, and sat up.

The lights came on in her room. Brett sat on the edge of her bed and drew her close. She was shaking, uncontrollably, but the screaming had stopped. He was still fully dressed, but he could feel her body shivering through the nightgown. He pulled a blanket from the bed and wrapped it around her.

The face she turned to him had never looked more lovely, but the expression was one of utter hopelessness.

"Brett, it's too late for us. I am quite insane." She knew that the girl in her nightmare had been the same one she saw in her mirror this morning.

Chapter 4

"How do you feel now, Linda?"

Linda was dressed again in her black-and-white caftan. She was in a large chair near the fireplace downstairs in the study. Brett had been sitting in the study when he heard Linda's screams. It had only been an hour since she had gone upstairs.

She looked like an ancient princess again. Her face was white and luminous, her eyes wide beneath dark, gracefully arched brows.

She didn't answer him but closed her eyes and leaned her head against the high back of the chair. She wanted to shut out the sight of his face. Never before had she been looked at with such love and tenderness, and she had nothing to return.

"Linda?"

"I'm alright now." She tried to smile.

He didn't return her smile. "Tell me about your dream—from the beginning. You were incoherent before." Brett turned his face away from her and leaned against the fireplace mantel. He poked at a log in the fire. Showers of sparks were like tiny fireworks.

She talked slowly without leaving out anything. She even told him about the image in the bathroom mirror that morning which hadn't belonged to her. He might as well know her for what she was.

"Brett, as the girl was being taken away, I could read her lips, although I couldn't hear her words. She was saying *mi amiga*."

"Doesn't that prove you were unduly upset with Dr. Tyler's words?" Brett reasoned.

"Upset? Of course, I was upset! I've been emotional since news of my father's death, but that wouldn't explain my nightmare!" Linda's anger had a touch of hysteria. "I must find out about my past. Perhaps, I am going insane. It may run in the family. The skeleton in my closet may have been a raving lunatic before he, or should I say she, died!" She stood before Brett.

She stared at Brett as he threw back his head and laughed.

"Linda, I'm sorry. It's my red hair. It gives me a terrible sense of humor. But don't you see, if you can be this objective, you are as sane as I am." His look wasn't apologetic.

"Do you think that would be an improvement?" Her retort was angry.

"Touché." His laughter was gone. "Linda, let's start looking for your past."

Brett pulled the trunk over before the fire and unlocked it. They spent several minutes going through the picture album again, but they found nothing new. There were a few other envelopes in the tray that held picture negatives, but nothing more. Brett lifted out the tray and set it on the floor beside the chair.

The paper had been folded so long that the creases were permanent. Brett let out an exclamation of surprise.

"What is it?" she demanded.

"This is a map I drew of the area of archaeological digs on my family's ranch. I sent it in with my first letter and résumé requesting entrance into graduate school as Dr. Grainger's assistant.

"Is this a public place?"

"No, it's our private property. Dad is an archaeological buff, and he and I had our own field. As a matter of fact, I'm returning home this spring to help with the ranch and teach. I've accepted a professorship at the university there."

"Why would father have put the map in here?"

"Maybe we'll find out." He pulled out a typewritten manuscript. The cover page was entitled *The Legend of the Crying Child*.

"So?" She waited, expectantly.

"It's a local story from my part of New Mexico. Adam and I never discussed it. I didn't know he was familiar with it."

"What does this mean?"

"Perhaps nothing, but it's too coincidental. *The Legend of the Crying Child* is a story of a burial mound not thirty-five miles from our ranch. There is no physical evidence there; the area is very remote. It was said a tribe of peaceful Indians fleeing the raiding Apaches were cornered. Rather than let their children be captured by the Apache, they killed them quickly. Then they killed themselves. One child remained alive for a short time. When the Apache war party arrived, the smell of death and the pitiful wail of a child met them. The crying child is said to be still heard from time to time."

"What a horrible story!"

"But just a story." Brett leafed through the manuscript. "This is a beautiful work. He actually has a complete log of his excavations there, even a grid plan. It was dated twenty years ago. I knew some archaeologist had dug there privately once. It wasn't funded by any group; it was just a summer vacation project taken on by some young professor. But it had been abandoned and thought to be a fake."

"You mean my father was the one?" Linda was struggling to keep up with Brett.

"Yes, so it seems. And, it also seems that the mound was not fraudulent. These graphs are detailed! Look at these sketches of jewelry he found and the bones! Many children's skeletons." Brett was engrossed in the work of Adam Grainger.

"This must be burned, Brett," Linda reminded him gently.

"But why? Why would he hide this? It should be published."

"We don't know why he hid it," she spoke, sadly.

Brett laid the manuscript carefully on the fire—a truly sacrificial offering. The tables had turned; she was now urging him to carry out her father's request.

"Linda, I've just had a new thought. Just suppose Adam had a personal reason for hiring me. At the time he did say he'd chosen me because I was from one of his favorite parts of the country. What if he brought me here because he was afraid of what I'd find? If I'd continued excavating, eventually I might have found some clue as to the authenticity of the Crying Child Burial Mound. He was trying to stop my work there."

"It isn't reasonable, Brett. He had far more to gain by publishing his work, and being accredited with such a find, than denying its validity."

"You're right. There's got to be more that we can learn."

The bundle Brett picked up was gray with age. He laid it on the coffee table and began to unwrap it.

"What a unique pitcher." Linda reached out and touched it with her forefinger. Nearly six inches tall, it was decorated with black on white. It was obviously functional as well as decorative. "Why didn't father have this on display?"

"Linda, we keep coming up with too many questions." He ran his hand through his hair. "I've never seen a piece of pottery like this, except in books or museums. It's incredibly old; it would date further back than the Crying Child Burial Mound—at least a couple hundred years."

Linda held the small pitcher reverently.

"The Apache raids that drove many of the peaceful, settled tribes further south came after nearly a quarter century of drought.

"The economic decline was caused by scarcity of rainfall. Even the springs dried up. Crop failure had weakened the tribes considerably, leaving them no alternative but to flee," Brett was excited over his subject.

"But my father knew the importance of these finds." Linda set the pitcher carefully back on the cloth. "We can't destroy this."

"He only said 'burn', so I guess he was concerned only with the written material and photographs." Brett turned to the trunk again. "Let's see what this portfolio has in it."

The portfolio was black, a dog-eared folder about 14"x20". It was held together with a cloth-covered rubber band which silently broke into two pieces when Brett attempted to slip it off.

"Brett, since father was there twenty-one years ago, he must have met my mother while he was in New Mexico. I'm twenty."

"Infant." His remark was accompanied by a mock-stern look. "I must have been six when he was excavating at the Crying Child Burial Mound. Then my interests were totally centered on being a cowboy. Rodeos were my life!"

"I'm quite adult, thank you. I have a college diploma to prove it." Linda wanted to keep this light; she knew her response to his kiss would label her inexperienced, if not adolescent.

"Only means you are a bright child. I thought you would be graduated in another month?"

"I'm a bright child, remember? My academic standing exempts me from the final exams; and I was given the option of returning for graduation, or not, because of my father's death. And, no, I don't actually have my diploma yet; but it will be mailed to me." She felt like she was giving more explanation to the subject that it warranted.

Brett laid the portfolio on the coffee table and opened it carefully.

"Linda, we've found your mother," he spoke reverently. On the margin of the photograph, a child-like scrawl read *Inez*.

Linda knelt before the table and studied the face looking up at her. It was like seeing a reflected likeness of herself, but there was a distinct difference. The girl in the picture was at peace with her world. Contentment and an innocent wisdom shone from her eyes and her smile. The photographer had glimpsed the girl's soul as she posed, head slightly back, lips parted in a smile. There was no coldness nor aloofness in this face.

Linda picked up the photograph and propped it up on the mantle, still unable to take her eyes off of the face in the picture.

"Here are more photographs." Brett spread the snapshots out on the desk. They showed the same girl in different poses. In one picture she was obviously pregnant.

"This one must have been shortly before I was born." She picked up another picture. "Brett, do you recognize any of this country?"

Brett looked over her shoulder at the one she held in her hand.

"No, I don't. I've roamed most of the area around our ranch, plus that shown on the map around the Crying Child Burial Mound."

"This shot looks exactly like the scene in my dream." She handed the picture to Brett. He walked over to the desk and placed it in a better light under the brass, crooked-neck lamp. He didn't answer her.

"Do you think I was born there?" she pressed him for an answer. "Could I have lived there long enough to remember?"

"Max said you were just two years old when your father brought you here. I suppose that could mean anything up to one-year old." He didn't want to remind her of this. He went back to the trunk and lifted out a basket. It was obviously handcrafted by an ancient artisan.

"From the same period?" She watched Brett run his forefinger carefully over the woven design.

"Yes. It's exquisite." His voice was reverent.

The clock in the foyer chimed like it was solemnizing his words. It was getting to be late. "Do you want to continue this in the morning?"

When she shook her head, he nodded his agreement and began laying out the items from inside the basket. Neither of them would be able to sleep.

"Linda, these things are almost like a story." Brett raised his voice in excitement. He lifted out a double-spouted black jar and looked at her expectantly.

"What does that mean?" She hadn't caught his excitement.

"It's a wedding jar!"

"Oh, and the double spout is a symbol?"

He nodded and held up a ceremonial sash.

"But what has this to do with my mother? Or me?" She waved her hand at the picture on the mantel, "or Adam?"

"I don't know, Linda. It's very puzzling. Your mother was Spanish, even Max told us that. But all these artifacts speak of relics from an Indian civilization, an old one."

"She was also Catholic, and these Indians are primitive, maybe even pagan," Linda stressed her words.

"That's a particularly good point. But remember, the picture album we opened first showed two distinct groups of people. We have unearthed some more questions that we can't answer." Some of his excitement died.

He drew out the last two items from the basket.

"Linda, the first items tell of a marriage: this double-spouted jar and the ceremonial sash for the man."

"What of the woman's wedding costume?" Linda looked into the empty basket.

Brett studied a moment. "These relics indicate strongly of Indians of the Southwest. I'd say pueblos. And, if I'm correct, the only time the girl wore her marriage costume was at her marriage and at her burial."

"So, you think the reason for the missing costume is because the girl died and was buried in it?"

"Perhaps," he conceded, "and as long as I'm surmising, I'd say she died in childbirth. This is a child's blanket and a doll." Carefully, he unfolded the child-size blanket.

The pattern was wide bands with a variety of complex weaving. Brett spread the blanket and laid the doll on it. It was a small figure. The feathers on the headdress had separated and crushed, but the lines marking the face were still sharp.

"This is too bewildering! These items tell a story that could be my own, except my parents aren't Indian? Tears of confusion glistened in her eyes.

"Yes, your mother was Spanish, and Adam was definitely not Indian, either," agreed Brett. He reached into the trunk and took out the final item from the trunk. It was a sturdy cardboard box that might have once held a thick textbook.

The box was full of notes and snapshots. But these pictures were of Indians. They were caught as they went about their daily work. Grain was being ground with stone implements and put into handwoven baskets. The faces were placid, innocent, and completely unafraid. The world was like another Garden of Eden inhabited by primitive Indians.

"Linda, the enormity of what these pictures suggest staggers me." Brett ran his hand through his thick red hair, reminding her of a rooster's comb. "This is evidence that Adam discovered a tribe of Indians that date far back to the Anasazi."

"*Anasazi* means 'the old ones', doesn't it?"

"Yes, it does. The *Anasazi* were the ones from which the tribes of the Hopi, Zuni and the Rio Grande people sprung." He chose a few of the pictures and handed them to Linda.

"The pottery in some of these pictures is the work of the Hopi. This piece in red and black on a white background with the deer motif is Zuni."

Linda nodded as he pointed out the differences. "So, you're saying that the tribe in these pictures is a group that somehow escaped being scattered and further divided down into smaller individual tribes?"

"It sounds incredible, I know, but this is an astounding amount of evidence pointing in that direction."

"And it must be burned." She was matter of fact, but she watched as anger flared on his face.

"It's not right!" He clenched his fist and then shoved it out of sight into his pocket. He read the sympathy on Linda's face and flushed hotly.

"Why don't you study the pictures a couple days before we destroy them." She knew that his torment was as great as hers.

"No." His temper had died. "If Adam wanted everything burned, then there's no use waiting." He fed the stack of pictures to the flame. The edges curled and blackened as the smiling faces of the primitive Indians disappeared. He turned his back on the fire.

"Brett, I must keep the picture of my mother." It was the pitiful plea of a lost child.

He slipped his arm around her waist and pulled her close to him as they stood facing the picture of Inez Grainger.

"Not even Adam could deny you that." He felt her relax.

Everything had been burned from the trunk that the fire would consume. Reverently, Brett put the things back into the trunk that they were going to keep: the wedding jar, the ceremonial sash, and the baby blanket with the doll. These things were like props from a play that had long been over.

The clock in the hall chimed again, reminding them that it would soon be dawn.

Linda said good night as they parted at her door. She carried the picture of her mother into the room and leaned it against the mirror of her dresser across from her bed.

She slipped off her black-and-white caftan and got into bed. The stimulant of their treasure hunt had worn off, and she felt the full effect of the light sleeping aid she had taken earlier.

The presence in the room with her was strong, but this time it wasn't overshadowed with evil. She was in a semi-conscious state and her eyelids were almost too heavy to hold open. But she thought she saw the figure of a girl, someone like her who's hair was black as a raven, standing at the foot of her bed. Instead of looking at her, the shadow girl was looking at the picture Linda had leaned against the mirror.

Linda wanted to speak out but couldn't. Somewhere in the distance she heard the noises from the valley—the rushing of the water and birds calling as they soared and circled.

Chapter 5

"Well, Miss Grainger, this shouldn't take long. Your father's will is not overly complicated." The lawyer's voice was nasal, which only aggravated its grating quality. There was some similarity to a sharp pointed object being scratched down a blackboard.

"Thank you, Mr. Rankin." She hoped she sounded calm. Not only did his voice grate on her tense nerves, but he talked in outline form. The combination of the two caused her to want to run from the room.

"Virtually, the will says: A. All cash, future royalties from books, and personal property except the house, be given to my only child, Linda Marie Grainger. B. The house is to be given to the University," he smiled apologetically. "I am, of course, giving you a simple translation of the document."

Linda met his eyes and raised her brows. "May I not read it?" Losing the house unnerved her. She was being thrown out on the street. Adam had never wanted her back in the house.

"Of course, Miss Grainger, we have a copy prepared for you." He indicated a brown manila envelope on his desk.

"Ahem." He cleared his throat. "There isn't much money, Miss Grainger. Everything that came in from his lectures and writing was channeled directly into the fund he had set up for your schooling. Originally, the fund was exceptionally large. He'd sold some art objects, I believe he said, to finance your education.

Now, it is nearly gone. What with, A. your schooling being so awfully expensive, B. your clothing allowance so generous, and C. the cost of boarding your horse. And to add to C., the purchase price of the horse."

She didn't know which upset her the most, his lapsing back into the outline conversation, his smirk, or the distasteful way he said *horse*. Edgar Rankin had handled the business of paying the bills of Adam Grainger's daughter with an accusing eye. She didn't trust herself to speak.

"I suppose a lovely young lady like yourself would make a lonely father very generous." He tried to smile. But the effort was too great.

"Mr. Rankin, if my father were lonely, it was his own fault. I never asked to be sent away and would have come back anytime. I never asked him for a thing. The horse was a Christmas gift." She kept her voice calm and well-modulated. It was a great effort, and she fought a painful tenseness at the base of her skull.

"Ah, yes, quite." He agreed politely, but it still sounded like an accusation. Her words had made no impression on him. He had disliked this unknown girl for years for draining the once-substantial account of his client. "Here is a balance sheet of the available cash. There is little. And, Miss Grainger, I have contacted the University. They have wanted this house for a long time and will take it over as soon as you can vacate. In addition, Miss Grainger, I am sure it would not be advisable for you and Mr. McAlister to reside in the same house too long. We are a small town, and the University is a smaller entity within that; so, there would be talk. His reputation with the faculty would suffer. Also, his students would suffer." The high-pitched voice softened, and his thin lips parted in a leer.

Linda glared at the poor specimen of manhood before her; dry, dull, and seeing things from only a twisted, male-dictated viewpoint. She knew he had never had a wife. The only Mrs.

Rankin would have been this man's mother, unless he'd sprung from the egg of some cold-blooded reptile.

"I'll have to see the furniture first." She was stalling for time.

Where would she go? The University would probably allow Brett to rent his room the remaining two months until his teaching contract was up, but she was an outsider. She had always been an outsider. Why had she thought that she could come back *home* and be welcome? Even from his grave, Adam was banning her from her childhood home.

"Perhaps the University will take the better pieces off your hands," he said. "It's a shame your father didn't include the gift of the house to include the furnishings," he continued matter-of-factly.

"Fortunately for me, he didn't." He felt the sting of her words and squirmed uneasily in his chair.

"One thing more, Miss Grainger." His voice took on strength as he abruptly changed the subject. "Shortly after news of your father's death was in the papers—and, Miss Grainger, it was noted in many papers across the country because your father was well-known in his field." He added his own comments in a forceful squeak. "Really, Miss Grainger, it was only a matter of hours until a telegram arrived for Miss Grainger, in care of Professor Adam Grainger's office at the school. Naturally, when it came to them, they hand-delivered it to me at my office."

"Naturally," she echoed. She was curious but wouldn't let this man know it.

He bristled." Well, Miss Grainger, it was perfectly logical. A. I am handling your father's estate, B. Your plane wasn't expected until the next day, and it was even late if you remember." He held the telegram but didn't extend it to her.

"Thank you for holding it for me." She stood and took the envelope from his slack fingers.

"Wouldn't you like to open it here before you go and see if it's something I can help you with?" His voice cracked in eagerness. It was probably an offer of sympathy from someone Dr. Grainger had worked with in New Mexico, but through the thin paper, he could tell it was a full paragraph of typing. He felt it was something more important.

Hardly anyone knew that Adam Grainger had a daughter. He was the one who called the newspapers with all the details; it was he who had been responsible for Professor Grainger's story being spread over the country. In life Professor Grainger's modesty had made him shy away from publicity; in death, Rankin wanted to make sure everyone knew the importance of his client.

"But I am sure you have helped me all that you can." She felt his eyes on her as she dropped the envelope casually into her purse. "When I've decided what to sell and what to keep, I'll phone you, so you may notify the University. If you have anything for me to sign, or if there is anything else you need to give me…", she let her voice drop as she prepared to leave.

"No, no need to keep you." His words were crisp now. He picked up the brown envelope and gave it to her. "I'll tie up the remaining loose ends."

"Thank you, Mr. Rankin." She even managed a smile which he didn't return.

She had spent most of her life covering intense feelings; it was no problem hiding hurt from this stranger.

Rankins' law office was within walking distance of the house. Brett had brought her, but she insisted she would walk back. Until the insurance company replaced her father's car, she would be without transportation.

She wasn't used to such inactivity. Back at school she exercised her horse for an hour every morning and every evening. With no outlet for the emotions raging within her, there was no wonder she was seeing things and hearing voices.

It was already April, but as Linda stepped out of the lawyer's office the rain still had the bite of winter. The cold felt good on her hot face. Her encounter with Rankin had cost her a great deal of strength. That despicable man had accused her of bringing her father financial hardship. He was saying she demanded exorbitant amounts for luxuries her father couldn't afford.

If she didn't work off some of her anger, she would explode. She even forgot the telegram that Rankin had given her so reluctantly.

It didn't take long to reach her father's house. She threw off her coat and undressed as she went toward her room. She stood in her underclothes as she searched in her suitcases for her jogging suit and sneakers. She'd run until the tension melted.

Her tears mingled with the rain as she stumbled out to the terrace and started toward the sidewalk that wound through the woods behind the house. She ran until her breath came in gasps, and she leaned heavily against a tree. When she regained her wind, she continued again at a slower pace. The rain and wind whipped at her hair. She could feel rivulets of water run from her hair down the neck of her jacket. The movement of her body felt good. It was a battle to run against the blowing rain. Her legs were beginning to feel heavy, and she was becoming overbalanced. She tripped and caught hold of a tree before she fell. There were concrete benches around a bandshell, and she sat down and put her head between her knees.

Her heartbeat slowed down and the pounding in her head stopped. She leaned back and closed her eyes. The rain was the only sound she heard.

"Is this a private torture session, or can anyone join in?" Brett's voice held no sympathy.

"You didn't have to come. How did you know where to find me?"

"I asked the paperboy who just came by on his delivery if he'd seen a girl. He said, 'Yeah, mister, if you mean the one with the gorgeous face and the body of wonder woman? She ran toward the woods in a jogging suit'." He did smile at her then.

"I'm glad you're here. I think I'll need assistance back," she said wearily. She stretched her hand toward him. "I'm too tired to fight with you."

He took her hand and pulled her against him, and she felt his lips hard against her own. That wonderful, heady feeling overcame her weariness.

He pushed her back and looked into her face. The rain had caused his hair to darken and a curl hung down on his forehead. Linda felt an odd stab in her heart. She raised her hand to his forehead and twisted the strand of hair around her finger, then lay her hand against the side of his face. She put her own lips against his.

He crushed her to him until she could hardly breathe. His lips were demanding. The intoxicating feeling seemed to fill up her whole being.

They stood in the rain, and he held her. She never wanted to move. When he spoke, his voice was unsteady. "You'll get sick out in this weather. You don't really have enough on." He unbuttoned his raincoat, took it off and slipped it around her. He kept his arm around her as they walked back through the woods to the house.

"I'm as strong as a horse," she denied. "I never get sick. I am getting cold, though." Her voice shook, but it had nothing to do with the cold.

They entered the kitchen and stood dripping water on the tile floor.

"Go get a hot bath and dressed up. I'll take you out for dinner." A smile played at the corner of his mouth. "I'm getting a little tired of warmed-over spaghetti." He kissed her quickly on the forehead and gave her a little push toward the door leading to the stairs.

The hot bath had been therapeutic. There was a sense of well-being and relaxation accompanying the physical exertion from the run in the woods. She had almost forgotten what had brought on the need for the vigorous exercise. She pushed the thoughts of the visit to the lawyer's office further to the back of her mind.

The realization that she might be falling in love with Brett gave her mixed emotions. With him, she felt too safe. When he kissed her, she wanted to cling to him and close out the world. Let him be her future, let her exist without knowing of her past. Just take his love and the family he offered and run.

But when she was alone, she knew that was impossible. What if she were unstable? She couldn't do that to Brett.

There was still the presence of the girl in her room. She hadn't seen her again, but she was there on the edge of her consciousness. Almost a part of herself. Brett had suggested she take her father's room downstairs, but she wouldn't run away. Once she'd been forced to leave by 'Uncle' Max, but she thought he had been wrong to suggest that her father send her away. It was something she had to face.

Perhaps, the only thing to face was her growing insanity. The possibility that Max had been right was becoming more and more evident. Removing her from this house only postponed her confrontation with the inevitable. With her limited knowledge, she couldn't ferret out the answer to her problem. Maybe somewhere in her past lay the explanation.

She stood before the mirror and fastened the coral earrings that matched her coral dress. She'd chosen the brightest color in her wardrobe to dispel the haunting feeling surrounding her. Her face in the mirror had the same shape and coloring, but her eyes were wide with a hint of shadow underneath. She had lost weight since she'd been in this house.

STANDING IN MY SHADOW

Brett was waiting for her at the foot of the stairs and held her raincoat for her. Then he handed her purse to her. "I found this on the floor by the door."

"I scattered several things in my hurry to change and get back outside." She smiled a little apologetically.

"Was the trip to the lawyer's office that bad?" he asked.

"That bad," she flared. "That Mr. Rankin is an infuriating man."

"Rankin has a reputation for disliking everyone except his clients. But he is the best in town." He locked the door as they left the house.

"Well, had the news he had to tell me been better, he wouldn't have enjoyed it quite as much," she retorted.

Brett laughed. It was an open, friendly sound, and she couldn't help smiling back.

"Brett, father left the house to the University."

"He what?" He was incredulous.

"It seems that when he sent me away to school, he never intended that I should come back to this house at all." The hurt in her voice registered on her face.

"Adam has gone to a great deal of trouble to hide something." Brett was thoughtful.

"Yes, probably that fact that my mother was insane. And the visions and voices that I hear in this house are due, somehow, to his thoughts of her!"

"Sweetheart don't be ridiculous," he snapped, bluntly. "You are being too hard on yourself."

"Brett," she said, suddenly gentle," maybe, you are the one deluding yourself. I've heard there is a fine line between genius and insanity."

"Are you a genius?" He asked. There was a hint of playful sarcasm in his voice.

"My intelligence quotient is high in the genius range." Her answer was apologetic.

"Well, personally, I think that old saying can be filed away with 'a whistling woman and a cackling hen are sure to come to some bad end'," he laughed. "Can you whistle?"

"Oh, Brett, be serious. I'm trying to begin to understand."

"Let's see if we can add some of my abundant common sense to your high IQ and come up with something reasonable. How about it?" He refused to take her seriously.

She sighed in surrender. "All right, you're on!"

"But, first things first. Such a heavy conversation can only be successful after we've eaten." He started whistling a tune and ignored her as she started to protest.

In the car, Linda leaned her head back on the headrest and closed her eyes. Brett was right. She was getting uptight again. She wanted to regain that relaxed feeling she had felt after her bath, but she couldn't very well jump out of the car and jog alongside. This would be all the evidence that Brett would need to be convinced she was crazy.

It was a little early for dinner, so the restaurant had few patrons. The waiter eyed Linda, smiled at Brett knowingly, and seated them in a back corner in a secluded area. Linda nearly giggled aloud when she caught the wink Brett gave the waiter.

She watched Brett lift the stained-glass globe off of the lamp on their table and strike a match to light the wick. When he replaced the globe, tiny irregular shapes of colored light spread over the white tablecloth.

"A little more atmosphere," he explained, tilting his head, and giving her his small, lop-sided grin.

Her heart did a funny flop, and she placed her hand on his. He turned his over and held her hand.

Linda had known instinctively that Brett would be a meat-and-potatoes man. His size would demand quantities of filling food. They studied the menus that the waiter brought.

"I'd like lamb chops, asparagus and a small tossed salad," she told Brett when he asked what looked good on the menu.

"That's not very much," he countered.

"But I'm going to have the strawberry shortcake for dessert," she said greedily, "with whipped cream."

The steak they brought Brett looked big enough for a family of four, and the baked potato must have been Idaho's biggest.

"You *are* hungry," she said in amazement.

"Hush, woman, and eat."

The meal was delicious. Linda found that her appetite was better than she had expected. Maybe Brett had been right about too much warmed-over spaghetti. The strawberry shortcake had been as good as she anticipated; and now they sat, contentedly, with their cups of coffee.

"Ok, tell me about your appointment with Mr. Rankin today." Brett was serious now. The tenderness in his voice caught her off-guard, and she had to wait until she could control her voice before she answered.

"It was really awful, Brett." She told him about the house again. She told him of the thinly veiled accusations from Rankin that she was the cause of her father being nearly bankrupt.

"Wait, Linda," he interrupted. "Those two actions conflict with each other. If on the one hand, Adam willingly spent everything he had to keep you in style in exclusive schools, why would he deny you ownership of the house. It makes no sense. The school would have been more than happy to buy it. He knew this, and he knew you would be able to use the money."

"But he didn't know that he would die so young. The accident caught him unprepared. He, no doubt, thought I'd be married and quite unconcerned with the house by the time he died."

"Or, he knew you would be finished with your schooling well able to support yourself," he reasoned.

"I have my diploma, but no defined career path," Linda said, bitterly. "Father wanted me to travel in high social circles. That is a little archaic for our modern age, wouldn't you say? I fought boredom as a constant foe. I overloaded my schedules, participated in the equestrian program; oh, Brett, I could go on and on. I've finished nearly half of my course work for a master's degree."

"Linda, you say you learned two things in Rankin's office: one, that the house is to go to the University immediately; and two, your father has very little money." He was counting the items on his fingers.

"There you go, talking like Rankin. Do you know that that despicable, little man communicated in outline?" Brett laughed at Linda's exasperation.

"Yes, I've heard him. He lectures on law as a guest speaker, occasionally."

"The powers-that-be at your University must be scraping the bottom of the academic barrel to come up with him."

"Many people, even the law students, sleep during the sessions."

"I can believe it," she sympathized.

Suddenly, Linda snapped her fingers. "Oh, Brett, I just remembered. He gave me a telegram that had been sent to Professor Grainger's daughter in care of the University. It had been forwarded to Mr. Rankin."

"That's rather a nebulous postal address. Who sent it?"

"I was so upset with the visit to his office that I forgot to look. Mr. Rankin was so curious that his eyes nearly bored through the envelope, but I dropped it into my purse right before his drooling stare!"

"You are a cruel woman," Brett moaned, as he rolled his eyes mockingly.

She bent over and took the yellow envelope from her bag and opened the seal carefully. She quickly scanned the contents, then started reading them again more slowly. "It looks like Mr. Rankin's suspicions were right. This is more than condolences from a far-away colleague." When she handed the telegram to Brett her hand was shaking.

Brett read the message aloud:

> To the daughter of Professor Adam Grainger. Until now unable to locate you to notify you of your inheritance from your mother, Inez Grainger: El ranchero de la casa amillaro, Dos Tigres, New Mexico. It is important that you come to Dos Tigres. Buyer interested in the property for developing dude ranch. Details to be worked out. Due to competition, it would be in your best interest to keep this secret.
>
> Please send reply as to time of your arrival to Straeder & Forest, Attorney-at-Law, P. O. Box 6441, Las Cruces, N.M.
>
> As soon as we hear from you, we'll arrange to meet you at the airport.

"Must have cost a lot to send this." Brett turned it over and looked at the back.

"This does answer one question. My mother is from New Mexico. A place called *Dos Tigres*," she spoke excitedly.

"But that's impossible." Brett's denial was flat.

"How can you be so sure," she demanded sharply.

"Don't look so stricken, Linda. Please?" Brett reached for her hand.

"But, how do you know? Is this your abundant common sense at work?" she snapped.

"There's no need to get a burr under your saddle, pardner," he drawled. "I'm on your side." His lop-sided smile softened his words."

She exploded. "Of all the conceit," Her words came out in a forced whisper.

Brett threw back his head and laughed until his eyes filled with tears. He wiped his eyes with the back of his hand. Linda couldn't resist smiling at his uncontrolled laughter.

"You don't mind telling me why Inez Grainger couldn't have come from *Dos Tigres*, do you?" Linda asked with exaggerated tolerance.

"How is your Spanish?" Brett asked.

"My French and Italian are fluent…"

"Don't brag, child," he interrupted.

"…but my Spanish is quite deficient. Enough for two tigers, though," she finished.

"Actually the 'tigres' mean mountain lions. *Dos Tigres* was a mining camp that got its name from a couple of prospectors. These two old fellows put up a shack, set up camp and worked the base of a mountain for several months. When they got back into town, the people asked them what they saw. One of the prospectors said they saw only two big cats. The other prospector was a Mexican, and he said '*solo, dos tigres*'. The name stuck. The skeletal frame of the prospectors' shack is all that remains to say they were there. About a mile around the base of the mountain toward the west is an adobe ranch house."

"Maybe this could be the one?" Linda asked.

"I'm afraid not, Linda. An old Mexican family has raised sheep on those scrubby acres for years. There were never any children there. And now they're gone. The only one whoever visited them was a priest from a Mexican village just across the Rio Grande."

"How far is *Dos Tigres* from your ranch?"

"Remember I told you the Crying Child Burial Mound was thirty-five miles from our ranch, the Circle Mc?" Linda watched him draw an imaginary 'Mc' within a circle on the tablecloth with his forefinger. "*Dos Tigres* is five miles further beyond that. What I didn't tell you is the thirty-five miles between the boundary of the Circle Mc and the Crying Child Burial Mound is nothing but desert—no road, no trail, just trackless sand. Beyond to *Dos Tigres* and the tiny ranch of the Mexicans, there is only enough scanty vegetation to keep a few sheep alive. I believe the lawyer to be mistaken as to the location. No one comes from *Dos Tigres*."

The waiter came to the table and asked if they'd like anything more. Brett accepted the check, "No, thank you. We're ready to go."

She could feel Brett close behind her as they left the restaurant. In the car as they started back toward Adam Grainger's house, Linda broke the silence.

"Brett, let me stay with you. I'll ignore the telegram from Straeder and Forest. We'll allow the secret of Adam Grainger to be buried with him and let the illusive memory of Inez Grainger be lost with her husband."

"What about the ghosts haunting Linda Grainger? How will we exorcise them?" Brett asked.

"I have to leave Adam's house anyway, and my ghosts seem to live there," she laughed a little shakily. She was glad for the darkness of the car.

"Linda, go to Las Cruces. Let Straeder and Forest show you the ranchero, wherever it is. See your mother's people, become familiar with her background."

Linda didn't answer. She couldn't. All she wanted were his arms around her, his voice urging her to stay. If she could only hear him tell her again that he loved her. But he was sending her away.

"Linda?" Brett's voice questioned.

"You're right, of course," she said, finally.

"I only wish that I could go with you. I can't now, but I'll follow when school is out." Brett's voice picked up strength as he made her plans. "We can both leave this place for good."

"I've no reason to stay since I have no home," she said.

"As soon as you find out the correct location of the ranchero, you can call and let me know. I know it can't be *Dos Tigres*. Then we can arrange our meeting place."

They were back at the house. When they walked in, Linda felt detached already. She was letting it go as she had been forced to do once before. Her father was betraying her from the grave.

And what did Brett want? She had asked to stay with him, but he refused. She couldn't believe it. Although he'd laughed when she told him Mr. Rankin was concerned over his reputation if she remained in the house too long, he seemed eager for her to go. She really had known him such a short time. But she knew that she could love him. His lop-sided smile tugged at her heart like a magnet. His slow way of talking and his soft slur that was sometimes a drawl were irresistible. Even the way he ran his hand through his hair was burned into her mind. The warm tender way he looked at her caused her defenses to melt. Yet, their conversations were lively and stimulating. Life with him would never be dull.

But maybe he had changed his mind. Perhaps, he was no longer willing to take a chance on her sanity. Dejected, she thought maybe he was giving her a chance to snap out of it or go on over the edge.

The look he gave her as he put his arms around her was full of love, but his kiss was restrained as he bade her goodnight. Coldness crept around Linda's heart. After holding men at arm's length all her life, the fear of losing the one she wanted left her desolate.

"Sleep well, darlin'." Brett kissed her forehead and held her against him a few seconds before he let her go.

As Linda turned to go up the stairs to her room, hot tears stung her eyes. She was uncertain now of his feelings for her.

There was a 'presence' waiting for her in her bedroom that was always welcoming. Linda walked to her room toward 'her friend' who would comfort her. With her she felt no terror. The one who called Linda *mi amiga* would always be faithful.

In the dark of her bedroom, Linda felt 'her friend'. She was in her mind reading her thoughts. Linda was communicating her plans to again leave this house—this time never to return. For now, this room was reality—all beyond the door was confusion and fantasy.

Chapter 6

How easy it had been! Although she thought it strange that Straeder & Forest instructed that a telegram be sent rather than a phone call, she sent one the following morning telling them which plane to meet in two days' time. With one phone call back to her school, she had arranged to sell her horse. Now that he was a champion, she had received a few offers. The last offer had been quite generous. The money would be wired, and it would be in her hands before she left. It would take all the cash she had now to purchase her one-way plane ticket to Las Cruces. The sale of the horse should give adequate funds for her immediate future.

The University would buy the house furnishings, except for the few things she was keeping. The money from the furnishings would at least pay for storage and shipping when she knew where to have the things sent. She wanted all of her father's books and the artifacts he had collected. She wanted the trunk in which they had found her mother's picture, and she was keeping her father's desk. No sentimentality about the desk, of course, but it had a roomy work surface, and the drawers were deep and spacious. She had liked how the light oak gleamed in the firelight.

Linda could see the sun glinting off of the wing of the plane. On past, toward the chain-link fence, she saw Brett still standing, looking toward the plane, searching for her in the windows. She waved, and she could see his answering smile as he lifted his hand.

It was all she could do to not run back down the ramp and beg him to let her stay. His body had been hard and demanding as he held her, and his kiss told her all she had longed to know in the past two days.

She was so shaken she couldn't answer him when she heard his husky, 'I love you' whispered into her ear. It was as though only at the airport, going beyond his reach, did he trust himself to speak again of his love.

The sun was riotous as it played in Brett's dark red hair. Linda watched him approach a flight attendant bound for her plane. He waved back at Linda as he handed the uniformed girl a large white envelope.

All the crew was on board now, and Linda watched as the plane turned its back on the airport and hurried once more into the sky.

Looking down, she saw the shadow of the plane on the ground grow larger and larger until it was stretched too thin to see—a smoky apparition blown away by the wind. The solid earth dissolved, and there was no support but the wings and the engine thrust.

The petite blond in her smart navy and white uniform had finished the oxygen mask demonstration, and the flight settled down.

"Miss Grainger, isn't it? I'm Ginger." The blond girl smiled.

"I'm Linda Grainger, yes." Linda returned her smile.

"A very handsome, red-haired man gave me this envelope for a Miss Grainger. He simply said, 'you can't miss her; she's easily the most beautiful creature you've ever seen.'"

Linda felt her face go hot with embarrassment, but the little stewardess just laughed.

"Thank you very much," said Linda, accepting the envelope.

Linda held the envelope for a few minutes thinking of Brett. She'd never expected to fall in love. Certainly, never this quickly. But she loved this man so much, it seemed unreal. Never had she anticipated such soul-shattering emotions. He hadn't even noticed that she never said that she loved him; he only wanted her to know of his love for her. She couldn't read the print as she opened the letter until she blinked away the tears blurring her vision. The writing was the familiar bold, black scrawl.

> **Linda, (did you know—with your 'elementary' Spanish that Linda means pretty?) I do agree, as you asked, not to tell my parents about you, but only until we meet as soon as I can get there. This may sound a little outmoded to you, but I'm anxious to introduce the woman I'm going to marry to my family. (They'd just about given up on me—Dad is despairing over the lack of a grandson to carry on the family name.) And what a grandson we'll present them! A very stalwart lad, inheriting his mother's beauty and brains along with his father's charm and common sense.**

Laughter escaped Linda, waking up the white-haired lady in the seat next to her. The lady frowned and closed her eyes again.

> **Seriously, I'm on bended knee asking you to marry me. I didn't ask you in person, because your responses are getting a little too much for me. We wouldn't want to shock poor Lawyer Rankin!**

Brett couldn't be serious.

The enclosed ticket is a claim check for a gift. It's on the plane with you. I hope you like the surprise.

Linda, I love you. I don't want you to think I'm shrugging off your problem. You aren't insane. We'll find the girl standing in your shadow. You've been under a great deal of strain and are entitled to mixed-up dreams and an imaginary friend or two for comfort. If we can't do it ourselves, we'll get help. Just let me be with you. Brett

Tears of happiness flowed softly down her cheeks. She lay her head back and closed her eyes. Never had she been so happy in her life; it was like a warm glow. She could have floated along without the airplane.

"Miss Grainger, are you all right?" Ginger, the flight attendant, asked softly as she leaned over the sleeping lady.

"I'm ecstatic, Ginger," Linda whispered back. She lifted the pages in her hand. "That handsome, red-haired man wants me to marry him."

"Congratulations!" She whispered loudly. The old lady stirred but didn't awake. "Are you going to accept?" she teased.

"You bet," she agreed. But as she said it, a cloud of doubt emerged.

Ginger winked like a conspirator as she brought their luncheon trays. Linda couldn't force down much food.

The layover was nearly an hour. First, Linda chose a postcard and mailed it to Brett. She couldn't put her feelings on paper. She would wait until she saw him again. Little shivers of anticipation tickled her stomach as she thought of what that would mean. Linda walked from shop to shop within the terminal. It felt good to move around, and it helped keep her mind off the meeting with Straeder & Forest in only a couple more hours.

Skyborne again, Linda was fascinated with the earth below. There was no preparation for the sight she was seeing now. The mountains below were red, their varying heights indicated by blackness splashed across in random patterns. If the plane went down, all could be lost forever on the edge of one of those shadowed valleys. The vastness was overwhelming. It was no wonder stories of unknown creatures like bigfoot living a secreted existence for a millennium in this endless red wasteland were never disproved. An exploration party couldn't live off these barren lands, and they could never carry in enough supplies to penetrate all the mysteries and secrets this land protected.

It held her origins secret. In thirty more minutes, the plane would circle a city and land. Then she would do battle to try and wrest the knowledge she needed from a long-dead past. Yet, in this ageless expansion, twenty years was merely a glance over one's shoulder.

The pilot interrupted her thoughts with the ground temperature and the time. Lights in the city below were like dim star pinpoints in a twilight sky.

Linda slipped into the matching cream-colored jacket of her pantsuit and adjusted the braided fastener just below the brown fox collar. She unzipped a compartment in the carry-on travel bag and found her luggage claim check. She held the 'surprise' claim check from Brett, too.

The pilot had given the time at 6 p.m., and now the clock in the terminal showed 6:20. Linda wondered if the man from Straeder & Forest who was meeting her minded working overtime. She walked up the blue concourse and looked around. Her fellow passengers were met in the usual ways—a kiss, a handshake, a hug, or a friendly slap on the back. Now, no one was left. The blue vinyl benches were empty except for discarded reading material that had filled in the time for those waiting.

"Paging Miss Linda Grainger. Will Miss Grainger please come to the Information Desk?" The message was repeated again before she could get to the desk.

"I'm Linda Grainger."

"There's a message for you."

"Thank you." This certainly was her day for envelopes.

The chubby girl at the Information Desk enviously eyed the expensive pantsuit on the slim figure of the beautiful girl who accepted the letter. She hated people who had everything: this girl could only be a model on her way to her next glamorous assignment. The clerk turned away abruptly.

The envelope felt a little thick.

Linda wondered when she opened it if an 'instant' man from Straeder & Forest would materialize. Inside, a few colorful brochures of the area were attached to a bus ticket.

The note was professionally apologetic. The type was crisp and clear:

> Dear Miss Grainger:
>
> An emergency has prevented me from meeting your plane. I do hope that you will excuse me. I have planned for us to meet with the potential buyer tomorrow evening. The enclosed ticket will get you to the town nearest your property. I'll meet you there.
>
> I have taken the liberty of making your room reservation near the bus station. You will find the address attached to the ticket.

Again, please forgive any inconvenience this may have caused you.

Sincerely,

Samuel Straeder

Well, that was that. Stranded. At least she wouldn't be out the expense of the bus ticket. It was a shoddy way to do business. But what could be expected of a law firm that had taken twenty years to find a missing heir?

A flash of red caught her eye.

"Porter?"

"Yes, ma'am." The young porter had been walking back and forth, hoping this great-looking girl needed help. She had been too absorbed in what she was reading to look up before.

Linda smiled. What she needed was to come in contact with another human being. She felt like she had been pushed out of a spaceship, free floating alone in an empty universe. "Will you get my luggage and help me find a taxi?"

"Yes, ma'am! If you'll wait here, I'll get your bags." He took the claim checks she held out to him, and she watched him disappear in the crowd milling about the claim area. She walked across the aisle to the bookstand and bought a couple of paperbacks and a newspaper.

She'd tried Brett's cell phone several times, and it kept going to voice mail. It only added to her confusion.

Linda saw the porter rolling her baggage toward a pair of double glass doors through which she could see a waiting taxi. He had wasted no time. Quickly, she went toward the door.

She tipped the young man generously and was rewarded by more smiles and 'ma'ams'. The young man made her feel as ancient as the Indians in her father's pictures. She couldn't be three years older than he.

It was completely dark now, and the taxi driver was silent as he drove through the rush hour traffic. The trip wasn't a very long one. The motel was a well-lighted, family type. As the cabby deposited her luggage in her room, she could hear the excited laughter of children in a vacation mood. It buoyed her own spirits.

A strange rectangular object was sitting next to her large suitcase. It was covered with a blue terrycloth wrapper with a metal handle sticking up through a slit. Brett's present? She bent down and carefully pulled off the blue cover. It was a cage and inside a white ball of fur was sleeping peacefully in a corner. A sign was fastened to the wire: *Hi, I'm an unnamed, eight-week old little boy. (I'm trained to a paper.) Sorry you had to sell your horse.*

She lifted the puppy out of the cage. "Oh, you darling!" At the sound of her voice, a little pink tongue touched her neck and a cropped tail wiggled. A button nose shone as black as his eyes. The tiny terrier was fully awake now and nibbled playfully at her fingers.

The dog was only a handful of white fluff with pale pink skin showing through the soft hair. A narrow, red leather collar was fastened around his neck. Linda had never held anything so delicate in her hands before that was alive. The backs of the small triangular ears were covered with black hair and a black marking on his face curved around the right eye, looking like a question mark. The inquisitive-looking face made her laugh. The puppy looked up and barked sharply at the sound of her laughter.

"Oh, ho, sir! I'm glad to meet you, too. It's a good thing this is a dog-friendly motel. Will you have dinner with me? Come to think of it, I'm starved. I'll be back shortly with our dinner." Gently, Linda put the puppy back into the crate.

After changing into jeans and a pullover, she washed her hands and splashed cool water on her face. Her spirits were rising.

The telephone sitting on the desk caught her eye. Maybe she'd try to call Brett again later. Just to hear his voice. She would opt for a postcard of thanks for the tiny terrier. When she finished brushing her hair, she sat at the desk and hastily wrote a note on the postcard provided by the motel.

> *Dear Brett, Slight mix-up in scheduling forces me to spend the night. But I am not alone—thank you very much for the friend you gave me. I'm naming him 'Cómo'. (Isn't cómo the correct word in Spanish?) He looks like he's asking a question when he looks at me. I'll try to call you again after my meeting with Mr. Samuel Straeder and the buyer. Love you, too. Linda*

She was able to buy a stamp and mail the postcard from the motel restaurant. The restaurant menu offered roast beef sandwiches; so, she ordered two, thinking of sharing with little *Cómo*. She added a carton of milk, coffee, and an apple. She asked for extra paper napkins and hurried back to the room.

Cómo was waiting for her and licked her fingers eagerly as she unfastened the latch on the carrying case. He tumbled out of the metal cage, righted himself to a sitting position and looked up at her questioningly. In the light from the lamp, the black hair in the configuration of a question mark stood out boldly on the white hair of his face.

"Oh, *Cómo!*" Linda couldn't help laughing.

He tilted his head to one side and barked once.

"I know, I know. It isn't nice to laugh at you, but you are such a curious-looking puppy, Mr. How?"

They finished their supper, and Linda snapped the braided leather leash to *Cómo's* collar. An attractive garden and dog walk were behind the motel. *Cómo* had proven he was trained on her evening newspaper, but it wasn't too soon to introduce him to the outdoors.

Cómo had no more endurance than any other baby puppy. He snuggled into a soft towel that she used to make him a bed and slept early.

The warm water from the shower was relaxing, and the heat from the blow drier made her drowsy. It took more time to dry her hair now. She had missed an appointment to have it cut when she rushed to her father's funeral, and her hair was longer than the brief cap style she had worn since childhood.

Her sleep was deep and restful, free from the valley scenes that had flashed into her dreams by an uncontrollable subconscious. She went to sleep with a smile of contentment on her lips thinking of Brett. Never again would she return to her father's house where voices and faces from the past haunted her. The last thing she heard as she drifted off was *Cómo* barking softly in his sleep.

Linda overslept. She had to dress hastily to have time to feed and walk *Cómo*. With another bus ride ahead of her, she decided on a tailored denim pant suit with a waist-length jacket. Beneath the jacket she wore a white, short-sleeved sweater that she hoped would be warm enough. The leather beret matched the vivid shade of red as that of her shoes and carry-on bag.

Cómo was allowed to ride in his carrying case safely tucked under her seat. The next leg of her journey by bus was made in relative comfort; but it was early enough yet, so that they left long before dawn. And as they left the station, there was little traffic on the streets, nor much activity anywhere. Linda's fellow passengers filed onto the bus in shadows and retreated into their own worlds. The large man sitting behind her slept immediately, snoring loudly.

The comforting thoughts of Brett that had lulled her to sleep dimmed in the cold darkness of morning. Reality was harsh. She was traveling several miles west to meet a lawyer and sell property that would cut her off from anything tangible that had belonged to her mother. But, perhaps, there would be someone she could find who remembered Inez Grainger. She didn't know her mother's name before she was married, and that would hinder her questioning.

The morning sky was washed in a pale, colorless light. Then, suddenly, the sun appeared from behind a mountain peak; and in its brilliant illumination the black and white landscape took on a wide spectrum of color. The rich, warm cinnamon of the sand stretched to the deep red wall of the mountains in the distance, and the jagged mountain tops cut into the vibrant blue curtain of heaven. Not a wisp of white marred the smoothness of the sky.

Linda had never traveled West. The desolate beauty of the desert struck a responsive chord, spreading within her a sense of well-being. She was glad that her fellow passengers were asleep, leaving her alone to revel in her new-found universe. Her self-assuredness and resolve came back to her strongly, and she felt in charge of herself and her destiny. She was more than capable of dealing with lawyer Straeder, and she couldn't be forced into selling the ranchero at *Dos Tigres* if she decided to keep it.

She hadn't much money after the expenses, but there were no debts. Perhaps she would just stay at the ranchero and wait for Brett; he would come and take her to meet his family. In a year or so, she would be ready to go back to finish her master's degree. But now in her immediate future, she could envision them researching her background and investigating archaeological findings on the Circle Mc while he taught at the nearby university. This could be another fantasy!

The bus driver called out as he swung out the door toward the restaurant.

They had been traveling for over an hour, and everyone was eager to get off the bus. For many passengers this was the end of their journey.

Linda waited until the bus had emptied and pulled the small cage from under her seat. She took off the blue terrycloth cover and was greeted by a yawning *Cómo*. The hum from the bus motor had kept him sleeping peacefully.

"Hello, little fellow. Are you ready for breakfast and a stroll?" She got the braided leash from her travel bag and snapped it to the collar of the drowsy terrier. The puppy blinked in the bright sunlight. The air was considerably warmer, and Linda left her jacket on her seat.

She walked *Cómo*, gave him a handful of dry puppy food, fresh water and put him into his cage where he chewed happily on the corner of his blanket. There was still plenty of time for her own breakfast.

The restaurant was part of the tiny bus station and by the time Linda got there, it was crowded.

"Miss, you're welcome to share my table." It was the bus driver. "It's pretty crowded in here this morning. The town is so small that if any of the locals eat breakfast here when the bus comes in, the place is overrun. And the bus coming, even this late in the morning, can be the highlight of their day."

"Thank you." Linda liked the driver. He was a medium-sized man that you might overlook in a group of people. His face was lined in pleasant lines that deepened when he smiled. The squint lines around his eyes were, no doubt, caused by his occupation.

The waitress brought a menu.

"The breakfast special is good," the driver said. His own plate was empty, and he sat lingering over his coffee.

"The breakfast special it will be then." Linda handed the menu back to the girl. "Hot tea, please, instead of coffee."

"A tea-drinker, are you?" The bus driver teased. "You must come from back East; we Westerners like our coffee hot and black."

"Of course, I guess it shows. This is my first trip West. And I must say that I love the country I've seen so far."

"I've lived here all my life, driven this route almost fifteen years; and I never tire of this country. The last leg of this route is the most spectacular. Here's your breakfast."

Linda moved her teacup back, and the waitress sat the laden plate before her. The steak and eggs were accompanied by fried potatoes and crisp triangular pieces of buttered toast. "It looks delicious. I didn't realize how hungry I was."

The bus driver was right. The beauty of the next hundred miles was like water to a thirsty man. There were very few passengers going on to the next stop, and Linda had the seat to herself. She kept her face turned toward the window and the unusual panorama it offered. The towns fell away, leaving only this gray ribbon of highway that allowed the bus to trespass through the trackless desert. A shimmering haze seemed to rise from the road with a mesmerizing effect. Linda slept.

She drew herself erect and looked at her watch. After such a heavy breakfast, she had slept through the luncheon stop. The bus was now pulling up in front of a small adobe café. The last stop on this bus's run was a tiny village hugging the border into Mexico; and a middle-aged Mexican couple were the only other passengers to get off with Linda. The driver quickly deposited the luggage from the bus inside the café that served as a bus station. He waved his hand in farewell as he headed back north toward the border.

She was in the desert so near Mexico! She looked at her cell phone. No service. How would Brett ever find her.

The sun was bright, but the heat wasn't too intense, yet. The poverty of the tiny village was on display in the harsh sunlight. In these rough surroundings, the denim pantsuit that Linda had thought casual, looked stylishly elegant. She took off the leather beret and pushed it into her travel bag.

"Well, *Cómo*, our journey's end," she sighed. The terrier sat close to her shoe, blinking in the bright sunlight. "Let's see if Mr. Samuel Straeder can be found inside the café." She scooped up the tiny dog and walked into the dimness of the adobe building.

The middle-aged Mexican couple that got off of the bus ahead of Linda were met by a swarm of children who had lovingly greeted them and followed them into the café. They all lined up at the bar and immediately engaged in animated conversation with the proprietor. The words were spoken so rapidly that Linda couldn't pick out one word of what was said. She noticed that they stole glances in her direction.

Two men were seated at a table; the one with his back to her wore a brown belted garment that could only be a clerical robe.

"*Señorita?*" The expression on the moon-shaped face of the rotund man behind the counter was as questioning as his voice. "May I assist you?" His drooping mustache spread in an accommodating fashion across his upper lip as he smiled.

"Yes, I hope so. I'm looking for a Mr. Samuel Straeder?"

"*Señor* Straeder? I don't believe I know an *hombre* by this name?" The man scratched his head in puzzlement. He looked over toward the two men and raised his voice.

"*Padre*, are you acquainted with a *Señor* Samuel Straeder?"

Behind her there was the sound of chair legs scraping against the plank flooring of the café.

"Thank you," Linda turned from the proprietor to face the priest.

Linda waited for the priest to speak to her, but he was intently studying her face. The color of his face was either that of illness or a face gone pale beneath a tan. The priest swayed slightly and his companion steadied him. Surely strangers in this town weren't that uncommon.

"*Padre,* are you ill?" The proprietor was instantly concerned.

"No, no, Pepe," he answered, but his voice wasn't very convincing.

"Father, I'm Linda Grainger and I was supposed to meet a Mr. Samuel Straeder in Las Cruces. But in Las Cruces I was further instructed to meet him here."

"I see." The priest's voice was completely steady again, but his face still had a strange pallor.

I'm beginning to think this is a big mistake." Linda felt anger rising.

The priest dismissed his companion, and the proprietor went back to the family he had been talking with a few minutes earlier.

"There's no mistake, Miss Grainger. If you'll accompany me to my house, you and I'll talk of Sam Straeder. Adella will fix us lunch."

"Then you are acquainted with the law firm of Straeder & Forest?" Linda was vastly relieved.

"Miss Grainger, after lunch you will meet Sam Straeder." Whatever shock the priest had suffered from the mention of the name Straeder had passed. He was in full control of himself, and he picked up her luggage. It was a short walk from the café to reach the neat, yellow house that nestled in the shadow of the small adobe church building. He opened an ornamental iron gate that led into a small courtyard at the front of the house. A tree shaded a stone bench, and there was a rock garden.

"It's lovely here, Father.""

"Thank you, Miss Grainger. I've been fortunate to be able to call this home for a long time," he answered.

Adella served lunch quietly. The priest spoke only in Spanish to her. She disappeared after the food was on the table, and Linda heard a door close.

"Do you like our lamb stew, Miss Grainger? It's one dish at which Adella excels." The priest was eating little.

"Delicious," Linda agreed, politely.

"Sam Straeder has arranged to meet with you at two o'clock." The priest was casual with his announcement. He must have given Adella a message to summon Straeder. He was evidently in town only briefly to meet her since no one but the priest seemed to know him.

"Oh, then, I haven't much time. She turned her wrist so she could see her watch.

He waved her back into her seat. "You will only need go next door to the church to meet him."

Linda now stood on the front steps of the church. She had left *Cómo* with the priest, and she felt strangely alone. But soon, very soon, she would have an answer to the question of the yellow ranch house that was supposed to be at *Dos Tigres*. The glint in the priest's eye had been enigmatic, and Linda thought he could tell her far more than he pretended.

Evidently, Mr. Straeder worked in town occasionally, so he rented a spare room from the church. The parish could probably use the money. Linda walked down the wide aisle between the pews. She turned left at the altar and went down a dim hall that led to a closed door. She used the key he had given her and went inside to wait for the lawyer.

It was definitely a law office. The bookshelves behind the desk attested to that fact. A framed certificate on the wall declared that Samuel B. Straeder was a graduate of a fine law school nearly forty years ago. The room was dim because the only illumination came from a skylight in the ceiling. The other door leading out was a solid paneled one with no glass, and there were no outside windows.

The room was sparsely furnished: there was a heavily carved desk with a lamp and between the desk and bookshelves, a leather chair. The only other furniture was a straight-back chair against the wall. Even in this poor light, Linda could see that everything was covered in a thick layer of dust. If Straeder were an itinerant lawyer, it had been a while since his last trip.

There was a scraping of a key being fitted into the door at the back of the room. Linda couldn't see the man's face clearly because he turned to relock the door. In the shadowy gloom she noted an average-sized man in a business suit with a small bundle in one arm.

He stooped and placed the wriggling bundle on the floor. *Cómo* ran to her barking happily.

"*Cómo?* What are you doing here?"

The figure came from the shadows to stand behind the desk and turned on the lamp so the light cut through dimness, clearly exposing the identity of the man who had come into the room.

"Father," Linda questioned," is this some kind of joke?"

He ignored her remark, but extended his hand, "Miss Grainger, I am Sam Straeder."

Chapter 7

"What's going on?" Linda stammered.

"No joke, I assure you, Miss Grainger. Let me explain."

"Please do."

"Maybe you should sit down," he indicated the chair in front of his desk. "I'm an attorney, but I no longer practice law. My last client hired me to find the daughter of Inez Grainger, so that the property could be settled. The task was never completed, until now, and so the case remained open."

"Why did it take so long to find me?" she asked.

"It was by accident that I've found you now. I saw the notice of your father's death. I recognized his picture, but he had changed his name from when my client gave it to me. I saw he was survived by a daughter. Then when I went looking for information on you, I saw your picture on a magazine cover."

So, was there a reason her father had tried to keep her out of the public eye? Did he want to keep her away from her mother's family?

She shoved these thoughts aside and thought of what the priest had confessed.

"But they called you *padre*?" She puzzled.

"I am also a priest. I actually do perform the tasks of a priest required by the people of my parishes. Maybe I'm not the best choice for a priest, but no one else wants to come to this desolate outpost. I do hope that you'll keep my little secret."

"I really don't care," Linda retorted. "And besides, I know no one to tell that they have a 'fake' priest among them. That's on your conscious."

Sam Straeder laughed.

"So true. But my conscious swallowed that fact a long time ago," he admitted.

"All that I'm interested in, Mr. Straeder, is the property left to me by my mother. I'd like to see it before I decide to sell."

"Yes, I have someone who has wanted to buy it for a long time. I had to find you first. She is unable to make the trip, so we'll have to go to her. But, as for seeing your property, that will be easy. It's the house next door to our little chapel."

Linda waited before she answered to let this information make sense.

"But you said it was your house," Linda protested.

"No, Miss Grainger, I said I had been privileged to live in it for several years. I was given permission to stay here until the heir was located. An unoccupied house doesn't fare well on its own. I hope you can see that I've taken the best of care of it. Left alone, the desert animals would have taken up residence."

"You said you have a potential buyer? It's so far removed from civilization that I'm surprised anyone knows about it," her remark was biting.

"Ah, Miss Grainger, what is civilization? Where can you find civilization?"

He gazed over her head for a few minutes.

"Civilization," he finally continued, "has many definitions. But, of course, I know what you mean. Access to technology and all that it can bring. Conveniences. People rushing everywhere."

"No need to be patronizing, Mr. Straeder. I know the definition of civilization. I know that it builds generation upon generation. One culture's civilization can be defined by parameters other than our own," she responded sharply. "And I'm not addicted to my cell phone."

"My apologies, Miss Grainger, I didn't mean to sound condescending. I don't get a chance to wax philosophical very often. Forgive me," he chuckled. "And to use the phrase 'wax philosophical' puts me in another generation if not another century."

"Perhaps, we should start again," Linda offered.

"Yes, let's. Let me change back into being a 'priest' and meet you outside. Would you like a tour of the house?"

"Yes, thank you. I'd like that very much."

Linda could hardly wait to look around the house for any clues. Maybe there would be pictures on the wall. She would like to find out as much as she could without asking this lawyer turned pseudo-priest. She didn't think she could trust him to be truthful with his answers. Would he be answering as a priest or as someone just trying to sell her house. If she sold the house, where would he go? More importantly, if she decided to keep it could she get him to move out of it?

It didn't take Straeder long to meet her in front of the house.

"I neglected to ask you about your family. Will there be other heirs? A brother? A sister?"

"No one. It was only my father and I. His parents were killed in an automobile accident while he was still in high school. I never knew them. And, he was an only child," she answered.

"And what about a boyfriend, a fiancé? A lovely girl like you," he pressed for answers.

Linda's suspicions gelled into a warning. She would keep Brett to herself. She didn't know why, but it seemed to be important to him that she be on her own.

"Quite alone. But I'm sure that I can handle my future," she kept her response light.

"I am quite sure you can. I sense fire along with determination. Shall we start our tour?"

A wide verandah fronted the house, traveling around the side toward the chapel. Six pillars of stacked sandstone acted as support for the roof of the verandah. Random stones had been sanded smooth and were fitted together to form an intricate pattern on the floor. Colors all blended from pale yellow to a dusty gold. Occasionally, the sun sparked off of a piece of gold quartz embedded in a stone, making the floor shimmer as in a mirage.

Linda looked at the house through new eyes. Had her mother lived here? Someone had certainly loved the place. The outside was not only in good repair, but the landscaping spoke of the best the desert had to offer. Because of an underground watering system, plants not native to the surrounding desert thrived.

Lunch had been served to them on the verandah, so she had not seen much of the house. They stepped off of the verandah through the wide intricately carved wooden door into the wide expanse of the living area.

"How cool it is in here," Linda commented.

"Yes. Here in the desert we use a different kind of air conditioning. We have what is called evaporative cooling that uses the fact that water absorbs large amounts of heat in order to evaporate. The temperature of dry air can be dropped significantly through what's called the phase transition of liquid water to water vapor," he explained.

"Oh, you are just adding moisture to this dry air?" she asked.

"Yes, that's about it," he responded. "I have an errand that has come up unexpectedly. Why don't you look around? Take notes. Just prepare to ask any questions that you have. I won't be long."

"I will, thank you. Don't feel like you need to hurry," she answered.

She was glad to have the time alone. So much called to her from the furnishings in this living area. It was like a museum.

Woven tapestries depicting tribal scenes from the lives of an ancient people. Brett had called them Anasazi, early Pueblo. Shelving lined one wall, holding tightly woven baskets decorated with dancing animals. Black and white seemed to be the colors of choice for these ancient artisans. There was another two-spouted pitcher like the one she and Brett had found in her father's trunk.

Pottery of different sizes and shapes filled one shelf. These were entire pieces without cracks, chips, or flaws of any kind. Some modern-day potter had adapted and excelled in these reproductions. Even as copies, they seemed museum worthy.

Polished pine flooring stretched through the main living area with additional tapestries woven with heavier threads for use as rugs. The furniture was masculine. A large, leather sofa flanked by two matching armchairs was positioned at a comfortable angle before the deep, sandstone fireplace. Throw pillows on the sofa again covered in woven cloth. Deep vivid colors slashed through these coverings, adding interest to the rich brown of the leather cushions of the furniture.

But something was missing. There were no personal touches. No pictures. It was as though a hand had come through and cleaned away any possible introduction to those who lived here. Maybe Straeder had no family. No one he cared to memorialize in pictures.

Adella wasn't in the kitchen. It bore no resemblance to the front of the house. Here nothing but modern appliances. Black stainless-steel appliances sat on a Mexican floor tile. Mesquite wood cabinets was the nod to their location. They had aged enough to have faded to their characteristic reddish baked sandstone color. Granite backsplash and cabinet tops were buff with corresponding flecks of sandstone.

Linda became more puzzled as she explored the hacienda. No expense had been spared, but where did the money come from. Surely, there was a mystery here. Another set of questions. But she couldn't ask Straeder where the money had come from. Her only business was to either sell the house or keep it.

The time change, the lack of rest and the unanswered questions descended all at once. She climbed the stairs at the back of the main area to the landing above. Her things had been taken to one of the two bedrooms. She walked into the bedroom closest to the chapel where her luggage still sat unopened. A noise drew her to the window that looked out toward the small chapel.

For whatever reason, she didn't want to be seen. Straeder, in his priest persona, stood talking with a small man at the chapel door. He was waving his arms, and the man stood his ground shaking his head.

Stepping close to the window, she could only hear bits of the loud discussion. An argument really.

"I told you I can't take any more right now!" The padre was adamant. "Zuni? Are you sure?" He was changing his mind. "Well, it will be risky. I will take them, but this has to be the last until I tell you it's safe to start again. We can only introduce a few new ones at a time," the priest conceded. "Bring them as usual, after dark."

"*Sí* padre. This will be the last until you say. It is getting harder anyway," the little man agreed.

Linda stepped back before they looked up at the window. She took off her shoes and lay on the bed. Her head began to pound. *What had she heard? Was he heading some kind of smuggling operation of Indian artifacts? Maybe this was why there seemed to be so much money! That would explain the items in the living area. They were genuine! What had she stumbled into?*

She closed her eyes against the evening sun streaming through the window. Weariness was stronger than her fear, and she slept.

A knock on her door awakened her.

"Miss Grainger?" It was Straeder.

"Yes, just a minute," she answered, then opening the door slightly.

"Adella has prepared the evening meal. We can talk while we eat," he suggested.

"Fine. I'll be down in just a few minutes," she agreed.

She was cut off. She was alone. There was no cell phone signal, so she couldn't call Brett. She definitely wouldn't be asking questions that would make Straeder suspicious of her. She would see the buyer in the morning, sell her house and let her own background stay buried. The girl in her shadow would just have to stay there unidentified.

The meal was an empanada. The dough was tough and the filling a mystery. He had been right when he said Adella's lamb stew was her best offering. But what did a Mexican peasant know of Spanish cooking? It didn't matter. She had little appetite. But the cool water and the fruit were welcome.

"I've decided to sell, Mr. Straeder. The house is lovely, but it is in too desolate an area for a girl alone," she began their conversation.

"That's probably wise. And, please, call me Sam," he offered.

"Sam, then," she agreed. "What time did you say we could meet with the client in the morning?"

"Ten o'clock. We can conclude our business, and you can still catch the bus back to civilization," he said, lightly.

She laughed at his attempt at humor.

"Sounds like a good plan. Before retiring, I'll walk to the cantina and purchase my ticket. *Cómo* would appreciate the outing. He's been neglected a little."

"Be sure and be back before dark," he warned. "I'm afraid we have predators around here that would make a meal of him. Some can come swooping down from the sky," he warned.

"I'm sure we'll be fine. We won't be gone long. The cantina can be seen from here."

She clipped the leash to the little red collar and walked across the verandah. She was sure she would be carrying *Cómo* back. His little legs would wear out just walking to the cantina.

When she opened the door to the little cantina, the proprietor was there alone.

"Señorita, did you find your Mr. Straeder?" He asked.

"Yes, thank you, I did. The padre had arranged for him to see me. What time does the first bus come by tomorrow? The padre said I could purchase a return ticket here," she asked.

"Manãna at two o'clock. Would you like to purchase one?" He pulled out his booklet of tickets.

"Yes, please. I won't be able to leave until two, anyway," she answered.

She pulled her wallet out to pay for the ticket.

A feeling of dread washed over her. *What if something prevented her from getting to the bus by two? The buyer could be late. Anything could happen.*

"Would you make sure this letter goes out on the bus tomorrow. Just in case I am delayed until the next bus?"

"*Sí* señorita. I'll be glad to handle that for you. It will be the last bus this week."

She handed him a tip along with the letter she had prepared. She hoped Brett would get the letter before he left. She would stay in Las Cruses and wait for him.'

"I should see you tomorrow," she said.

She waved goodbye and picked up *Cómo*.

"Manãna, señorita," he said. Then he turned back to the bar, stuffing the money into his pocket.

She returned to the hacienda before dark. It was a pleasant site. The house gleamed in the last rays of sunset, shimmering as gilded in gold.

Her inheritance. Her link to her past. She would sell. If Brett had changed his mind about her, she would find another future. After all, they had known each other such a short time. Oh, he had declared he loved her through her father. But after he met her, he said, there was no doubt. He had said that he thought God had created her just for him. Did she believe anything like that? He had a vibrant faith, but would that even be possible? She did have strong feelings for him, but maybe it was her longing for security and family. He was offering family. Five sisters!

Sam wasn't around, so she went to her room to pack. Little *Cómo* was snuggled in his cage. The trip to the cantina and back was exhausting for him.

She slipped out of her room and went down the stairs and outside on the verandah. The sun was down. Coolness had descended with the sunset. She pulled her jacket more closely around her shoulders.

"Beautiful this time of evening, isn't it," Sam said.

She was startled.

"Sorry, if I scared you. In this time of evening, one doesn't need to speak loudly," he apologized.

"I guess that's true if you're expected," she retorted.

"I'm sorry. I did frighten you," he apologized, again.

"Not really. Just lost in my own thoughts."

"Shall we go in? I'd like to go over the points of the sale."

She walked in through the verandah door that he held open for her.

A small fire was in the large fireplace, taking the chill off of the room. They settled in the chairs before the fire.

"The sale is simple, really. The buyer is a woman by the name of Elena Cortez. She owns adjoining land, and she has always wanted to add this property to hers. She was, actually, the client who sent me in search of your father over twenty years ago. When she knew your father, he went by the name of Alan Griffin. It seems he kept his initials, but for whatever reason, he changed his name. He was lost to us."

"He must have had his reasons," she defended.

"Yes, I'm sure he did. But it's no matter now. We have found you."

"So, it seems," she agreed.

The night was turning into one full of mystery. She would not let him know how deeply this had affected her. *Had she known her father at all?*

"Well, back to the terms of the sale. It will be a cash sale, and the offer is quite generous," he continued.

He offered the sales contract to her.

"The offer is quite generous. I wouldn't think that a property this far out in the desert would attract many buyers," she puzzled. "But it is a lovely home. The furnishings and artwork are quite outstanding."

"They're not genuine, you know," he explained. "But the reproductions are quite beyond reproach. It has taken years for me to collect even these replicas."

Something in the tone of his voice wasn't right. His tone was heavy with the guilt that he felt downplaying these copies. Suddenly, Linda knew that they were originals. Not one of the artifacts displayed was an imitation. Fear gripped her. She wanted tomorrow to be over. She wanted to leave this place.

"I knew your mother quite well," he began.

Linda turned to him. He was offering to change the subject.

"Please tell me about her," asked Linda. She didn't want him to know how desperately she longed to hear.

"Lovely girl," he mused. For a moment he stared off in space. "You look somewhat like her. You seem to lack her gentleness. What I mean is, that you seem made of sterner stuff. She married your father quite young, and she died in childbirth. But I'm sure you know all of that."

"I'd love to hear about her from you. From another person who had known her," Linda encouraged.

"As I said, she was gentle. Good with animals, quite an equestrian. Like you, I guess. I read the article about you very carefully. It helped with identifying you. I couldn't bring the wrong Linda Grainger here."

Linda was confused. Her identity seemed to hold a fascination for him.

They sat quietly for a while, each in their own thoughts.

Adella came softly into the room. She carried a tray with two ceramic mugs that looked like museum artifacts. She set the tray on the table between them and quietly left the room.

"Hot chocolate. Adella does this tolerably well," he explained. "But she has her own recipe if it tastes strange to your palette. But it should lull us to sleep."

They drank in silence. He was right. Adella's drink was an acquired taste. But it was warm and soothing.

"I think I'll retire," Linda said. She placed the mug on the tray and stood to leave.

"Goodnight, my dear," he answered. "Tomorrow will be an eventful day."

She undressed and showered for the night. As she wiped the steam from the mirror, a familiar face appeared. A face like hers, but yet not hers. She held to the edge of the sink to keep her balance. This image was much clearer than ever before. The girl in the mirror was saying something. As Linda watched her lips, she read 'go back, go back.' Linda wanted to ask what she meant. A hand from behind the image in the mirror grabbed the girl's arm and pulled her out of view. The mirror misted over again.

Linda sat on the bed to catch her breath and regain her sanity. *This was so close. Was it because she was in her mother's house? A connection with her mother somehow? Oh, she needed Brett. His calm spirit, his arms around her.*

A noise outside got her attention. She slowly made her way to the window, and again saw the small man. This time he had two small bundles. Sam took the bundles and handed them to Adella who was standing with waiting arms. They looked like babies.

Was Sam into human trafficking as well as smuggling museum pieces? Her brain couldn't absorb the scene she was witnessing. She was groggy, her knees were weak. If she could only make it to the bed. The chocolate! There had been something in the chocolate. No wonder it tasted different. She wasn't supposed to witness the scene out by the chapel. Brett, oh, where was Brett!

Linda made it to the bed. Her last feeling was the warm comfort of an unseen presence in the room.

PART 2

Chapter 8

Brett looked around the rooms. The house held only the things that the university had purchased from Linda. The moving company had picked up the furniture that she was keeping only this morning and taken it to the storage facility. It felt empty even with the furnishings that were left. And the rooms were adequately outfitted. But without Linda, it was empty.

The moment the plane was out of sight, there was an empty space within him.

Oh, Lord, what have I done. You finally showed me the girl you have for me, and I have sent her off into her unknown future alone. What will she find on the other end? With everything she's been through lately, she needs someone with her. Please take care of her.

His prayer was fervent, but the ache without her remained. He hadn't been able to reach her cell phone, and he had been in class when she tried reaching him. Now when he tried, it went to her voice mail.

He was already packed and his luggage stowed in his car. Directly after class he would head to the airport. But he had this night to get through and his last responsibility at the school tomorrow.

He slept fitfully and the time at school the next day dragged unmercifully. He had to turn in final grades and check with the dean before leaving. He had to return his house key and check the mailbox one final time. He hoped she had sent a second card.

The first one didn't put any of his fears to rest: Her meeting was moved to another destination and a bus trip to who knew where.

When he finally got the mail, he sat in his car studying the letter.

Dear Brett,

It's all so mixed up. I've decided to sell, and I have a ticket to leave here tomorrow at 2 o'clock. Sam Straeder is a mysterious man. Hasn't practiced law for twenty years but has been masquerading for some time as a padre in this desolate backside of the desert. That's a story I'm sure you'll enjoy when we meet. The little cantina that serves as a bus depot has a faded 'dos tigres' sign lying on the ground, so I guess there is such a place. I'm heading back to 'civilization' tomorrow. I'll meet you in Las Cruces. I'll call you when I can once again get a signal.

Love, Linda

He just sat there with his head propped up in his hands. The letter that he thought would answer his questions did nothing but add more questions. So, she'd been in a dead area. That would explain the lack of communication. The letter had sounded rushed. It certainly didn't give him much reassurance.

But he would be in Las Cruces this evening. Even traveling by bus, she could have been there two days. He should have received a call from her by now. It wouldn't have taken her long to recharge her phone after she booked into a near-by motel.

He put the car in gear and headed toward the airport. He'd have time to make a call when he got there. He would call in reinforcements. His family.

The phone rang once.

"Hello," the voice said.

"Dad, it's Brett."

"Son, so glad to hear from you. I guess we'll be seeing you soon."

"I'll be there in Las Cruces late this evening," Brett said.

"Ok. I know you won't have a car, so we'll come meet you," his Dad offered.

"Great. The plane should land around six-thirty this evening. But I have a favor to ask," Brett said.

"You only have to ask, son, you know that," Mr. McAlister said.

"Well, Dad, I hardly know where to start. You see, there's this girl..." Brett began.

There was a whoop at the other end of the phone. "Finally," his Dad said.

"Yes, Dad, finally. But I've lost contact with her. She should have arrived in Las Cruces yesterday, and I haven't heard from her. I feel very uneasy, like something may have happened. She had been traveling by bus, so she would have found a motel close by. Would you have time to call the nearby motels and see if they have a Linda Grainger registered? She'll have a little dog with her," he explained. "Then we can pick her up after you meet me."

"Sounds like a plan, son. See you this evening," he agreed.

Brett closed his eyes as the plane lifted off. He felt a weight removed from his shoulders. No doubt his entire family would be calling every motel in fifty miles of the bus station. He smiled as he drifted off to sleep.

They were all there to meet him: mom, dad, and the five sisters. He wasn't fooled that he was the main attraction.

"Son, we called everywhere. No Linda Grainger. One ticket clerk remembered her," he added.

"How did they remember her?" Brett asked.

"They recognized her picture," he explained.

"Where did you get a picture of her?" Brett asked.

"You know Katie subscribes to *Women Equestrian Champions* magazine. Keeps every copy. It seems Linda Grainger was in vivid color on the front of the issue two months ago. Your sister, Katie, remembered the name right away. All the girls insisted they come, too, and help," he apologized. "Brett, I saw her picture. Are you sure she's interested in an ole cowpoke like you?" He slapped Brett on the back affectionately.

"I guess she thinks I'm only a college professor. Hasn't seen me all dirty yet," he said. "She sure is something. Wait 'til you see her in person."

Brett's face turned red with embarrassment. His Dad might be right. Linda didn't know about ranch life. She had been sheltered in private schools. Could she be happy with him?

"Everyone is waiting in the van. What do you want to do?" Mr. McAlister asked.

"I think we've done everything we can tonight. Let's go to the ranch, and I'll start looking tomorrow. The bus may have been delayed somehow. She'll probably call me tonight," he explained.

That's all that could be done tonight. The clerk at the depot had told them he recognized her picture, and he had sold her a ticket to the little town sixty miles west. She would change buses there. That bus was just a small private line that only runs two days a week. And that was if the nearby river didn't flood the road. And at this time of year, flooding was a danger.

At the ranch they got out a map to trace Linda's trip. Sixty miles west would put it close to a small town that they located, but the next leg of the trip an hour further west would be close to the Mexican border. No towns were identified. No *Los Tigres*, for sure.

He'd shared the events with his family, but he couldn't escape the guilt that he felt for allowing her to leave alone. He did have responsibilities. Ends to tie up before he could leave the university, but he should have tried to find a way. If she had asked him, he would have dropped it all and left with her. But she seemed to want to do it on her own. Perhaps, she'd been alone too long. But her world had been encapsulated. She hadn't had to deal with circumstances beyond her ivy-covered walls.

He was a little chagrined when he thought of the chip he had put into the small red collar around the puppy's neck. Such an insignificant action. He would have to be within a short distance of the little animal before the device could signal its location. It was all he could think of to do on the spur of the moment when he'd purchased the dog. But it was something that kept him from feeling totally helpless.

Brett was the first one in line at the ticket office the next morning. He purchased the exact tickets that Linda had bought, going to the same destinations. He'd left the ranch early. His family had gathered around him and prayed for his success. No one wanted to think of the girl traveling alone in the desert to an unknown destination.

Brett slept the first hour of the journey. The restless night had left him exhausted mentally as well as physically. He was looking forward to getting back into the swing of ranch work. His muscles had rested too long as a professor. Gym workouts just weren't the same.

The vehicle that pulled up to the small bus depot that would complete the last leg of the journey looked inadequate to make the trip. As Brett stepped up into the bus, he sat on the front seat close to the driver. He wanted to find out as much as he could. There was no air conditioning and a light coating of dust had filtered in the windows, settling on the seats and floors. Brett closed his window against the grit. His fellow passengers were Mexicans, locals returning to their villages.

"I'm looking for a girl that may have been a passenger a few days ago," Brett started the conversation with the driver.

"Oh, yeah? What kind of girl would you like?" the driver joked.

"Well, actually, this is my girl," Brett admitted. "She had to leave a few days before. I was to follow her."

Brett felt a swell in his heart. He hoped beyond reason that Linda was 'his girl'.

"What did she look like, mister?" he asked.

"Short black hair, ivory skin, shining dark eyes…"

The bus driver laughed. "You got it bad, mister."

"I guess so," Brett admitted. "She is a beautiful girl. If you saw her, you would remember."

"Oh, I remember," the old driver admitted. "I just had to tease you. She had a little dog with her. I've driven this route for many years, and we don't get many young, beautiful girls traveling alone. I know most of my passengers. They have regular schedules."

Brett began to feel a little relaxed. Maybe he had worried for nothing. He would find her house, and they could return together.

"But, funny thing," the driver continued," she missed her return trip."

"She bought a ticket to return?" asked Brett.

"Yep. She bought her ticket. She gave the clerk a letter to mail in case she didn't make it. She said she had a meeting to sell her house and wasn't sure if she could get back to the depot in time."

"But she could have left the next day?" Brett asked.

"Nope. I only make this trip two times a week. But she could be at the cantina waiting for us right now. We should be there in about fifteen more minutes."

"Ok. Thanks."

Brett settled back, trying to roll with the bumps in the road. The bus seemed to hit all of them.

A stranger on the bus was at least easy to track. The driver was sure of what he knew. So, he was definitely on the right trail.

He pulled out his cell phone to report back to the ranch. No signal. The screen was black. So, this was why he hadn't heard from her. No communication was possible. The driver had a two-way radio, so the signal towers were nowhere close.

No passengers waited to board the bus for its return trip. Brett grabbed his backpack and got off of the bus. Before entering the cantina, he looked for, and found, the faded sign lying on the ground that read '*dos tigres*'. So, such a place did exist.

Before the bus driver left, he accompanied Brett into the dimly lit cantina.

"Hey, Pepe. This young señor is looking for that pretty girl that came in a few days ago," the driver explained. He smiled his big smile. He loved his jokes.

"Welcome, señor. *Sí*, a very pretty girl stopped here," he was playing along with the driver's sense of humor.

"Have you seen her lately?" Brett asked.

"*Sí*, she came to buy a ticket. And gave me a letter," he explained. "Let me guess. The letter was for you?"

"Sure was," Brett admitted. "When did you see her last?"

"Two days ago. She missed the bus."

"She was supposed to meet a Mr. Sam Straeder. Do you know if she did?" Brett asked.

"No. I didn't know a *Señor* Straeder. But our padre did. Your girl left with our padre. So, see, all is well."

Brett hoped all was well. Linda called the padre a 'fake priest'. He wished he knew what that meant. Did it mean no credentials, or did his actions indicate less than honorable intentions?

"Where do you think they went?" Brett asked.

"The padre said they would meet *Señor* Straeder at the padre's casa. You can see it from here. It's an easy walk to the yellow hacienda."

The bartender brought a plate of burritos to the table and placed it before Brett with a bottle of water. "Eat, then walk."

He couldn't refuse the food. He might need this man as a friend and a source of information. And, who knew when he'd eat again. The food was authentic. Very good.

His boots kicked up dust whorls as he walked. The trip had been drying all the way here, so there was no threat of the flooding that could have caused danger. He pulled his Stetson further down on his head to shade his eyes. The house in the distance glimmered in the sun. As he neared, he could see the verandah and the intricate detail of the wrought-iron railing around its edges. If this were Linda's inheritance, it was a beautiful house. The locals couldn't afford a house like this one, so the buyer must be someone special.

There didn't seem to be anyone around. The doors were locked. The shades were tight against the windows. The occupants were gone, and they had closed up tight. A small chapel sat close by.

Brett entered the chapel. No one here, either. No loving parishioners cared for this chapel. No flowers at the altar, just a dusty cloth. Sunlight struggled to push rays through the dirty windowpanes. Dust motes were suspended in the sunbeams that did make it through. But it was functional. Perhaps the padre did meet with his worshipers here.

A hallway led to the left. A rug was fastened to the floor. One corner of the rug was turned back slightly, uncovering what looked like a trap door. Someone's secret was accidentally revealed. There were footprints and evidence that someone had pulled something along the floor.

Brett looked more closely. It was indeed a trap door. Quite a large door for such a small chapel. He lifted the door. The hinges had been recently oiled; it opened smoothly. Dampness curled up from the space. A sturdy ladder led from the top to the earthen floor beneath. Brett pulled a flashlight from his backpack and lighted his way to the bottom. The floor here was covered with the same markings as on the chapel floor.

He turned away from the ladder. It wasn't a room; it was an entrance. An entrance to a tunnel. The walls had been reinforced with timbers. Someone had wanted this passageway to be safe and to last a long time. He adjusted his backpack to a more comfortable position and climbed the ladder just far enough to close the trap door.

The beam of his strong flashlight guided him easily through the shaft. The path inclined gently upward. Then it began its ascent sharply. He could see light at the end of the tunnel. Sunlight. He turned off his flashlight and thrust it in his backpack. He needed both hands to balance himself on the rocky floor.

What was he doing here? Just satisfying his curiosity. No, he was suspicious. Not sure what he was suspicious about, but he had to know what was at the end of this passageway.

Brett felt a vibration on his leg; then, he heard a faint beep. It was the tracker that he had inserted in the little red collar around the puppy's neck. He had checked out the sound at the pet store before he added it to the collar. Maybe Linda was up ahead with the little dog. He hurried.

The beeping got louder as he neared the egress. He stepped into the clearing. He looked for the collar. It was caught on a low-hanging overhead branch of a scraggly pine. As he reached up for it, he noticed that it was covered with blood, dried now, but definitely blood. It looked as if it had been wrenched from his neck. The clasp was broken. He took a few minutes to search for the body of the little animal. He breathed a sigh of relief when he found nothing. He turned off the beeper and stowed the damaged collar in his backpack.

A few more steps and he spied a golden hoop earring shining between two small rocks. Linda had worn earrings like this when they went to dinner with Max. His heart caught in his throat! But there was no blood on it. He put it in his backpack, too.

He was concerned with the tracks that he found outside of the tunnel: boot prints, wagon wheels. Evidence showed that two trails converged at the tunnel's opening. One trail was just outside the tunnel and the other trail came from a slope to his right. It looked like some sort of buckboard. Hoofprints showed that a horse had been tied along behind. Maybe two horses. Of course, horses couldn't have come through the tunnel from the chapel, but if he could read the tracks correctly, a party had left the chapel, traveled through the tunnel and were met at the other end by further transportation. But where were they going? The sky, the path, the mountains all looked empty. The road they had to travel was no more than an unused logging-type road. Weeds grew, nearly covering the rutted lane.

This was no country to be without protection, and he longed for his rifle. The mountains were full of predators. Mountain lions hunted, panthers roamed, screaming at night, and bears lumbered throughout the day foraging for food. His Dad had told him that the livestock on the ranch had been attacked by a pack of wolves lately. A pack of wolves might just be his greatest danger.

But now he was a predator. Someone had taken Linda. She was out there, and she would be expecting him to find her.

He had never prayed harder in his life than now as he followed faint wheel tracks on the grassy slope. *God, please keep her safe! Help me find her before it's too late.*

He walked several feet further up the path and heard a soft whimper. Hidden in the weeds, the tiny puppy struggled to get to his feet. Carefully, Brett lifted *Cómo*. A tiny pink tongue licked his finger.

"What's the matter, boy. Are you hurt?" Brett crooned to the puppy.

As he washed away the blood with the water from his canteen, he saw the tear in the dog's neck from where the collar was ripped loose. Someone was either unaware that the puppy had been lost, or it had been left to fend for itself. Linda would not have left this small animal to die. Someone had her. Someone whose plans did not include rescuing the injured animal.

The bleeding had stopped, but now he had another dilemma. He couldn't leave the dog, and he couldn't take it with him until it was thoroughly cleaned of all blood. He didn't have enough water for that. But if he didn't clean it, he might as well ring a dinner bell for the meat-eaters in these mountains.

The bus wouldn't return to the cantina for two more days. He couldn't wait, nor could he get word to his family. The bartender at the cantina didn't know the priest was an imposter, so he would never believe that he had kidnapped Linda. But Brett was convinced Sam Straeder was behind it. He had to go on his own. He had no other choice. Linda wasn't alone, and it looked like she was in dangerous company.

His decision made, he headed back down the trail to the tunnel entrance. He needed to be better equipped. It would be dark soon, and he had preparations to make. Back at the chapel, he was able to wash the dog clean from all the blood stuck in its hair. He bandaged the wound to keep out the dirt that they would pick up from the trail. The altar scarf made a sling in which to carry the dog. A woolen blanket had been left on one of the pews, and he stowed it in his backpack. He knew that his father would not just sit and wait too long for him to return. He left a note to his father, pointing the way to the trapdoor. Just in case he got this far.

He made his way through the passageway again and positioned himself just inside the tunnel's exit. He built a small fire. From a thicket nearby, he found a green sapling that looked to have been recently torn away. He sat before the fire and carved both ends of the sapling into a spear. He left just enough of the bark on the shaft of the spear to act as a grip. Carefully, he turned the points of the spear above the flame until they were barely toasted. The heat would speed up the drying process, hardening the tips. His backpack had included a sharp knife, but he would have traded it for his rifle.

He collected a thinner sapling from which he could fashion a bow. He knew that almost any material for a bowstring could be used in an emergency. He'd be on the lookout tomorrow for any fiber that could at least be used for a one-time shot. He had fashioned six arrows out of the birch that he found, so he was nearly ready. Brett just prayed that he wouldn't need to try these implements. He knew that he would have to be close to his target for penetration of the tough hides. He was digging deep into his Eagle Scout background for survival techniques, stepping from his present into his past.

With the campfire located between him and the trail, he settled against the tunnel wall and tried to sleep. He tucked the woolen blanket around him and the puppy in the altar scarf. The dog had drunk a little water and snuggled back to sleep. He rested fitfully until the first rays of light pricked at his eyes.

Brett collected his things. He stomped out the last glowing embers of his fire and checked on the puppy. It hadn't made any noises during the night.

"How are you, boy," he asked. "Your nose feels too hot. What's wrong?"

But he knew what was wrong. Infection had set in the gash in its neck. Its pulse was strong if a bit rapid. He forced cool water into the dog's mouth and readjusted the sling. They'd both go as far as they could. Linda's life could be in danger. He would mark his trail just in case someone from the Circle Mc came looking for him.

The path became steeper. Snows from the mountains had begun to thaw, and there were little streams running from above. He would have plenty to drink. He stopped at a wider stream and splashed the icy, clear water on his face. He wet a corner of the altar scarf and patted the dog's nose and underbelly. He only hoped it would help.

At the broader parts of the stream, he had been able to identify some prints. Wide paw prints were distinctly cat tracks. Big cats. Many smaller ones had been made by other nocturnal critters. He again picked up the slight indentation that the wagon wheels had made in the grassy lane. He kept himself at a steady pace, always upward. The air was slightly thinner, and he could tell that his breathing was somewhat labored. He'd lived too long at a lower elevation.

Sweat stuck his shirt to his back. He stopped again at a small stream and splashed water on his face and neck. He forced some water into the little dog's mouth. His watch showed he'd been on this upward trail for nearly three hours. The sunbaked rock he rested upon was uncomfortable. He stood. He'd have to be watchful. Sun this hot would wake the rattlers and invite them out from under the rocks for basking in the heat. His hiking boots didn't come up around his calves.

He unwrapped jerky from his backpack and chewed slowly. The saltiness was not unpleasant, but it would require a lot of water. At this altitude it would be easy to dehydrate. He chewed a piece of jerky into a soft wad, and he placed it at the pup's lips. A little tongue flicked at the intrusion, then nothing.

"Boy, you're going to have to fight to survive," he urged the puppy. "Linda wouldn't like it if I arrived alone."

He applied his cold-water treatment to the little body again and rewrapped it. Adjusting the sling, he started back up, following the faint trail. Brett's footsteps were slowing. He needed to rest more often as the path continued to ascend.

After another hour, he came to a small clearing. The wagon he had been following sat to the side, abandoned and empty. Steps had been crudely cut into a wall that led up to a small tabletop. A mesa, actually. The rough stairway had been used recently. Scrape marks clipped the edges from something having been bumped step by step to the top. Occasionally, he could see a hoof print. The horses had been led up to the top.

From his vantage point a little higher, he looked over from where he had come. The trail was hidden by a canopy of scrubby pine. Above the timberline, the good hardwoods were gone. As he scouted the tabletop, he spied a trailhead. If he hadn't been looking for the entrance to another path, he would have missed it. Its entrance had been covered by limbs of pine, carefully placed to look like a scraggly bush.

It took a while to pull away the brush covering the trailhead. Someone knew how to hide the entrance to make the tabletop to look like an enclosed circle. When the way had been cleared, he could see that there was no steep wall going back down. The path continued upward.

Hoofprints were easier to follow now. Melting snow from the higher elevation had made the ground softer. Three horses had come this way. The first horse's hooves sank deeper into the ground, indicating a heavier load. The other horses had followed with lighter packs.

Dusk was beginning to fall around him. Darkness would descend soon. He had to find shelter. One more night. He wondered where this trail would end.

A shadow played on the ledge above him. Was it a shadow? Or did it have substance? As he stared, the shadow took the shape of a big cat. There was just enough light to see its eyes gleam yellow. Clutching his spear, he knew there would be just enough time to throw it before the cat would be upon him. His aim would have to be true. He positioned himself below the cat and hurled the spear. It plunged deep into the cat's chest.

His foot slipped and he tumbled backwards just as the cat's body lost momentum and rolled close to him. He could see its fangs as they gleamed white in the dusk. Blood trickled from its open mouth onto its neck. As he covered his face, he heard the whisper of a missile through the air. He turned and saw the cat stretched out in death; an arrow buried beside the spear in its chest. As he turned back to the top of the rock, a figure of a man arose. It wasn't like any man he had ever seen. This man could have sprung out of the pictures from Dr. Grainger's drawings of an ancient race.

As he tried to stand, his boot slipped in the mud. His ankle twisted and he went down hard. His head struck a rock, and his vision became blurred. The last thing he saw before everything became totally dark was this large man bending over him with his weapon in his hand.

Chapter 9

"*Ella esta despertando!*" Adella warned. "*Aún no puede despertar.*"

"No, Linda, we can't have you awake yet," he sympathized.

Above her head, Linda could see Sam Straeder's face. His features were blurred, and his head had no firm definition floating above his shoulders.

"No," she tried to protest.

"This won't hurt," he answered her.

She felt a small prick in her arm, and he disappeared.

"How are the babies, Adella?" Straeder asked.

"Like little angels. They are perfect," she answered.

"I didn't want to bring them since we had the girl. But the opportunity was too great. Two Zuni babies. They'll live in their new home and never remember the outside. But we can't risk anymore 'adoptions' for a while," he explained.

His role as priest gave him access to unwanted babies. Elena would be especially pleased with these Zuni babies. Authentic blood lines to strengthen the family. New blood to enrich the tribe.

He watched Adella rearrange the babies' blankets and pat their faces. She was getting soft. With Linda's abduction, there could be no loose ends. No one could speak out of turn. Adella saw very few people, but she was known among the Indians across the border where they found most of their babies. Babies headed for orphanages, or worse. She couldn't be allowed to leave the valley again.

To him, they were favors. Something to please Elena. Elena was his life. He had sold his soul for her many years ago. She had become his religion. Tonight, he would present to her the Zuni babies. More importantly, he could now give her what she wanted most in life. A granddaughter worthy to be her successor. One with spirit, fire, and determination. Not like the other one.

He would present these gifts to his wife, Elena, and she would make love to him, welcoming him home. Then everything would be alright again. His conscience would be buried even more deeply. He quickened the pace for the last mile of their journey.

This would be his last journey. He didn't intend to go below again. He would stay with Elena. His task of finding her granddaughter was complete. The house he'd left would stay abandoned. In his role as priest below, he was known to go on a circuit that included many villages across the border. He just would never return. In this wilderness, things happened. His acquaintances would mourn only a short time. They'd not mourn, exactly. It would be an item only for conversation, speculation. Others before him had disappeared in this area. He didn't like to think that he was responsible for some of them. Maybe with time, the memories would fade.

The trail was narrow as it slipped behind a waterfall. The horses splashed their way through a dim cave-like tunnel, taking their hoofprints with them. Their trail visibly ended several yards back before getting to the waterfall. It was a perfect way to disappear. It had served well for generations before he came into the picture.

How long had he lived this double life? It was nearly forty years now. He had only been twenty-three years old at the time. He let his mind go back. The harbor had been teeming with ships, emptying their passengers out onto the boardwalks. One girl stood to the side of the crowd. She stood tall. Tendrils of hair had escaped the black coil of hair at the nape of her neck. Her dark eyes scanned the crowd and looked in his direction. He held her gaze as he made his way to her. Behind her stood a young woman he would come to know as Adella.

"I'd like to help you," he offered.

It didn't matter what she wanted. He knew at that moment he would do anything that she asked. He had never changed his mind. After a month in San Francisco, they were married. His parents were dead, so he had no family. He left with her and never looked back.

Her story wasn't an unusual one for her people. Her Spanish father had taken her back to Spain for an arranged marriage. She was just fifteen. Her mother stayed to take care of their holdings in the new world. Elena had been married into nobility and lived there a year. A girl child was born. Her husband had contracted a disease that was raging in their city at the time. When he died, Elena and her father started back home, bringing Adella with the baby. On the boat, the same sickness took Elena's father.

When Elena and Sam returned, she had taken him to a small casa on the land where he now had his home. At first, there was nothing there. No cantina, no bus route. Just Elena, Adella, the baby and him. Elena had christened the baby, Inez. They didn't need anyone else. Occasionally, there would be a mysterious visitor, bringing a letter from Elena's mother. He never saw the messenger. And, Elena never shared her letters. One such letter was different.

"Sam," started Elena, "my mother is coming."

"That's good," he agreed. "I think it's time I met her. She probably would like to meet her granddaughter."

Elena was very hesitant. She said nothing for a while.

"She isn't coming to visit, Sam. She is coming to get me. There is nothing that can be done about it. It is my destiny. I have to be prepared for the responsibilities. I don't expect you to understand. You are free to go. But only if you go before mother knows of your existence. After that, I can't answer for what will happen."

"You mean you haven't told her about me? About us?" he asked. "She doesn't know we're married. Does she think you've been alone?"

"She knows Adella is here and the baby. I've been away from the valley nearly two years. That's all the time she allowed me."

"Allowed you?" He shouted. "What is she?"

"Our society is Matriarchal," she tried to explain. "After my mother, Consuela, is gone, leadership will fall to me. I must be ready. As my great-grandmother and my grandmother were ready."

"I don't pretend to understand, Elena, but you know I'll never leave you. And I love your daughter as my own," he exclaimed. "She will just have to accept that."

"Alright, Sam. If this is your decision," she agreed. "You may not like the consequences."

Consuela arrived. Her eyes all flash and fury. Inez had done her duty in producing a female heir with the correct bloodline. Sam was just a mistake to be dealt with. The death of Consuela's husband was never mentioned.

Sam's first trip from below to their destination in the high mountains was made blindfolded. He spent hours on horseback hooded in darkness until they reached their home.

Home? It could nearly be called a kingdom. The sprawling hacienda hugged the top of a hill, looking down on the village below. Well-tended garden plots lined the backside of the hacienda, abundant with vegetables and flowers of all varieties. They had traveled from the dry desert to a verdant countryside. A lush paradise hidden in the shrouded mystery of the mountains.

Sam had been dealt with. As the years passed, it became his way of life. A life that included Elena and little Inez. So, it could be tolerated. With Elena's father gone, Consuela needed an emissary. She needed a contact with the outside world. The gold from the mine had to be sold. Some things had to be bought and brought in from the outside. The years proved that she could trust him, so she chose to put these tasks on Sam. She knew he wouldn't fail her. She had control of what he loved most—Elena and Inez. Threats of harm to them would keep him in line. And the threats were real. As an added precaution, Adella would accompany him as his housekeeper.

Sam had some conditions. He would build a hacienda with modern conveniences to replace the small casa. It was to be deeded to Inez. He hoped someday to be allowed to return with his little family. It was Consuela's idea for him to enter the area as an itinerate priest. No one would question the times when he was gone from the community. Sam wasn't catholic, so he didn't feel any sacrilege. He learned rites and rules as he was called upon to act out his role.

Sam built a small chapel to conceal the entrance to the trailhead that led to the hidden valley. He had just passed the bar exam when he met Elena. All he had from that life were his diplomas. He hung them on the wall in the small office he built within the back of the chapel. All his law books were lined up in the bookshelf behind his desk. He had no regrets. Elena had captured him body and soul.

Consuela had finally told him how they came to be keepers of the tribe that lived with them in the valley. That's what she called what she did—keeping. He never mingled with the villagers, but he knew they were Indians from an ancient tribe, living secluded under her guardianship.

Her story told of a family of a Spanish Grandee that immigrated from Spain to Mexico. It was a time of Indian unrest in the area. One particular battle was bloody with Apaches completely overrunning a group of the old ones, the Anasazi.

The tribe scattered, fleeing into the hills. The Grandee's family found them, tended their wounds, and let them live on their lands. The Apaches again attacked. But this time it was an attack upon the Spanish that were sheltering the Indians. Together the Spanish and the Indians on their land stood them off until dark. During the night, the Grandee herded everyone together and set out quietly into the unknown.

He had a map that had been given to him by the chief of the Anasazi. It was believed to be an ancient place of safety. A place where they could live and not be found. The Grandee had explored the map only a short way, but he was pushed for a way of escape. He led his small group and a few pack horses on the path laid out by the map, brushing out their footprints as they went. They found the place on the map marked *Paraiso*, paradise. The Apache would attack again at sunrise. But they would come upon an empty compound and the trail invisible. Their tracks had been swept away by the brush, but the rain that came in the night had finished the job.

In the hidden valley, the Indians had quietly slipped back into their familiar way of life as builders and agricultural people. Together with the native plants they found in the valley and the seeds brought by the Spanish, neither group wanted for anything. Mountain sheep were caught and tamed. They furnished hair for spinning, skins for tanning for clothing and moccasins. Their meat was dried into jerky or roasted.

The Spanish assumed the roles of protectors and guardians. Over the years, the lines had become more defined with the Spanish in complete control. They kept the exit to the valley secret. No one wanted to leave this land where crops abounded and game was abundant.

In the years that followed, the Spanish explored the caves and tunnels throughout the valley. They found gold nuggets in a stream flowing from the mountains. They followed the stream back into a cave where gold winked at them from the crevices in the walls. Plans were made to make use of it. One trusted by the Spanish leaders was commissioned to take a small amount of gold to an assayer's office below. He was given a list of tools to purchase. Thus, the community flourished in secret.

The only lack was the way to replenish the Spanish leaders. Keeping their bloodlines pure took planning. As a daughter from the Cortez family became of marriageable age, a jovenes from Spain was purchased from an impoverished family. The revolution in Spain left many of the wealthiest families in want. When this youth was old enough, he became husband to the daughter. After a daughter was born to the couple, the young man could choose to return to his family in Spain, with gold in his pocket, or remain in the valley. In reality, did they return home or were they lost to the elements in these rough mountains between their hidden valley and lower civilization? No one knew for sure.

"And then there was Elena," Sam said aloud to himself.

He had no fear of waking his traveling companions. Adella was exhausted, and Linda was drugged.

"Elena was indeed Consuelo's daughter. Fire, fury, and a will of her own. She wanted to go to Spain and choose her own mate. She loved the valley, but she wanted a little freedom before taking over her destiny," he said. "Or perhaps, before her destiny took over her."

He remembered what Elena had told him.

"She gave me two years," she explained. "Two years to find a mate, produce a daughter and return. I wonder what I was supposed to do if it had been a son?"

Her desperate laughter still floated in his memory. Her father was along to chaperone and see that orders were followed. Fate had taken a hand when her husband died in Spain. His family had received their gold, and they wanted nothing more to do with her or her child. Then when her father died on the boat home, she was alone with innocent Adella. Alone and unfamiliar with the outside world.

He continued to talk aloud to keep himself alert.

"She was so alone. Her fire and spirit came from her surroundings in the mountains. Now she needed someone. And he was there for her then. And he was still here for her now."

They stopped. He dismounted and checked the straps around Linda's waist. He didn't want them too tight. The babies were still snuggled in their baskets mounted on either side of Adella's mule. He remounted, and they slipped behind the falls for the last few miles before journey's end.

He had loved his adopted daughter, Inez; but Elena counted her as her one failure. He wondered if Elena had ever loved Inez. He knew she was disappointed in Camila, the baby girl Inez had left behind in her death. Now Elena clung desperately to the existence of Linda, her other granddaughter.

Alan Griffin had stumbled into the Indian village in their valley. Before Elena learned of his existence, he and Inez had fallen in love. A marriage ceremony had been performed at the Indian village by their religious leader. By the time Elena found them and could intervene, Inez was with child.

As the months passed, Inez and Alan lived quietly. Alan studied the Indian ways, took pictures, and cared for his pregnant wife. He found time to help Elena in ways that he thought would appease her. But Elena knew that he was not the kind of man to stay secluded in her valley. She knew that Alan planned to take Inez and leave the valley. Sam knew that Elena would never allow them to leave. He also knew that she would do nothing until after the baby was born.

That part of their lives was over. He was back now. Never again would he leave. And he had brought her what she wanted. Her last granddaughter. When Alan Griffin had run off into the night immediately after Inez died in childbirth, they thought that chapter was closed. Elena had a baby girl to groom as successor, and Alan was gone. His body was never found. He never returned to claim his child. Through the years, Elena had urged Sam to keep looking. He subscribed to a wide number of news magazines to keep in touch. They knew he was absorbed in the Indian lore that he viewed first-hand in their valley, so that was a lead.

He never would have found him if Alan hadn't become well-known. He had changed his name to Adam Grainger, but the picture with his obituary was easy to recognize. The years had marched gently across his face. When the article had listed an only child, the pieces fell into place. Then he saw her picture on the magazine cover. He knew. Inez had given birth to identical twins as she died. Adam didn't know of the second child; they had not known of the first. It was easy to lure Linda here. She was alone, searching for family, a connection.

"You're home now, Linda," he told the sleeping girl.

Elena was waiting for them. A gleam of satisfaction lit up her face as she watched Sam carry the girl to the room prepared for her. She removed Linda's boots and covered her gently.

"At last, you are home," Elena whispered.

Linda couldn't open her eyes, and her limbs felt weighted. But twice now she had heard someone tell her she was home. Home? The last her fuzzy brain could recall was just making it to bed at the house she was going to sell. These voices seemed sure that this was her home.

The two vague figures left her room and it was quiet. Slowly, she was aware of a door opening. The girl standing in her shadow was bending over her. A face bent to place a gentle kiss on her brow, leaving a teardrop on her cheek. Linda relaxed in the warmth of the affection she felt coming from the presence. She slept.

Chapter 10

The light coming in the window was still weak, giving items in the room outline but no detail. Linda lay still trying to remember the past day. She had gone to sleep in Inez's house. Snatches of scenes played in her subconscious. Voices of Sam and Adella, patches of sunlight through hovering trees. She had swayed in rhythm to a horse's gait, the familiar scent rising from the warmth of the animal. Saddle was western, not her Eastern one. She had definitely been on a horse in her blacked-out time.

But, now, where was she? There had been two shadowy figures, and she knew they'd left the room. The last memory was very vivid. Someone had kissed her brow. A tear had fallen to her cheek.

Now she knew. The girl standing in her shadow had appeared!

She turned quickly in bed, and the girl was still there. This was no ghost. She was real. And it was like looking in the mirror. Except for the hair. The figure before her had one thick braid that fell over her shoulder.

"You're real?" Linda whispered.

"I'm real. And so are you." Her voice was soft and held warm humor.

"But what is going on?" Linda asked.

"Shh," she whispered. "They must not know that I'm here. I'm not allowed."

"Not allowed? I don't understand," Linda continued more softly. "Who are you?"

"We'll find a time and place to talk later. Please don't tell them that you saw me," she warned.

There was a noise outside Linda's door. She looked toward the door, and when she looked back, the girl was gone.

"Good morning, Linda. Did you sleep well?" Sam asked.

"One usually does sleep well when drugged," Linda snapped.

"Oh, I like her, Sam," a voice behind Sam said. "Some spirit!"

The woman stepped close and examined Linda's face.

Linda's first look at the woman triggered familiarity. She looked like the picture of Inez that she'd taken from her father's box of keepsakes. This woman appeared to be in her forties, but the classic beauty was in the bone structure. Slight gray winged the sides of her hair, adding a natural sophistication. Her figure was that of an athlete half her age.

"Are you Inez's mother?" Linda asked. It had to be.

"Yes. But more importantly, I am Elena, your grandmother. And I have brought you home."

"Where is home?" Linda commanded. "I had thought that the house that was left to me might become my home."

"Oh, that house is yours, but you won't live there. We used that as an attraction to bring you to us. Sam had been searching for your father many years; finding you was just a bonus. If he hadn't met his untimely death, we might never have known of you. You have no other family now, no close friends." Elena explained.

This woman must be mad.

But she didn't know about Brett. He was a secret that she would hold close to her heart. Even though she had known him only a short time, she believed that he loved her and wouldn't stop looking until he found her. As she struggled to hold on to these thoughts, she prayed they were true.

"I don't think I'll stay here," Linda said. "I have questions to ask, and then I want to be taken back to the yellow house."

Linda saw her grandmother's eyes narrow. There was a little space of silence, then Elena continued.

"You'll learn all in time. You may change your mind. Now, dress. You will need to eat," she ordered. "Adella will bring up a tray, and after breakfast you will need rest. The drug you were given saps the strength." She started for the door, then turned back. "Sam and I'll be gone most of the day, but we'll talk more this evening."

Sam and Elena left the room, closing the door before Linda could raise any further objections.

If Elena thought she would happily agree to stay here, she would learn differently. Grandmother or not. She owed her no allegiance. She'd lived this long without her; she didn't need her now. Especially after being tricked, lied to, and kidnapped!

Linda sat up and her knees buckled as she tried to put her feet on the floor, holding on to the bedpost. Her energy was indeed sapped. She needed to move around. Her grandmother had told her to dress. Dress in what? She hadn't brought any clothes. Had she?

She made it across the room, opened the closet door and rested against the doorframe. Clothes hung neatly on hangers: loose trousers, tops, and a few dresses. The dresses were long with intricate western patterns, some vivid, some muted.

She opened the top drawer of a nearby chest and found underclothes. Nothing fancy. Soft, white cotton. Grabbing what she needed, she went to the connecting bathroom. She stripped off the clothes she'd worn for two days and stepped into the tub filled with scented water. She soaked in the hot water, and finally rinsed out the shampoo that smelled of gardenias. She toweled off with the thick material.

Her movements still weren't smooth, but she managed to slip into a pair of black trousers and a rose-colored cotton top.

Miraculously, everything fit. There were no shoes in the closet, no jacket. Her trips outside were being restricted! She was being held prisoner.

A soft knock found Adella entering with breakfast. "Elena ordered a breakfast tray for you," Adella said as she set it on the table by the window. Adella's footfalls were silenced by the moccasins she wore.

"You startled me," Linda said. "But how kind. Thank you, Adella."

Adella had been with these people since she was incredibly young, and she didn't suppose that she could win her to her side. But she didn't want to make her an enemy spy. Spy? Where did that thought come from. She was already thinking in terms of who was for her and who was against her. So far, I'm a group of one!

Linda sat in the chair by the table. She picked up a fork and started on the western omelet. The vegetables in it were brightly colored and fresh. These people must eat well. She poured a cup of hot tea into her cup.

"I'm not sure I'd drink that," a voice said from the corner of the room.

Linda wiped at the tea that she'd spilled on the tray at the sound of the voice.

"You! It's you again. You are real." Linda spoke to the girl now standing in the shadowy corner of her bedroom.

"Yes, I'm real. You aren't seeing spirits!" the girl said.

"Well, you look like me. But since I think that I am still me, you must be someone else!" Linda retorted.

The girl's laughter floated softly through the room.

"Yes, I'm me. And you are you!" She countered.

"How did you get in here?" Linda said. This conversation was going in circles.

"This used to be my room. There's a secret way in and out."

"Let's back up. Who are you?" Linda asked.

"I'm your '*amiga*'," she explained.

"*Mi amiga?*" Linda echoed." I remember."

"The first time I was able to reach out to you we were almost six years old," the girl went on.

"Reach out to me? But who are you?" Linda pressed.

"My name is Camila. I'll answer your questions, but we need to leave this room."

Linda wanted more, but the girl wouldn't be rushed.

Linda picked up her cup again and looked at the liquid.

"So, you think I shouldn't drink this tea?" she asked. "What's wrong with it?"

"Sam and grandmother will be gone until dark, but they want to make sure you don't leave this room. What better way of assuring this, than to have you sleep while they are away?"

"How do you know how long they'll be gone?" Linda asked.

"Whenever Sam returns, they always ride off for the day. I don't know where they go. I was just always glad they were gone. Sam has always treated me kindly, but grandmother has been extremely disappointed in me. That's why she brought you here when she learned of your existence."

"So that's why, whenever I saw you in my visions, you warned me to 'stay away' or 'go back'."

"Yes. I also warned you because I don't want you here. I want to be the next Matriarch. It is my right." Camila said.

"Camila, believe me, I don't want to be the next Matriarch. I don't know where I am, but I know that I don't want to be here. I was brought here against my will. I want to go home."

Camila ignored Linda's protest. "We need to leave this room. Adella probably won't come back since she's busy with the two new babies, but she might hear us," Camila whispered. "We have to lock the door."

"The babies?" Linda questioned.

"Not now. Later," Camila said.

"I can't go," Linda said. She held up her bare feet. "No shoes!"

Camila reached into a deep pocket of her long skirt and pulled out a pair of leather sandals. "I came prepared. I know their tricks. Come."

Camila led the way into a deep closet. Bending down, she pushed the back wall gently. It clicked, loosening a panel. Camila pushed it up, leaving a space large enough for the girls to enter. When they stepped through. Camila lit a candle that she took from a wooden wall sconce, lifted a lever, and the wall closed softly.

The flickering light from the candle revealed the dirt floor and the packed earthen walls. Camila moved forward slowly and Linda followed.

"I don't live here any longer, and it's been a while since I've used this tunnel, so we must be careful of the path. Some of the ceiling may have fallen," Camila explained.

Nothing more was said as they made their way forward. When Camila blew out the candle's flame, the glow from the outside threw its light onto their path. They stepped out into the brilliant sunlight.

"Oh, I've never seen such a place!" Linda exclaimed.

Their path was at the beginning of a vast meadow carpeted with a thick green turf. Not too far was a herd of brown and white goats, at home and unafraid of the newcomers. A far field was a blanket of blue still sparkling from the morning dew. The aroma carried by a gentle breeze was spicy and clean.

"The blue flowers are horsemint. Because of the aroma, it's also called wild oregano," Camila explained. "Our valley is thick with beautiful flowers."

Camila led the way to a crude bench sitting on a small rise overlooking the wide expanse of the meadow. "We can sit here. I'll answer the questions that you have. I'll tell you what I know."

Linda looked at the girl. She read innocence on the face that looked so much like her own.

"Who are you?" Linda asked the burning question.

"My name is Camila. I've always lived here. My mother died at my birth and my father died shortly after. Elena told me my mother was her daughter, so I was her granddaughter. She would tell me nothing of my father, except that he wandered out of our valley and was killed by a wild animal in the surrounding mountains. There's a grave with his marker beside the one for my mother."

"Did she tell you your mother's name?" Asked Linda.

"Inez was her daughter's name," Camila answered.

Linda showed no emotion. It was all too confusing. If what Camila said was true, this would mean that she was her sister. But Linda could think of no explanation where this could be true. This all had to be a trick.

"You said you reached out to me? How did you do this?"

"I wasn't reaching out to you exactly. I was reaching out and you appeared."

"How did you do this?"

"When I was small, I was allowed to play with the Indian children who live in our valley. They have many dances and rites that are fascinating, even to a small child. When I was five, I watched a playmate of mine do a Spirit Winging Chant with her mother. She danced, did a chant, and journeyed for several hours while asleep. When she awoke, she told me it was like someone calling for her to come to them. Her family was quite pleased with her. She told me of it over and over. Children aren't encouraged to do Spirit Winging Journeys until at least twelve years of age."

"So, you tried it?" Linda asked.

"Not then," she answered. "But one day I was in my room and I felt a sad presence. It was wanting help."

Awestruck, Linda listened as Camila continued her story.

"I got up and did the dance as I remembered and repeated her Spirit Winging Chant word for word. In my spirit I entered a strange room. A little girl, who looked like me, sat at a small white table with beautiful dolls sitting in chairs around it. She had her head on the table and was sobbing. Her puppy was gone and wouldn't be back."

Linda tried to keep her face from registering any expression, but her heart beat wildly in her chest.

"I walked over to the table and sat in the empty chair beside the girl. Then she saw me, and her sadness left. I told her I was *'su amiga'*. I don't know how long I was there, but one day the little girl told me to leave because she was going away."

All the feelings that Linda experienced at that time as a small child rushed back over her. Tears flowed down her face and dropped onto her shirt.

"It was you?" Camila asked.

"Yes, when you reached out, you came to me," Linda admitted. "What happened when you left?"

"When I awoke, Elena and Sam were in my room along with a spiritual healer from the clan. It seems I had been asleep for nearly a week, and they were worried enough to contact the clan's healer, Spirit Warrior."

"What did you tell them?" Linda asked.

"Nothing. I couldn't share with them. I told them I had fallen and when I lay down my head was hurting. Grandmother just decided it was from the fall."

"So, what happened?" Linda asked.

"Grandmother made me stay in bed for a week to rest," Camila admitted. "But as Spirit Warrior left, he looked into my eyes and I knew that he knew the truth."

"Did you try again?" Linda asked.

"I never felt your spirit cry out again for many years. But later when you became sad and mixed up yet again, I was able to reach out once more to your room. I saw your reflection in a mirror. But it frightened you."

"Yes," Linda admitted. "I was afraid that I was losing my mind. But I was home for my father's funeral and I was troubled, wounded really. I saw your image and it was a shock to me. You must have been able to reach me because I had returned home."

"The spirit journey had been made once, and the way was familiar," Camila reasoned.

"But the last time I saw you, I was in a different place," Linda said.

"I did travel a different path, but you were close and the connection was an easy one. You were very distraught. I tried to message you to stay away from here."

"I did get the message, but it was out of my control," Linda said.

Linda looked out over the peaceful valley. What looked like paradise held many hidden secrets that might never come to light. Many serpents might still linger, taunting with forbidden fruits. The sun shone brightly, but even its brightness couldn't unveil all the mysteries that could be uncovered here. She wasn't sure that some of the hidden truths should come out into the light of day. What was the expression? Let sleeping dogs lie.

They sat quietly, each alone in their own thoughts. Their own lives had been lived so separately, but somehow, they touched. If not sisters, then theirs was a close relationship.

"You said you weren't allowed at the house? I thought it was your home," Linda asked the second question that teased her.

"I had told you that I was allowed to play with the children of the clan. That abruptly stopped when I was fifteen years old. Grandmother said it was time that I was groomed for my destiny. She said there were many things I had to learn before my trip to Spain. Trip to Spain? That was the first time I'd heard of it. Sam had taught geography to me along with my other lessons, and I knew that was from where our people had ultimately come.

I had some interest in travel, so I learned all I needed to know. Well, almost all."

Linda felt her tone as well as heard it. Even now rebellion rose up in Camila's story.

"But at the same time, I resented being cut off from all my friends. The ones I played with were more of a family than Grandmother and Sam. My friends helped me to build an escape route—the one that we took to get out today. So, I continued to meet my friends when I wasn't at my lessons. My special friends were Alo and his sister, Acoma. Especially Alo. We secretly planned to marry when we were old enough. The clan has a beautiful marriage ceremony."

Linda could feel the tension build as Camila continued her story.

"Then I learned the rest of the reason why I was being groomed to travel to Spain. I was to meet and marry into the nobility. It seems the women in our family had been doing this for generations. Whether they agreed to this, I wasn't told. It was just to be. Our family is quite wealthy and the Spanish nobility had suffered much monetary loss. The trade is simple."

"Did you tell them you wanted to marry Alo?" asked Linda.

"That wouldn't have been safe. Grandmother would have quietly removed him. To where I don't know. But people who displease her have disappeared before. I was now seventeen and had only one year before being taken to Spain," Camila explained. "I wanted to marry Alo who was one of the clan; but, also, I wanted to stay here and become the next Matriarch. I love the clan; they are my family."

Linda began to piece things together. With Camila on her Grandmother's blacklist, she would be the next one expected to carry on the tradition.

Well, that would never happen. She had to get away. Brett had to find her!

Camila looked over Linda's shoulder as though bringing back memories. Her features formed determined lines from the past.

"When I told Alo, the boy I loved, we didn't know what to do. We secretly married," Camila said, softly. "Soon I became pregnant."

"And what did Grandmother do when she found out?" Linda knew the answer.

"She put me out of the house and told me to never return. The clan took me in, and Alo and I were happy. He was killed in a rockslide before the baby was born. I'm still not welcome in the hacienda; I live in the village. I have a beautiful little boy. If the baby had been a girl, I think Abuela would have taken her as my replacement. I don't know how it was arranged, but I think somehow, she killed Alo. I only hope my child is safe. But now that you are here, she will continue the arranged marriage and trip to Spain."

"Camila, she thinks that she has me for a replacement!" Linda said. "But it won't happen."

It wouldn't happen. She had Brett. He would find her. He was her secret, and she had to keep him secret. In the meantime, she would go along with their plans for her here in the valley. But she would not go to Spain.

Linda and Camila walked over the meadow. Although Camila showed her special hiding places for birds' nests, tracks of certain animals, she still felt a real suspicion from Camila. They wandered until the sun began to set. Linda thought of the dog that Brett had given to her.

"Camila, did Sam bring a tiny dog with him?" Linda asked. "There was one at the hacienda before we left on the trail."

Camila's face lit up. "Not Sam, but Spirit Warrior found one and gave it to my son, Ahanhu. It had an injury on its neck that he treated with an elderberry poultice. I guess Sam was bringing a gift to Ahanhu and lost it on the trail."

"Oh," said Linda. "So, I assume that the dog's well now?" She guessed that Brett had rescued the puppy from the trail. Seems she'd lost the gift from Brett, but she knew that the puppy would be taken care of.

"Yes," Camila answered. "Ahanhu loves the puppy. We have never had such an animal like this before. And speaking of Ahanhu, my little one will be missing his momma, and it's time to get you back to your room," Camila ended.

For a moment Linda sensed Camila's withdrawal and feared she would leave her alone to be lost in the fast-coming twilight. Alone in the darkness, she would be easy prey to the dangers of the night. But Camila led her back to the path that went to the tunnel, pointed to the opening, and disappeared. Nothing else had been said. Linda stumbled through the tunnel. Her fingers were clumsy on the door latch, but she managed to open it and slip through.

The plumbing in the hacienda was a mystery to Linda, but the warm water was in abundant supply. She guessed that Sam had installed solar power here in the hacienda, and the bathroom had access to all the heated water one needed for a hot bath.

After bathing, she slipped into bed, weary from the activities of the day. Her head hurt from trying to make it all come together.

Suddenly, she jumped out of bed and picked up the shoes lying on the floor. It wouldn't do for anyone to find them. She slipped the flat sandals under her mattress at the foot of her bed. She giggled at her actions, feeling like a guilty schoolgirl. But this wasn't funny; she was not caught up in a joke. She was entangled in the plans of a strong-willed woman, determined to have her own way.

Chapter 11

It was the odor that drew Brett from unconsciousness. Gentle smoke wafted into his darkness and teased his senses. Numbness still wrapped around his muscles, and he had to fight the cold tendrils entwining his physical powers.

Before Brett could open his eyes, he could feel he was lying on a cot. He wasn't on the hillside under the big cat. He had been able to throw his spear that killed the cat. But in his mind's eye, he saw an arrow plunged in the cat beside his own spear. Then what?

The man! He had seen a man standing up the hill. The man held a bow in his hand. Brett tried to stand, but his twisted ankle couldn't hold him and he fell. That was the picture his unconscious had thrown up on his visual awareness.

Slowly, he opened his eyes and turned toward the cause of the smoke. He knew he was awake, but the sight that reached him was from something from someone's past. Not his past. A clay pot rested on a low fire, bubbling, sending the aroma of meat cooking. A meat that he couldn't identify. The tall figure was covered in primitive Indian dress, his plaited hair adorned with a few colorful feathers. As he attended the mixture in the pot, his back was to Brett. A sharp, wicked-looking knife was sheathed at his waist.

When the figure turned, Brett could only stare. It was a man directly from the picture collection of Adam Grainger. There was no doubt in his mind that Adam had been here. He had known this man. Brett felt some degree of safety.

Brett sat up and tried to stand. Pain shot through his ankle and forced him down again. His ankle was encased in some primitive cast that looked to be made of clay.

"It'll be a while before you can walk without help. I've made a walking stick for you," the Indian spoke good English.

He walked toward Brett holding out the walking stick. It was actually fashioned more like a crutch with a piece to fit under his arm. The padding on the piece was of the softest leather that Brett had ever felt. Expertly worked deer hide.

"Thank you," Brett said.

It was all he could say. Now where would the conversation go? It was all so surreal. It was like a play staged in the woods, and Brett hadn't been given his lines. And his costume was all wrong.

The frame of the cot was held up by wooden limbs and tightly woven together with rawhide straps. Boughs of soft pine were covered with more of the supple deer-hide leather. A lean-to under which he sat was made to butt up to the mouth of a cave. To Brett this was the Hilton of the Hills.

The Indian went to a nearby stream and filled a glazed, clay cup with water.

"You will be very sore. You've had a shock, and I know you have a lot of questions," the Indian said. "First," the Indian began, "my name is Spirit Warrior."

He handed the water to Brett and extended his hand. Brett took it.

"I'm Brett McAlister," Brett answered.

"You rest and I'll tell you a little about myself. It may answer many of your questions."

Spirit Warrior lowered himself to the ground close to Brett.

"I am the clan elder of our people. We live in a valley not too far from here." Spirit Warrior eased into his narrative. "A man, not unlike yourself, came to our village many years ago now. He stayed with us and taught us many things, and he learned much from us. He taught me and my family to speak what he called 'English'. He taught us of his God. Our people knew gods came from the sky, so Allen Griffin told us how this happened: Jesus birth, his death, his resurrection. This Jesus will come back from the sky and take us to a new village in heaven. His God spoke to the hearts of many of our people. This Holy Spirit speaks to my heart every day."

Brett sat awestruck. From his Bible he remembered reading how the sky points to God's glory. *"The heavens declare the glory of God; the skies proclaim the work of his hands. Day after day they pour forth speech: night after night they display knowledge. There is no speech or language where their voice is not heard. Their voice goes out into all the world."*

"Yes. I, too, know and worship the same God as Alan Griffin."

"Do all the people where you come from worship this God?" asked Spirit Warrior.

"No. They know of him, but some will not worship," Brett admitted.

"Yes, it's the same in our village. Some will not accept," he answered sadly. "Alan Griffin said that all creation was the first missionary: look at what God created and see God."

Brett remembered Adam/Alan saying that he thought God met people where they were and led them to himself if they were seeking.

Brett didn't know how long Adam Grainger, aka Alan Griffin, had lived here, but he hadn't wasted any time. He had shared his knowledge of language and the salvation of God, through Jesus Christ. He was seeing and appreciating more and more the man he thought he had known.

Spirit Warrior abruptly ended the conversation. He went back to the fire and moved the pot to one side. He laid a small wooden plank over the coals. He then laid four small trout on the plank and sprinkled them with some seasonings he took from a leather pouch. He had cut small pieces of potato and added them to the plank. Mountain trout freshly caught from the stream. Brett's stomach sounded its anticipation. The hot drink that Spirit Warrior had given him smelled like coffee. Tasted like coffee. So, he guessed they grew coffee beans in his village. It was beginning to sound like El Dorado.

The food warmed him and he lay back to relieve the pressure on his ankle. His mind was awhirl with so many questions, but his strength wasn't enough to keep him from falling back into the darkness that beckoned him.

When Brett opened his eyes again, he was staring at a mountain lion. It was lying, belly up, on a huge sheet of deer hide. The animal had been relieved of all his intestines and lay open for further preparation. With a sharply-honed knife, Spirit Warrior began the process.

Cutting the skin on the leg above the hind paw, he carefully followed a natural seamline up the leg to the belly. Moving steadily with a deft hand, Spirit Warrior finished his cutting until the skin could be laid aside attached only to the four paws and the head.

"You killed a very large mountain lion," Spirit Warrior said. "I think this is the one that has been raiding our goat herds. He has eaten well, and he is very fat. His meat will be a treat for the next feast."

"Is lion good to eat?" Brett asked. Even as he asked the question, he guessed the answer. He was glad he'd get the chance to try its meat, not be eaten by it.

The hindquarters, shoulder, tenderloin and backstrap were being rinsed in the flowing stream. When Spirit Warrior was satisfied that all the blood was washed off, he carefully stored them in a large leather pouch.

"Big cats have good meat," said Spirit Warrior. "We thank God for the food, but we honor the sacrifice the animal has made to nourish us and don't waste any part of it. This skin will become a soft rug for you."

With its neck down and hanging over a pole, Brett watched as Spirit Warrior began the process of fleshing the animal by using a slab of pine with a long handle. Careful not to puncture the skin, he pushed down and away to scrape off all the meat and fat particles. He turned the cat end over end, scraping until he was satisfied.

He'd watched while Spirit Warrior removed the brains from the lion's head and warmed them in a pot over the fire. When cooled, he had worked them into the animal's skin. He told Brett that each animal had a quantity of brains to do the job of leaving soft, useable fur. Or it could be used when removing the hair and tanning into leather. The coating with the brain material also stopped deterioration. He had talked as he worked: a master craftsman sharing his knowledge.

I'll certainly research brain tanning when I get home!

When Spirit Warrior was finished, he burned all the leftovers that would attract predators, leaving only a pungent charred odor. Smoke from the burning made their eyes water, but it was protection.

Earlier, Spirit Warrior had gathered root vegetables from their surroundings and added them to the small clay pot that had been simmering meat on the coals for hours. The smell was now more tempting. Spirit Warrior ladled the stew into two bowls and handed one to Brett. Brett couldn't have described the vegetables or identified the meat, but it was a gourmet's delight. If nothing else, Spirit Warrior was a pleasing host.

The sun was beginning to lean westward, and Brett watched Spirit Warrior stow his meager pack inside the cave and move their fire to a place at the mouth of the cave, between them and any outside intruder. Brett's spear was beside him, and Spirit Warrior had put his bow and arrows within arms' reach. The sun dropped behind the mountain, and suddenly it was dark.

As he drifted off to sleep, he wondered when he would be able to walk out of this forest. He had to admit that his injured ankle was feeling better tonight, but he hadn't tried to put much weight on it. He still had a lot of questions, but maybe tomorrow he would learn more. He would ask about Linda.

Chapter 12

Brett was dreaming of the big cat and woke with a start. He felt a wet tongue on his cheek. With a cry, he sat up. The sun was just offering enough light to dispel the fear of a mountain lion in the cave. Another lick. It was Linda's little dog that he'd found on the trail. He had long decided that it was a victim of its injury. But the smell from the poultice could only mean that Spirit Warrior had treated the dog. Whatever had been applied to the wound on its neck had done the trick. The gash was still noticeable, but it was closing and a scab was beginning to form. Its hair would grow over the wound and it would disappear entirely.

He petted the dog's head gently. Seemingly content, the puppy snuggled again into his bedding and went back to sleep. Brett could see crumbs from the puppy's breakfast.

Spirit Warrior had again built a cooking fire and the smell of trout again was tempting. He had made flat cakes of cornmeal, roasted to a delicate crispness. And again, the coffee.

"We'll stay in camp another day," Spirit Warrior announced. "Your ankle will then be strong enough to get you to our village. And, the mountain lion's skin needs another day to dry."

Brett doubted the statement about his ankle, but he knew they couldn't stay here. He had to find Linda.

"You have many questions still." It was a statement.

"Yes," Brett agreed.

They finished their meal in silence. The silence was not an awkward one, but companionable. Spirit Warrior had accepted Brett at face value: a wanderer lost and in need of care. He offered his help with an open hand.

"How did you come to be here?" Spirit Warrior asked, his hand gesture taking in the scene around them.

"I was following the trail of a man whom I think has kidnapped the woman I plan to marry," Brett answered. "I got as far as where I encountered the mountain lion."

"Yes. I tracked them, and I recognized two of the three. I've never seen the young woman, but I know of her. She must be the one you seek."

"Does she seem to be okay?" Brett asked. His mouth suddenly became dry. He took a drink of his now-cold coffee.

"She seems to have been given something to make her sleep, but she still sits her horse well," Spirit Warrior offered.

"Yes, she's a champion rider," Brett agreed.

"She is with two people that I know well. They'll not harm her. She is the granddaughter of the Matriarch of the Mountain. She is the daughter of Inez, the Matriarch's daughter; her father is Alan Griffin. The one you call Adam Grainger," he explained.

"Who are the ones who took her?" Brett asked.

"Sam Straeder is the Matriarch's husband. The woman traveling with them, holding the babies, is Adella. Adella is from the household of the Matriarch. When Sam Straeder is away from the valley, she travels with him," he explained. "She brings the babies."

"What about the babies? Where do these babies come from?" Brett asked.

He wanted to know about Linda, but since Spirit Warrior mentioned the babies it must be important.

Spirit Warrior was quiet. His features took on a determined expression. He seemed to be wrestling with the answer to the question. Many secrets lay hidden in the lines of his face.

"Our clan is growing small, and we need more children. On the outside of the Mountain, he holds the position of priest. When he encounters infants without families or unwanted babies of other tribes, he brings them to the Matriarch who then gives them to our clan. There is a presentation ceremony and a feast of thanksgiving. Our people think the gods give these babies to the Matriarch as blessings to our clan."

Who was this woman that would soon have Linda?

"I refused a child once, and I never saw the baby again," he explained.

"Surely she would not kill them," Brett was outraged.

"I cannot have that on my heart. God's Spirit would not be pleased with me," Spirit Warrior confessed. "We take them in, and I teach them the way of the True Spirit that came from the sky. The One who is coming back to get us one day to live with him forever."

"In my Father's house are many mansions, if it were not so, I would have told you. I go to prepare a place for you, and if I go and prepare a place for you, I will come again, and receive you unto myself; that where I am, there ye may be also," Brett quoted.

"You know our Father, too?" Spirit Warrior said. "That is good."

"Why do they want Linda?" asked Brett.

Fear rose up in his heart. The circumstances were becoming so entangled. One question's answer did nothing to make things clearer. The outcome of Linda's kidnapping was beginning to sound ominous. His resolve was firm. He would fight for her. He turned his thoughts to what Spirit Warrior was saying.

"I must start at the beginning. Alan Griffin came to our village by accident. He was quite an adventurer, and he wandered into our midst exhausted and delirious. It only took a week until he was up and about. His curiosity knew no bounds. He wrote many words in his book, he took what he called pictures and memorized his surroundings. One day Inez visited our village. After they met, they had eyes for only each other."

Brett could imagine. After meeting Linda, he could never love another. But for Adam to see a girl such as Inez in her natural surroundings, there would have been no other choice. He could never regret the path not taken.

"Our marriage ceremonies are simple affairs. Everyone gathered around while the Chief Clan Elder bound them together with a simple prayer said aloud in unison. Alan added something from his Holy Bible: *What therefore God hath joined together, let not man put asunder.*"

"So, you performed the ceremony?" Brett asked. "You were Chief Clan Elder?"

Spirit Warrior simply nodded.

Brett could visualize such a ceremony. Out under God's sky, surrounded by innocence.

"The newly wedded couple were led to a freshly-prepared dwelling furnished by those who knew Inez and had come to know Alan. It was two days before the Matriarch sent for Inez. She, of course, didn't know of Alan. Inez often stayed with the girls of our village. But Inez had no choice but to obey the summons. Alan would not let his new bride go alone."

Hurrah for him. Yes. He could see him here. He could see his courage. That same courage that had, for whatever reason, kept Linda away from his house all those years.

"I, of course, don't know what his reception was. But I know that he stood up to the Matriarch, although he willingly agreed to live with Inez here. But after Inez became with child, I knew he wanted to go back, taking his wife and child with him. He told me these things. I feared for him."

"What could the Matriarch do if he wanted to leave?" Brett asked.

"I told him to guard his secret," Spirit Warrior said. "I've seen strangers wander into this valley who disappear, never to be seen again. If they were injured and put outside the valley, the animals would descend on them."

"But that's the same as murder," Brett protested. "Is Linda safe?"

"For now," Spirit Warrior assured him. He continued his narrative.

"As the time for the birth grew near, they set a time to sneak off of the mountain. I was to lead them to the path that descends to Alan's world. No one can find their way out of our valley alone. It is a secret handed down from Chief Elder to Chief Elder. It is one of many secrets handed down.

"But it was too late. The Matriarch protested but Sam went for his own medicine man called a doctor. It was a long journey there and back, and Inez became very weak. She was near death, and the couple knew there was no hope. Sam and Elena left the lean-to, leaving only the doctor with the couple. A baby girl was born with Inez's last breath. The doctor shoved the baby in Brett's arms and told him to run. But there were two babies. When Sam and Elena came back into the lean-to, the doctor handed the second one to Elena, telling her he didn't think it would live. She handed the tiny baby to Sam. In a fit of anger, Elena plunged a knife into the doctor's back."

"But why?" Brett exclaimed.

"Her anger was fed by a number of things. She hated Alan, she hated strangers in her valley, she hated that Sam had brought in the doctor when Inez died any way, she hated the small scrap of a child that would someday take her place as Matriarch."

"How do you know this?" Brett said.

"I followed and watched," he said simply.

He then told Brett how he had followed Adam as he ran out of the valley into the forest. He knew the babe couldn't survive out there. When he saw Alan fall and become unconscious, he loaded Alan onto the burro he'd brought. He wrapped the baby in soft deerskin and started back to the village. A village mother had secretly wet-nursed the infant, and Alan soon recovered. He kept Alan and the babe hidden until he could slip them out of the village to a place where Alan could find the path back to his world.

"Did the other baby girl live?" Brett asked.

"She lives. Her name is Camila, and she is Linda's twin sister."

"Why does the Matriarch, Elena, want Linda?" Brett asked.

"Camila is no longer acceptable. She is disgraced, and she has been put out of the Matriarch's hacienda. It is because she refused to marry the one chosen for her; she married one of our clan. She gave birth to a boy. Maybe if it had been a girl, the Matriarch might have been appeased. This still left no heir for the future rule.

"Somehow, the Matriarch found out about Linda's existence. Sam only agreed to help bring Linda here if she would leave Camila alone. Sam is probably the only one that Elena has ever loved. Sam has always done what Elena wanted; except he has never killed for her."

It all came flooding in on Brett. Somehow that other girl had a link to Linda's mind, her spirit. There was no explanation for it. But she had to be the girl standing in Linda's shadow.

It was quiet. Brett didn't know what Spirit Warrior was thinking, but he was coming to believe that there could be more that he could learn from the Clan Elder. Answers that would make things clearer.

"Linda has felt the presence of another person at stressful times during her life. A few times she has seen an image much like herself through the mist in the mirror. She has been afraid her mind was becoming weak. She has even doubted her sanity. Linda knew nothing of Camila," Brett explained.

"Her father didn't tell her of his life here?" Spirit Warrior asked.

"No. He changed his name to Adam Grainger and lived quietly with his daughter for a few years. He became a teacher many, many miles from here. After Linda's first vision, she was sent away from the house. She went to school far away from her father. He visited her when he could." Brett's explanation was sounding weak in his own ears.

"Camila didn't know of her sister, but from time to time she felt lonely. She wandered all over the valley, always searching for someone. She played with the clan children, but she was often seen on her own, talking to an unseen playmate," Spirit Warrior remembered.

"Camila was with the clan children most of the daylight hours. She could have learned of The Spirit Winging Chant. It has been practiced in our clan," explained Spirit Warrior. "I don't encourage this any longer because I cannot find such a practice explained in the Holy Book."

Brett was impressed with Spirit Warrior's determination to follow the teachings in the Bible. He was learning every day with an obedient attitude.

"Spirit warriors are not trained to hunt or to do physical battle. We are trained to do battle on the Unseen Plain of the Spirit. I have only learned how to do this from words from the Holy Bible: '...*be strong in the Lord, and in the power of his might. Put on the whole armor of God, that ye may be able to stand against the wiles of the devil*,'" he explained. His face took on a light of understanding.

"Yes," agreed Brett. "The whole armor of God is given to us."

Spirit Warrior continued to quote, "*Stand therefor, having your loins girt about with truth, and having on the breastplate of righteousness; And your feet shod with the preparation of the gospel of peace; Above all, taking the shield of faith, wherewith ye shall be able to quench the fiery darts of the wicked. And take the helmet of salvation, and the sword of the Spirit, which is the word of God.'"*

Brett felt humbled. This man, cut off from institutions of theological learning, had been taught by the Holy Spirit from God's word. The people of his clan were certainly in good hands.

He went on to explain that a personal spiritual journey was a basic belief of their clan. An individual was freed from their physical confinement to the ties of this earth. Their spirit was set free to travel for productive purposes. Never for any light-hearted reason. Camila would have repeated the Spirit Winging Chant that she'd heard in the village. She wanted to reach the unknown part of her that was missing. If what Linda says is true, Camila must have been successful.

"It is an explanation," Brett said. "Camila's desire must have been extremely focused. Her mind must be quite strong. I do believe what Linda says she experienced is true."

Brett knew of Linda's intelligence. He expected that her twin sister's intelligence would be no less.

"I learned this chant from the beginning of my Spirit Warrior training, but I didn't know its true meaning until I met the True Spirit, Jesus Christ, the Son of God. It was meant to be a chant against dark forces," he explained. "But I say it as a prayer to the Only True God.

Oh, Great One Above.

Shield us from the face of the Dark One.

I am not afraid to fight.

I must have your power.

I am Spirit Warrior of the People.

I guard my people from the dark ones.

I will protect with my life.
Oh, Great One Above.
I will shield with The One's Light.
I am not afraid to fight."

Spirit Warrior spoke it forcefully, but with a deep reverence for his new beliefs.

They moved on, ever upward, stopping only to let the puppy move around a bit. He was still weak, but the little exercise was doing him some good. His small bark was still just a squeak from his throat injury. He could swallow only tiny bits that he was given.

Brett, too, was glad to stop for the rest periods. His leg screamed with pain, and his arm pit was raw from the rubbing of the cloth. It was soft to begin with, but it had worn down to the wood. It was getting dusk, and Spirit Warrior had said they wouldn't reach the village until tomorrow at dusk. He said he wanted to enter the village under the cover of darkness.

So, he was being sneaked into the village. That was okay with him. It would give him a chance to get to Linda before her captors knew he was here. Spirit Warrior knew who held her, but he was reluctant to say whether or not getting her out would be easy. Or, if it would even be possible. He did say that it wouldn't be safe.

Safe or not, my love, I'm coming for you. Just don't give up.

The same scene played the second night. Another small fire before a cave entrance, but this time they ate roasted rabbit that Spirit Warrior's bow had bagged for their supper. Rubbed with spices from his pack, its taste was superb. Spirit Warrior had strung Brett's own handmade bow, but he didn't think he could exhibit the skill he'd seen from this Ancient One, this Anasazi, this ancestor of the Puebloan people.

Chapter 13

Brett didn't think he would be able to sleep for the pain in his leg. Also, he felt that his shoulder had become nearly dislocated from the weight he'd had to put on the crutch. He lay still, giving in to the pain, and listening to the night sounds. No voices could be heard, but owls hooted in rhythm to the barking of the coyotes. But soon, the hot drink that he'd been given caused all the sounds to stop.

He awoke at first light. The room he was in was small, walls smoothed with adobe colored red and ochre. Furnishings were minimal: the bed he lay on and one small table with a chair. Light was furnished by the first rays of the sun and allowed in through a square-cut window. His backpack lay on the floor beside him.

Someone had been in during the night. His shoulder had been rubbed with an unfamiliar-smelling salve, relieving the sting of the chaffing. His boots had been removed and cleaned. He was no longer wearing his own clothes, but he was dressed in an embroidered shirt, loose over buckskin leggings. His ankle still wore the cast, but the trouser leg was wide enough to hang over it. His crutch leaned against his bed. The crosspiece at the top of the crutch was padded with what looked like cotton and rewrapped with more soft buckskin.

"Spirit Warrior say I attend you." His English was broken, but his voice was soft and musical. "Me, Tohopka." He pointed to his chest.

"Tohopka," Brett repeated. "My name is Brett. Thank you." He indicated his clothing.

Tohopka nodded and helped Brett to go with him into the adjoining room. It looked just like the one he slept in, except it had a basin for washing and what Brett guessed was a chamber pot. Looks like he had an adjoining bath.

Brett hobbled back into his room aided by Tohopka.

"Eat," Tohopka said.

Brett hadn't noticed the food. On a ceramic dish, there was a roll, cheese, and a cluster of large, purple grapes. A ceramic mug held a steaming liquid.

"Spirit Warrior say rest. No walk today," he carefully relayed the instructions. "More food later." Then he was gone.

The roll was made from a wheat flour as far as he could tell, and the cheese was made from goat's milk. The grapes were sweet.

Brett used his crutch to make it to his adjoining bathroom and came back to his room. He sat on his bed, sipping his hot drink. Not coffee this time, but a flavorful cocoa drink. His vision was blurring, the cocoa drink had an added ingredient.

When he opened his eyes, he felt rested. Tohopka had brought food again. This time the drink was clear, cool water. He ate slowly and tried to gather his thoughts.

What did he really know? It was dark when he came, and he hadn't even looked out the window since it was light. There was only one window in his cubicle, so it would be a one-dimensional view.

Brett hobbled to the window. It was magic. He'd come from the sandy desert, traveled for two days up a rock-lined path of pine and deciduous trees, to this carpet of green that lay before him. As far as his eye could see up the incline to his left, all was green. Terraced gardens marched up the hillside where, at the top, gabion-like structures would protect the plants from rushing water during hard rains. Whatever grew there was thick and flourishing. It was too far away for him to identify any of the plants. If it were a vegetable garden, it would certainly feed a lot of people. There would be herds of goats to produce the cheese he ate today, and there must be vineyards and fields of grain. Somewhere they produced coffee beans and cocoa beans for the chocolate he drank this morning.

The ceramic dishes he had eaten from had to be fashioned and kilned. Artisans had to be adept at preparing the clay, molding, and firing. The design had been black on white with a pattern he'd seen on Dr. Grainger's artifacts. He'd seen cotton firsthand. Cotton for the shirt he was now wearing, and cotton pads on his crutch crosspiece. His trousers were of soft deerskin, so there was game. They could grow cotton, and someone had to know how to spin and weave, make patterns and sew clothing.

This tribe, or clan as Spirit Warrior called them, had to be quite large. It wasn't the nomadic, tepee-housed Indians that he had expected. This was an advanced civilization of intelligent people complete with much knowledge for being self-sustained. A dedicated halidom for worship. People who weren't wandering. They'd settled here so many years ago that not even the eldest knew from whence they came.

Where would he begin to look for Linda? He certainly wouldn't be of any help in her rescue until his ankle healed. And how would he find her? There must be hundreds of inhabitants in this valley. No wonder Spirit Warrior had been reluctant to give him an easy answer for getting Linda out. He needed to talk to Spirit Warrior. Would the Indian even have time for him now that he was back with the load of responsibilities that he must have?

Brett thought back to his middle-school years. His father had taken the family to the Chaco Canyon where his interest in the ancient Indian civilizations had really started to take root. He and his sisters had explored ruins from previous ages. They stepped through odd-shaped doorways that led up and down the stairs of multi-storied buildings. From the top floors, they could look out windows into the desert sky, a sea of blue that went on forever.

From the top floor he took pictures of the layout below of building complexes that he later came to know was called great houses. These great houses had hundreds of rooms, a central plaza, and kivas. He had romanticized the kivas into places of mystery, home to past spirits of the Anasazi. The ruins spoke of an advanced race of superb engineers and builders. Builders of roads that led to unexplained destinations. But since no evidence of a written language had surfaced, much of the life of these settlements were shrouded in the mists of antiquity.

The interest had consumed him and he couldn't seem to learn enough. Getting the scholarship for his Ph.D. work with Dr. Grainger had been a dream come true. Grainger had been the foremost authority in North America. Now he knew why he'd been chosen. Dr. Grainger was not only protecting his discovery, but he was protecting his family. The paper that he had submitted to the professor had told too much. It had come too close to raising academic questions that would need investigating.

The ancient ruins and roads in the desert were all that was left when they toured Chaco Canyon. Rubble left to make paths uneven, and debris to cover secrets of the buildings below the earth. But what about where he was now?

It was true that with his injury he hadn't been able to explore, but what he could see out of his square window did not lay in ruins. Besides the terraced gardens where lush growth marched upward as far as he could see, to his right were fields of grain fenced in by rock walls. The agriculture knowledge here was awesome. The snow-capped mountains he could see cutting into the blue of the sky must provide for irrigation. They had channeled the course from the melting snow to a useable flow that could be harnessed and directed.

"Spirit Warrior come see Brett tonight," Tohopka announced. He had entered the room with lunch: a whole baked fish and boiled potatoes. The fish was seasoned and there was butter for the potatoes. An apple and slices of cheese completed the lunch.

Room service with gourmet food! It couldn't get much better. Except he had to get out of this room. He'd have to explain to Spirit Warrior his need to find Linda. Maybe Spirit Warrior had some news of her.

Again, the hot drink had something extra added. He slept and woke up to darkness.

"Brett?" It was Spirit Warrior. He held a candle which he placed in a ceramic holder shaped like a deer.

Brett instantly sat up and looked toward the sound of the voice.

"Yes, I'm awake," he answered the Indian. "Just still groggy from your sleeping aid!"

"It will help you heal," he didn't apologize. He sat in the chair beside the bed. "I know you have even more questions now."

"Yes, I do," Brett hastily agreed. "Linda? What about Linda?"

"As I thought, she is here. She is with the Matriarch of the Mountain, Elena, in the hacienda on the high hill. I haven't seen her, but Camila has reported to me. Camila tells no one else for fear of her own safety. And Linda's safety."

"What would she do to Linda?" Brett asked. His features took on lines of determination.

"I do not know. But only Sam Straeder stands between Camila and Elena's wrath. The Matriarch feels like her power to direct her family has been taken away with Camila's rebellion. Our clan holds the Matriarch of the Mountain up as the source of god's favor. If she dies without a successor, god's favor may be taken from us."

"How did this start?"

"At the beginning…we do not know the time, our clan was nearly destroyed by an enemy tribe. A nearby group of Spaniards came to our rescue, and the war-like tribe fled. The next day, the tribe returned to fight the Spaniards and the rest of our clan. They were again driven off, but some of ours were killed."

"In our past, I believe the incident was named 'The Legend of the Crying Child'," Brett added. He was beginning to get the picture.

"Yes, the story said many children cried. The Spirit Warrior at that time had a map. It was called the map of escape."

"The valley where we are now?" Brett interrupted.

"Yes. He showed it to the Spanish leader. They planned their way, and the entire band set out by cover of darkness. By dawn, the group had traveled, covering their tracks, far enough to be safe. After several days, the map led them here."

"How do you know this?" Brett asked. He knew there was no written language from the Ancients.

"It is passed down from Spirit Warrior to Spirit Warrior through the ages," he explained. "We also have a chant for it. The chant tells the story, and we repeat this once a year when we gather in the kiva. It is a chant of remembrance. This chant blesses the Spanish for their guidance. The one in leadership at the time was a woman. A woman has been in power every generation: Matriarch of the Mountain. Our band grew quickly in this protected place, many children. The elders of the clan remembered the ways of building, planting, and the ancient wisdom. The Spanish had brought much seed for planting. Through the ages, it has become as you see it."

"That's another thing, Spirit Warrior," Brett retorted. "I've not seen much. I have to get out of this room!"

Spirit Warrior's eyes gleamed in the candlelight and a small smile changed his countenance. "I have brought the other walking stick for you." He rested the second piece of the crutch on the bed. "You'll be safe as long as Elena does not know that you are here to take back her granddaughter."

"Who would tell her?" Brett asked.

"She is held in great fear. No one speaks to her from our clan except me. Of course, Camila would not tell her. So, unless Sam sees you and reports to her, you should be safe."

"Safe?" Brett asked. "What would she do to me?"

"Kill you. Or have you killed."

Chapter 14

Brett was well-rested after sleeping most of the day. The full moon bathed his cubicle, luring him outside. No pollution obscured this sky. The platinum light edged everything silver. The far mountain peaks reflected a shiny, lively gray.

It took a little while to get used to the crutches but slowly he could use them. He was totally unfamiliar with the terrain which made going slow but the path was smooth and light. Obviously, it was well traveled. Just seeing things from a perspective other than his cubicle window was inspiring. This civilization showed depth—agriculture, construction, halidom. His room was just a small room in a larger complex. The roads running from the building where he had been staying were not unlike spokes in a wheel. Buildings like his own each had a spoke that ran to a large stone enclosure. Between the spokes, gardens of flowers scented the night air with mystery, looking as though they'd been cut from tinfoil.

It seemed a luxury for such a civilization to cultivate something other than that which would sustain life. But how was he to know? Perhaps these people had gone beyond just needing that which sustains the body, longing for the ethereal. The intangible that feeds the hunger of yearning.

Curiosity beckoned him on down the path toward the center building. Although he saw no others out in the night, he proceeded quietly. When he approached the doorway leading to the interior of a large, round building, he heard the voices. He slipped through the opening and hid in the shadows.

An elevated dais made of stones was at the other end of the space. This was not unlike a raised dais part of the floor at the end of a medieval hall for dignified occupancy. Two chairs, not unlike thrones, sat in the middle of the dais, flanked by two chairs on each side.

Brett recognized Spirit Warrior occupying one of the thrones with a woman sitting beside him on the other. Brett knew that this was the Matriarch of the Mountain, Elena, Linda's grandmother. Here on the platform were the two leaders of this civilization.

On the other side of the woman stood a distinguished man in black. Brett decided this must be Sam Straeder. Beside him was a woman cradling a baby in each arm. On the other side of Spirit Warrior were leaders, no doubt, under his tutelage.

The woman rose. Standing wasn't a good enough description for what she did. Her movements were fluid, and she just seemed to float upright. She was tall, regal, and robed in scarlet. Her hair was coiled in a coronet around her head. Her voice carried even to the back where Brett hid in shadow. The voice was spellbinding, commanding the attention of all in the room. Not loud, but with a timbre that was mesmerizing.

"Welcome, people of the clan. I'm privileged to bring gifts. Once again, we are blessed with the addition of two new members to your number. The spirits of the crying child are honoring us with new life."

The Matriarch beckoned the woman holding the babies to stand beside her. With her head kept down, she stood in subservience to the Matriarch. Elena took one of the babies from Adella and stood in front of Spirit Warrior. He stood and accepted the little one. The two who had been sitting by him were now erect by his side. He gave the babe to one of the men and turned to accept the second child that Elena surrendered to him, then gently handed this babe to the other man. The two men holding the children bowed before Elena as she chanted,

> *"Spirit of the Crying Child,*
> *We accept these little ones*
> *From those who wish to atone*
> *For the wrong done so long ago.*
> *Merged into the people of the clan*
> *They will grow strong*
> *They will fulfill the destiny*
> *As was theirs in the beginning."*

She turned and those with her followed in her wake and disappeared silently out into the night.

Spirit Warrior stood before the men holding the babies and raised his arms. No sounds were made as he lifted his face upward. Then he began his prayer.

"Heavenly Father, the one True God, we thank you for these precious babies that you have given into our care. May we teach them your way as we have learned from others. Bless the families into which they will be blended. In Jesus' name, amen."

The power of his simple prayer settled on the clan. A musician with what looked like a gaita began to play. Brett knew that this instrument was an ancient type of bagpipe from somewhere in Spain.

The clan picked up the melody which reverberated from the rock walls. The song was a doxology. *"Praise God from whom all blessings flow, praise him all creatures here below…"*. Never had the words touched Brett as they did here in this place. This cavern became a cathedral. Adam Grainger had been blessed to do mission work among such a receptive clan. But he had heard many add their voices to the pagan chant of the Matriarch, and he remembered Spirit Warrior saying that all did not accept the True Way. Spirit Warrior had told him that the spirit warriors were not trained to be skillful hunters or physical protectors. They were trained to protect the clan from the spiritual dark forces on a higher plane. And this had become clearer after he accepted God through Jesus. It came about with prayer and living his life according to the holy book that Adam Grainger had left behind.

A couple came forward to claim the babies. This way may not be legal, but it was a good alternative to an orphanage. These little Indian babies would know love and acceptance before they could remember anything else, and they wouldn't end up experiencing hunger and rejection.

Brett stayed hidden, watching the crowd file out. No one was looking for a stranger in their midst, so he felt safe.

Suddenly, there she was. Dressed differently, but it was Linda. He was ready to go to her, but as she turned directly toward him something seemed different. The face was the same but the expression was all wrong. The hair was too long. She walked close to a group whom she was obviously a part of. A young child was asleep in her arms. Brett knew that if he went to her, she would not know him. This was Camila, Linda's sister.

The disappointment held his heart in a vice. Where was she? Had something happened to her? Brett didn't think she would be expected to attend this ritual, but those who had her were in attendance, leaving him to speculate that she was locked away somewhere.

When the great house was empty, Brett stepped from his hiding place.

"This is the way the babies are introduced into the clan." The voice came from behind him, and he almost lost his balance.

"Spirit Warrior," Brett acknowledged. 'I thought everyone was gone."

"I always stay to leave last. And," he added, "I knew you were here. I could feel an alien presence. Not an evil one, but a questioning one."

"It was all quite impressive," Brett said. "I thought I saw Linda," he continued, "But it turned out not to be."

"No, it was Camila. She went through the marriage rite with my son. His name was Alo. It means 'spirit guide' because he would have become a spirit warrior. But, my son, the child's father, was killed in a rockslide. It was a strange accident."

"And the baby?" Asked Brett.

"A boy. His name is Ahanu which means 'he laughs'. He's always been such a happy child. We wait to name our children until they show signs of their personalities. His laughter became bubbly and loud." The pride on Spirit Warrior's face was the same as grandfathers everywhere.

"How did the Matriarch accept their marriage?" He remembered the implacable look on Elena's face.

"Not well. There were consequences. Camila's belongings were burned, and she was put out of the hacienda on the hill and told never to return. Sam Straeder still stands between Camila and the Matriarch's wrath. It's been nearly three years, so Camila's life may not be in danger now; but when Sam Straeder is gone, Camila stays hidden among the clan. If Camila's child had been a girl, Elena may have been somewhat appeased, thinking she would take that child as a substitute."

"So, that's why Linda is in such jeopardy," Brett said.

"Yes. The Matriarch will not willingly let her go. When she found out that Linda existed her fate was settled."

"Settled only in the Matriarch's mind! I will not go back and leave Linda here. She belongs with me. She belongs to the world outside." His face burned.

"Elena is desperate for someone to take her place. And there must be time for them to be prepared. The journey to find a proper mate would be the first step," Spirit Warrior said. Then he added, "She must not find out that you are here. Linda would disappear beyond our reach."

Brett stumbled slightly on the path back to his cubicle. Spirit Warrior put a guiding hand to Brett's elbow.

"You aren't strong yet," Spirit Warrior said. "You must rest until you are. You will not be a help to Linda until your ankle is healed completely. And we must pray for guidance."

Brett realized just how weak he was when he lay down on his cot. The trip to the round house had taken its toll. Most of the weariness could be attributed to the helplessness that he was feeling. He prayed, but his last words before falling asleep were said to Linda.

I'll not leave without you. Please just hang on.

Chapter 15

Weak sunlight escaped around the mountain peaks to awaken the new day. Brett immediately opened his eyes. He felt rested and stretched cautiously on the cot. He had found, to his hurt, that he was just a little longer than his bed. He raised his arms and smiled as he anticipated the new day.

He knew that he would need to talk to Spirit Warrior and see just what his boundaries would be. The clothes he had been given would blend in with those living here, but the color of his hair contrasted to those around him. He couldn't draw attention to himself for fear of putting Linda further out of his reach. Although, he desperately wanted to find a way to tell her he was here.

"Good morning, Tohopka," Brett said. Again, the young man had brought his breakfast and put it on the table beside his bed.

Tohopka nodded to him. "Spirit Warrior say that you rest one more day."

"I'm wanting to get out and walk about in the daytime," Brett answered him.

"He will come soon. Spirit Warrior know best," Tohopka said.

"Ah, yes. No doubt that he does," Brett agreed.

Tohopka smiled and left quietly.

One more day. Could he hold his curiosity one more day? Well, there was no complaint about the food.

Brett looked at his food arranged again on a bright-colored ceramic plate. The goat cheese spread like cream cheese on a piece of toasted flatbread, and there was fruit, butter, and honey. And, again, their delicious coffee. Coffee beans must do well on these surrounding hills.

Brett finished his breakfast and was savoring the last of his coffee when Spirit Warrior entered his cubicle.

"Good morning. Is there anything that you require?" asked Spirit Warrior.

"Tohopka has been more than helpful," answered Brett. "But he says you want me to stay in one more day?"

"Even with your walking sticks your movements should be limited. When you leave this mountain, your ankle will need to be strong, and you were unsteady on your sticks last night."

"Yes, but I want to get outside in the day, but I'm concerned that I don't blend in very well. I can dress the part but when the sun hits my head, my hair color will give me away."

"Spirit Warrior chuckled. "Yes, your hair shines. Our clan would think you are a gift from the sun. No, we have never seen hair this color, so we must make you fade into our people. I have prepared a potion for your hair. Tohopka will apply the dye, but it will be several hours before the hair is dark. That is another reason for you to stay hidden. After today, you may roam around outside as long as you stay out of view of the Matriarch's house on the hill."

Spirit Warrior left and Tohopka came in carrying a small pot of liquid, smelling of some type of berry. Brett couldn't place it. The liquid stung his scalp just a bit, but then there was a cooling sensation that made goosebumps on his head.

The hot chocolate that Tohopka served must have had another sleeping aid in it, because soon Brett was asleep in his cot, breathing a little heavily. Was Spirit Warrior not taking any chances that Brett's need to find Linda would drive him outside too soon, or was he protecting Brett from the Matriarch's uncertain reception?

The sun seemed brighter here, the new day fresh and the air free of the man-made pollutants that existed below. It was probably his imagination, but the sky seemed a purer blue and the few wispy, white clouds unblemished.

Tohopka had told him that breakfast would be with their family clan this morning. Spirit Warrior had prepared Brett's way by saying he was a wandering visitor. No one would question his presence. He felt adrift, but he was a wanderer with a purpose; and he itched to get started on it.

The meal was in the round house that he'd visited the night before, and he could see that it was central to six houses at the ends of each of the six stone-covered paths at equal distances around it. From his cubicle window he had seen the domes of four other round houses to the east. If he assumed there were five other such layouts to the west, it had to be quite a thriving community. He quickly took a rough census of those at his table and multiplied it by ten, making it a well-populated area.

Brett was welcomed with shy smiles on open faces. Breakfast was family style with large platters of food passed around. He was familiar with the toasted flatbread, goat cheese, butter, honey, fruit, and coffee, but one platter held strips of meat that had been beaten, seasoned and grilled. It smelled spicy and enticing. Spirit Warrior gave thanks for the food and the meal began.

When breakfast ended, each person took his plate to a tub of hot, sudsy water and washed it, rinsed it, dried it and put it on a shelf that lined the wall behind the long, meal table.

The table was scrubbed and the area beneath the table was cleaned of any debris. As soon as the children could reach the tub, they cleaned their own plates. Brett watched in amazement. It all worked smoothly and the families scattered to what, he assumed, were their jobs for the day. Tohopka took Brett's plate and cleaned it for him.

Tomorrow I'll find a way to do my own dishes—even on walking sticks!

Again, Brett saw Camila. In the morning light, she looked even more like Linda. Her laughter was the same as he heard her banter with her companions. The food he had eaten suddenly turned into an unwelcome lump in his stomach.

The laughter and talking ceased, and Brett looked around to discover he was the only one left at the table. Spirit Warrior must have meant it when he said that he was free to explore. In the far distance, he could see the hacienda of the Matriarch perched on a hill overlooking the entire valley. That was his destination, but not yet. He couldn't very well see himself running away on his crutches with Linda thrown over his shoulder.

Meanwhile, this entire world was of immense interest to him, and he knew when he finally left, he could never return. It might put this innocent civilization in danger. He now completely understood Adam Grainger's protective feelings for this valley. He would wait for Spirit Warrior's plan.

He started his inspection with the closest garden plot, clumsily making his way on the paths. Vegetables that he knew, and many that he did not, marched in long well-tended rows as far as he could see. Workers were pulling weeds and tossing them into the baskets they carried. He'd seen enclosed compost piles, so nothing was wasted. He saw orchards and vineyards. The east side of the valley must be set off for the growing of food. Somewhere the sound of a goat's bleat echoed back to him. A hungry baby kid looking for its momma. Perhaps the west side were pens and enclosures for their livestock.

Somewhere cotton and grain fields were laid out. He had seen evidence of an irrigation system for the vegetables; so, no doubt, they harnessed and directed the waterflow from the mountain streams for their use. The irrigation system must extend its benefit to all that they grew.

Awkwardly, he lowered himself to the ground in the shade of a blossoming tree, smelling of orange. The climate here must be exactly right for many things. Brett closed his eyes soaking up the peace in the air around him. Gentle breezes blew warmth and sweet smells, lulling him to sleep. He hadn't had any of Tohopka's spiked chocolate, but he hadn't needed it this time.

He thought he was dreaming. A wriggling bundle sat on his chest licking his cheek. The tongue was tiny and wet. A little boy sat beside him, giggling at the antics of the small dog.

Brett tried to open his eyes. "*Cómo?*" he asked. Linda's dog sat on his chest.

Again, the little boy giggled.

Now Brett was trying to wake. The dog was sitting on his chest licking his face much to the boy's delight. A taller figure stood over him, bending down to retrieve the boy and dog.

"Leave the man alone, Ahanu," she said. "Come with me."

Her face was now only slightly shaded by the tree.

Was he dreaming? "Linda?" Brett asked.

He heard a sharp intake of breath as the girl picked up the child and the puppy, turned, and ran.

Chapter 16

Linda could only imagine what her life would be if she couldn't find a way back home. So far, she'd been given strange clothes to wear, and all her meals had been brought to her on a tray by Adella. Her one trip outside had been when Camila had introduced herself from the shadowed corner of her room and led her out for an introduction to her present surroundings. But that had been nearly a week ago now. *Oh, where was Brett? Why hadn't she asked Camila if any strangers had wandered into the valley?*

The door opened and Elena entered the room.

"Linda, I do trust you have rested from your trip here," said Elena. "I am hoping that you are strong enough to join us for dinner this evening."

Linda was puzzled. Was she supposed to be sick, an invalid, or in some way handicapped? She didn't know how to respond. Just perhaps it would be best to go along with her grandmother. Pretend to be what she wanted. Act as though she was a person that Elena could easily control. Act as though she had been drinking the tea with the sleeping powders dissolved in it.

"That sounds very pleasant," Linda said. "I look forward to leaving this room for a while."

"Of course, you do," Elena answered. "When you are stronger, you may venture outside and enjoy our gardens. We have a lovely waterfall garden with flowers and colorful fish. After dinner you may visit our library and select some books if you wish."

"Thank you," Linda said.

"Well, you'll have time to bathe and dress for dinner. Adella will come for you." With her speech delivered, Elena left, closing the door softly behind her. At least she was getting out of this bedroom.

Thank you! All I said was 'thank you'! I wanted to scream 'let me out of here'. I'm not made for such inactivity. I'd try the secret door again if I could learn when she and Sam will again be gone. I don't want them to learn I have a way out. I could leave, but where could I go? I don't even know where I am. Oh, Brett, where are you? How can you ever find me?

Linda went to the closet in her room. She chose a white dress with black goat-like figures marching along the band at the bottom. It brought her again to the time in her father's library with Brett. There was a picture of such a dress.

Linda answered the knock at the door and followed Adella out of the room. She had been carried to her room while asleep, so this was her first look at the house. It was like a lodge, wooden beams and large windows set in horizontal paneling. The walls were natural pine. With the light coming in the windows, it would be bright and airy when the sun was out. Now the sun was dipping behind the mountains, and a wedgewood blue twilight shimmered over the landscape. Gray streaked over the leafy trees binding them together with cobweb-like fingers.

The staircase led to a large open greatroom. The table was placed by a wide window, allowing the outside to become a mural. Sam stood at the deep, stone fireplace, and Elena was seated in a chair facing the fireplace. She and Sam were talking in low tones. The conversation stopped as Adella led Linda into the room.

"Ah, Linda, you are looking well," Sam smiled as he greeted her. Elena just eyed her, saying nothing to welcome her.

What were all these comments about her health? Were they trying to convince her that she was on the edge of a breakdown?

"Shall we eat?" Elena said. Sam went to the head of the table and pulled out a chair to seat Elena. He sat to her right, and a place was set at her left that Linda decided was for her. Linda sat and pulled her napkin into her lap. The table was set with museum-quality ceramic dishes color-coordinated with the woven mats under the plates.

"You have a lovely place here," Linda said. The silence was becoming unbearable.

"Yes, Linda. And this will be your home," Elena said.

"Oh, no," Linda answered. "I must go back. I have some schooling to finish, and…"

Elena interrupted and waved away Linda's words.

"That won't be necessary here. With your father gone, you must stay here with us. We are your family now. Sam has researched your background. You excelled in school, but you had few close friends, none that will sound an alarm when you don't return to school."

"But I have plans," Linda protested.

"They cannot be as important as your destiny here. You will become the next Matriarch. You will travel to Spain with Sam, marry the man I have chosen, and be expected to produce a daughter to follow in your footsteps. It was good fortune that we found you."

Linda couldn't believe her ears.

"But…" Linda started. She could feel the heat burning her face.

"We will talk of this later. For now, let's enjoy our dinner," Elena said.

A maid entered with the food and served the Matriarch and then Sam and Linda. Adella had disappeared, so Linda guessed her cooking wasn't appreciated here either.

"It will be quite a good life, Linda," Sam said. "You will have great respect and honor."

"I don't want respect and honor. I want my freedom," Linda kept her voice controlled.

"Enough, young lady," Elena's voice was like a steel blade, cutting into Linda's protest. "We will talk of this later. Sit, and eat your dinner."

Linda obeyed, but rebellion raged within her.

Who did she think she was? Did the Matriarch think she could even command the sex of a child?

But she was hungry, and Linda found that she could eat her dinner. She couldn't identify the dishes she was served, but they were excellent. She would control herself. If they didn't think that they could trust her, she would never be allowed any freedom except what she could steal sneaking out through the secret door.

She raised her chin and looked at her grandmother. "Perhaps, I will stay a little while and see how I like it but going to Spain to marry a stranger seems out of the question," Linda said. She couldn't give in all at once. That would be suspicious.

"We'll take it slowly, and you will see the wisdom in my plans. It's not just my plan but the responsibility is passed down from mother to daughter throughout several generations. Unfortunately, my own daughter, your mother, died and you are the next in line. You had a twin sister but she, too, died," Elena was warming to her subject. "I know you won't be a disappointment to your ancestors."

If Linda hadn't talked to Camila herself, she might have accepted the fact that her sister was really dead.

"No doubt I have much to learn," Linda forced out her words.

"After dinner we'll go to the library and choose the books that will explain to you our demesne," Elena had seemingly forgotten Linda's reluctance.

"Demesne? You mean all the people here are your tenants? You are over all of this estate?" Linda asked.

"Exactly," Elena agreed. "They would be helpless without our guidance."

"They have no leader?' asked Linda.

"They have a leader called Spirit Warrior. He performs all the rituals, rites and keeps the peace. Together, he and I oversee this realm. He comes here to report once a week. He is due in two days, and you will meet him." Elena was already enmeshing Linda deeper into her web.

They finished the meal in silence, each in their own thoughts. Linda looked at Sam, but he didn't seem to be opposing anything that Elena said. He wouldn't be any help to her.

"In the morning, we'll ride out and you can view the land," Elena said as she stood. "Now let's go to the library."

Finally, Sam spoke to Linda. "My dear, life here won't be so bad."

"But make no mistake, Linda, your life will be lived here," Elena said.

The grip Elena had on Linda's arm underscored her words. There would be bruises.

Linda followed her grandmother to the library. One book that Elena handed her was entitled *Legend of the Crying Child*.

Linda spent a restless night and was awake when the early dawn outlined the mountains in the far distance. Her soul longed to walk on those mountains away from this house to freedom. For now, she couldn't even escape this room. Her grandmother had told her to feel free to ask the maid for anything she needed, but the maid actually lingered at her door. Linda knew it wasn't to supply any need but to report back to her grandmother if she tried to leave. Her bedroom and bathroom were well stocked.

Linda was summoned early. After breakfast, she, Sam, and Elena mounted their mountain horses and started out. Linda sat easily in the English saddle, feeling the comfortable rhythm of the gait from the gelding she rode. The chestnut's mane and tail were pale while the color of his coat reflected red in the sun, and she smiled thinking of Brett's hair. The warmth and scent from the horse were familiar, and she relaxed for the first time since she had been kidnapped and brought here.

Elena positioned her horse beside Linda and acted as guide. There was much to see. It was like an enchanted kingdom with well-tended gardens, a large lake and a waterfall that sparkled as it bubbled down the far mountainside. As they rode down the valley away from the Matriarch's hacienda on the hill, Linda could see wide-spread agriculture that was the lifeblood of the clan.

Large fields of grain, seemingly endless rows of vegetables and fruit orchards were tended by the members of the clan. As they rode by, not one worker looked their way or lifted his head. This feudal system had long been established, and there was no guessing who was 'lady of the manor.'

Could it be that Elena felt the burden becoming too heavy? By casting out Camila for her betrayal, was her grandmother desperate to find a replacement? Someone to fill this role and thus free Elena to escape this valley? Linda recognized a cunning look on Elena's face, and she knew she was right. She, Linda Grainger, was to be the substitute. Or sacrifice.

Chapter 17

It was about noon when they returned to the hacienda. Sam had indicated to the waiting groom to take only the chestnut that Linda had been riding back to the stable. The other two horses were left tied to a hitching post close to the hacienda. So wherever else Sam and Elena planned to go, Linda could see she wasn't invited.

Lunch had been prepared; and as they ate, Elena continued talking to Linda about the vastness of her realm and how they hadn't seen even a third of it. Her eyes took on fierceness as she explained the importance Linda would have with her new position here in the valley.

"The clan will accept you as my heir and things will continue as always," she said. "Spirit Warrior will continue with the rites and rituals of the clan, and you will govern over the laws of the population. I will thoroughly brief you on what is, and what is not, allowed to keep the sanctity of this realm. I'll teach you the chants that are expected from you at our combined meetings."

"You're giving her too much at one time," Sam interrupted. Linda noticed he was gentle with her grandmother. And only when she talked to him, did she stop to consider her actions.

"Perhaps you're right," Elena answered. "But she must be ready."

"But you're not old," Linda protested. "You don't need me!"

"Maybe not," Elena snapped. "But I will make you ready for when you are needed!"

Linda knew there was something wrong. Elena would not allow Linda to be ruler as long as she was in the valley. Was she ill and afraid of leaving the clan uncared for, or did she have another agenda? She must learn to keep quiet and not rebel too strongly and make her grandmother suspicious. She will let Elena think she was convincing her.

With another comment about Linda needing to rest, Elena escorted Linda to her room, explaining that it was important that she read the books they'd chosen from the library. There was the inevitable cup of hot chocolate in a tiny mug that Elena set on Linda's bedside table. Elena left the room, closing the door softly behind her.

"No way, lady. No more spiked drinks!" Linda said after Elena had gone. She poured the drink into a potted plant.

There was soft laughter from the corner of the room, and Linda whirled in surprise.

"Ah, my friend standing in my shadow again," she spoke to Camila.

Camila stepped out into the light coming in the window.

"Yes, I'm here. Abuela and Sam will be gone this afternoon. We must talk," Camila seemed agitated. "It's safe to go out again."

No other words were spoken as Linda followed Camila through the door in the back of the closet out into the garden of the hacienda. The peacefulness of the garden belied the situation in which the two sisters had found themselves.

"What is it, Camila, with all these sleeping potions put into my drinks?" Linda asked.

"Control. Mi Abuela must be in control. When she thinks you are no longer planning your escape, she will ease up a little. But you will always have eyes upon you. Adella is supposed to give Abuela reports, but she takes much sleeping potions herself."

Again, Linda followed Camila through the shaded garden to a bench in the sunlight.

"I'm afraid there will be trouble," Camila began.

"Trouble, how?' asked Linda.

"A new man showed up in our clan," Camila said.

"Is this unusual?" asked Linda.

"It doesn't happen often. Spirit Warrior will find a lost one wandering in the wilderness outside our valley, and he will bring him in. Many times, they are near death. The clan thinks he is a visitor from above, coming so that Spirit Warrior may heal him. Who is to say the clan is wrong? Strangers that come into our valley who don't die just seem to disappear. I, too, rebelled against Elena to marry one of the clan; so, you are her last hope. I wanted to be the next Matriarch: I loved my husband, our little boy, and the clan, and I never want to go away. But she has found you, and she will not give you up."

"Why do you think this new stranger will cause trouble?" asked Linda.

Could this stranger be Brett?

"My son had wandered off with his little dog and found a man asleep in the shade of a tree. When I went to get him, the man opened his eyes and called me 'Linda'."

"Brett!"

"What is Brett?" asked Camila.

"A friend. He has come for me," Linda said. She could feel her words tumbling out as she felt relief.

"He won't be safe," Camila said.

"He will stand out that's for sure. His hair shines like bronze in the sun." There was laughter in her voice.

"This man's hair was not bronze. Just dark," Camila said.

"Then he must have dyed it! I have to see him, Camila. I must," begged Linda.

"We'll have to be careful. If Elena knows of him, he will disappear," Camila warned.

"He won't be taken so easily. I think he knows there's danger," Linda said. "Oh, Camila, please tell him I'm here!"

"I will find him, and I will tell him. I don't want you here." she said.

"And, I don't want to be here. Oh, thank you. Hurry, oh, hurry."

Spirit Warrior had been close enough to witness the brief encounter between Brett and Camila and her frightened reaction. He was aware that Camila knew of Linda through the *Spirit Winging Chant* that she learned and practiced as a child when she was feeling loss. With her twin torn from her at birth, she hadn't felt whole and was restless until she had *Winged* her spirit out to touch the spirit of the other child. The gentle breeze had blown her thin, tentative plea back to him as she entered her request for a spiritual journey:

> Spirit Within
>
> Breathe the Power.
>
> Open your eye.
>
> See the lights.
>
> Spirit Within.
>
> Breathe the Power.
>
> Open your ears.
>
> Hear the sounds.
>
> Spirit Within.
>
> Breathe the Power.

Spread your wings,
And rise up free.

    Spirit Warrior couldn't find anything like this in *The Holy Book* that Alan Griffin had given him, but the experience had given the girl peace, so he had never spoken to deny her. But he no longer encouraged this practice.
    He found Brett still sitting in the shade of the tree by the vegetable-growing field, listening to the workers as they planted new seeds. It was a song that had been passed down from the old ones. He stood quietly and listened to the chant. The chant had a musical quality that helped ease the burden of the labor.

Oh, gentle, gentle wind
Blow gently over the land
Sing your song through valleys and plains
Scatter the seeds. Scatter the seeds.

Oh, gentle wind
Scatter seeds upon the land,
Take them far. Take them far.
Bring them near. Bring them near.

Little seeds. Little seeds,
Burrow deep and safe.
Drink the rain. Drink the rain.
And grow to reach the sun.

With little effort, he bent and seated himself beside Brett and waited to speak until the younger man acknowledged his presence.

"I thought I saw Linda," Brett said.

Spirit Warrior nodded. "Yes, they look much alike."

"So, it was Camila?" asked Brett.

"Yes, with her son, Ahanhu."

"Do you think she has seen Linda?" asked Brett.

"Yes, she came to me. I told her the story of her birth, of her mother and father. She is aware now of why she could reach out to her 'shadow' self."

"We must make a plan to get Linda, so I can take her back with me to our world," Brett was forceful.

"In time," Spirit Warrior agreed, "in time. I must think upon it. In the meantime, you must be kept hidden among our people."

"We may have another problem," Brett said.

"And what might that be?" asked Spirit Warrior.

"My family. I know that my father will follow my trail, and he won't rest until he finds me or my dead body."

"He knows you came here?"

"No, we never knew of this place. But he knows my trail from the time I left our home. Then, I marked a trail for him after I came into the wilderness outside of your valley. But after I was injured, I could no longer mark the trees," Brett explained.

"This is good, so he won't find his way. One more stranger coming into our valley would be difficult to hide from the Matriarch. We have four separate groups in our clan, but I can only promise safety to the stranger that I can slip among the planting people. The sowers of seeds are the farthest from the Matriarch's hacienda. She rarely comes to inspect the vegetables since there is always an abundance that can be delivered to her household."

"I am his only son, Spirit Warrior. He will never stop looking until he finds me. He will be like the shepherd looking for his one lost sheep."

"Yes, I read this in the *Holy Book*. Is he wise in the forests?" asked Spirit Warrior.

"Very wise," said Brett.

Then, I must go to him and stop his journey before he finds us. A stranger rarely stumbles into our valley, but a wise one may find us. You are the first one since Linda's father found us many years ago. A duty of a spirit warrior is to keep the clan pure from the outside. Our people do not know there is an 'outside.' They think you are a visitor from above. But if too many strangers open the door into us, then that door may remain open. When you leave, I must make your footsteps disappear.

"While I am gone from the valley, you may explore as you wish. Tohopka will guide you where you wish to go. Tohopka often makes inspections for me at each village, and he rarely travels alone, so it will not cause questions. There are caves and markings that Alan Griffin found interesting. You may find them interesting, also. Just keep out of sight of the hacienda. When I return, I will find a pathway out for you and Linda. You neither one belong here with us."

Brett watched Spirit Warrior stand and walk away from him. Spirit Warrior had not asked for reassurance that Brett wouldn't look for Linda. But with the faith he had put into him as he talked, Brett almost felt as though a promise had been extracted from him. He was given permission to explore, and he would use this time to satisfy the curiosity that was building more each day that he was here. His backpack still held his camera and recorder.

His cell phone was useless without a signal, so he couldn't let his family know he was safe. But then, again, was he safe? The Matriarch would not hesitate to kill him if he stood in her way. But he was forewarned. He would be careful.

Brett stood and leaned only lightly on his crutches. Whatever Spirit Warrior had done to him was astounding. He found only this morning that he could walk without aid, but he was skeptical that it would last, and he'd brought his crutches.

He walked in the direction of his room to collect his backpack. He wouldn't put the clan in danger by disobeying Spirit Warrior's unspoken command, but if an opportunity presented itself, how could he not give Linda some hope.

Brett had no idea how long he would have to explore before Spirit Warrior returned, but he had a willing guide in Tohopka. Tohopka had finished his inspection of the seed planter village this morning while Brett was watching from the tree shade where he was sitting. After lunch and rest, Tohopka said they would go to the fruit planter village. Lunchtime included a two-hour siesta for the entire clan; and from the quietness that descended in the valley, Brett could tell that it was strictly observed by everyone, escaping the hottest part of the day.

Oh, well, when in Rome. But he was becoming impatient to use his time in this valley wisely. So much of the ancient past was playing out before his very eyes, and he wanted to jump into the middle of it. But he closed his eyes and joined in their sleep time.

Tohopka's little burro was outfitted with two large, empty baskets hanging one on each side below the short animal's belly. Tohopka held the reins loosely and went toward the shelter that housed the vegetables. Selecting only perfect specimen of all the vegetables, he motioned for Brett to follow. Brett guessed that the fruit planter village was to the east of the seed planter village with the length of a football field between them. As they neared the orchards, the old almond trees were in full bloom, showcasing little white balls. The buttery, honey-like aroma drew in hundreds of bees, pollinating the entire orchard. When he was a kid, Brett remembered giving his mother a body spray mist with an almond fragrance for her birthday. Ever since, its delicate scent had been her favorite.

Workers in a near-by shelter were working with stored almonds, pounding the dried nuts into a meal-like substance. The white almond flour was pounded from nuts without the brown skin. Brett watched as Tohopka chose the readied containers of the almond flour, the almond meal and shelled almonds and stow them carefully into the carrying basket. Pale yellow almond oil was carefully poured into ceramic jugs and sealed. Brett knew that almond oil could be the vehicle for many ingredients, those for health or beauty treatments. Other containers held shelled pecans which he added to his basket.

Many questions sprang to mind and Brett wanted to linger in this area. So much to learn. But Tohopka had worked quickly to obtain the necessary items, and he was ready to move on.

"We'll only have time to get to one more village before delivering supplies to the hacienda of the Matriarch," Tohopka said. "This isn't our regular delivery, but she sent word that extra things are needed. We must get there before dark. It isn't safe to travel after dark."

"Will we stay at the hacienda until morning?" asked Brett. Here was a chance to see if Linda were really in the hacienda. Tohopka was supposed to show Brett the caves and archaeological sites, but Spirit Warrior couldn't have known of the request for the immediate trip to the hacienda.

"Yes, there is a place to stay behind the hacienda."

Brett could hardly contain his impatience as they started on the trail again. The last visit was to the village of the goat herds where Tohopka loaded milk, cheese, and meat. Baskets full to overflowing, he seemed satisfied to lead the way up the hill to the hacienda, keeping the burro at a slow walk and the load balanced. The activities at this village alone would have kept Brett fascinated for an entire day but for the excitement of the trip to the hacienda where he would perhaps catch a glimpse of Linda.

Tohopka was unaware of Brett's real purpose here in the valley. As far as he knew, Brett was just an injured stranger that was sent to Spirit Warrior to heal. It didn't happen often, but it was a great honor for Spirit Warrior, a sign of approval by those up above.

Chapter 18

Mac McAlister knew his son Brett well. It was true that he had been away from the ranch for nearly four years, but some things never changed: Brett's deep-seated loyalty to his friends and his faith in his God. His interests never wavered.

Brett loved the ranch, but he had loved archaeology as long as Mac could remember. His Eagle Scout troop had scoured the desert for signs of ancient tribes and artifacts. Their search had not been fruitless; Brett had quite a collection still displayed in his old room at the ranch. He had been keenly interested in *The Legend of the Crying Child*. He had researched all the articles in their library, and he even had gone so far as to interview a chief on a nearby reservation for his high school paper.

After the vacation the family had taken to the ruins in Chaco Canyon, there had been no stopping him. He devoured all the archaeology books in the town's library and kept mail order delivery hot with books on the ancient tribes. When he had finished his master's degree, he had applied for the position of graduate assistant to finish his doctoral studies under Dr. Grainger. When he was accepted, his enthusiasm knew no bounds. His letters home were filled with the admiration he had felt for his mentor. When Brett learned that Dr. Grainger shared his strong faith in God, he knew that he had been led to the right place to study.

When Brett had spoken of Linda, Mac knew that what his son felt for this girl was real. He may not have known her long, but with Brett, it was long enough to gauge his feelings. Now she was lost to him, and Mac knew that Brett wouldn't stop looking until he found her again. The loyalty he felt was strengthened by the love he felt for her.

Now it seemed that Brett was gone. He hadn't contacted them in any way, and his cell phone no longer went to voice mail. He was either out of range, or his battery needed recharging. The whole family was getting uneasy. News reports telling of slight tremors in the surrounding mountainous areas were causing more concern. If a strong earthquake hit, it would most likely open chasms in the terrain, perhaps seemingly bottomless abysses. He remembered his grandfather telling of a mild 'quake that hit when he was a boy, opening wide ditches in their pastures. These ditches had been filled in and grasses planted over them, leaving no trace. There was an unnamed fault running through the surrounding mountains, but it had never risen as a threat.

It would be at least three weeks before he could follow Brett. The spring calves had to be branded and the hay in the fields cut, baled, and stacked in the barns, so Mac knew he couldn't leave the ranch in the hands of his family and the hired help just yet. There were always a few hitches that required his attention.

It had been nearly a month since Brett had left the ranch to look for Linda, and now when the ranch chores could be left with his family and the ranch hands for a few weeks Mac had to search for Brett. His inner radar was beeping. The backpack that Brett had taken with him wasn't well stocked with food, so what he had taken wouldn't last long.

Mac loaded the four-wheel drive truck with what he thought he might need for his trip. He wouldn't expect the worst, but he would be prepared for it. He threw in his bedroll, extra blankets, food, and water. His rifle was in the rack above the back window.

The places Brett's tickets were taking him wouldn't offer much in the way of comforts.

The depot where Linda had purchased tickets was the place to start. She was remembered there. No doubt she would be remembered at every stop she made.

Mac trailered his Rocky Mountain horse and left shortly after dawn. The road was empty of vehicles. Sagebrush grew up to the roadside, and tumbleweeds danced and whirled in front of the wind, brushing out the tracks of the night-time predators. He loved this land with its starkness, the endless sky, limitless desert inhabited by the long-eared jacks and loping coyotes. Big cats roamed that fed on the deer and smaller game, occasionally raiding the ranches. But it was a land like no other. It was his home.

The sky was beginning to darken.

That's all he needed! Rain! If the river flooded, his road would be covered.

The last stop was a small cantina. The bus had reached it before him, and the driver was standing by the café door.

"Morn'in to you," the driver called to Mac.

"Morn'in. Looks like rain," Mac called back.

"Hope I get back before the road gets all muddy," the driver added.

"I'm looking for a passenger you might remember," Mac said. He walked up to the driver.

"Do you remember this girl?" Mac held the picture of Linda out to the driver.

"Sure do. Nice little thing. She had a wee dog," the driver answered. He swung up into his bus, preparing for his journey back. "Ask inside. I know she talked to the proprietor."

Mac went into the cantina. No one was there except the clerk. Light struggled to come through the dust-covered windows, leaving most of the room in shadow. Mac ordered coffee and laid the picture of Brett on the counter. "Can you help me? I'm looking for my son?"

"*Sí*, your son." The man looked at Mac for a minute. "*Sí*, he looks like you. He came looking for a girl. A beautiful girl." He winked at Mac.

"Yep," Mac said, "the girl he plans to marry."

"The girl was looking for a Sam Straeder. He isn't known around here, but our padre knew of him. Padre took Linda to meet him at the yellow hacienda down the road from here. The padre lives there. This is what I told your son. If she is with the padre, she is safe." He shrugged his shoulders and waved his hands outward.

"I'm sure. I'm sure," Mac agreed.

The owner pulled the shutters together and prepared for closing. Mac was puzzled.

"Sorry, señor, I'm closing. The clouds we see will bring much rain. This area will flood and I'll not be able to get home. My little ones will be frightened. I must leave now," he explained. He hung his apron on the back of a chair. "Just go down the road to the yellow hacienda. The padre will know of the young people. I wouldn't stay long though; the road is impassable when it rains."

Mac drove down the road the short distance to the house that the man had pointed out to him. It was on a higher elevation, so maybe if it rained, he could wait it out safely. He could leave the truck on the highest level behind the house. Although the truck made a rumbling noise as it came down the road and neared the house, no one had heard or come out to meet him.

He parked on the rise behind the hacienda in the shelter of a copse of native pinyon and juniper trees. Chunky, little cones hung heavy on the pinyon pine. Mac could tell that it was an old tree and would have many tasty nuts inside those cones.

The Rocky Mountain horse was backed out of the trailer. Mac had trained him as a colt, and he couldn't have a trustier mount.

He had named him Benj for no reason that he could think of; he just liked the sound of it. The surrounding area didn't look too truck friendly, even a four-wheel drive. He put a bridle on Benj but mounted him bareback and scouted the area around the house. Outside of the close perimeter of the house, nature had been allowed to go wild. Scrubby growth, cacti and sagebrush were in a tangle. If the floods did come, the rattlers would be on the move. Another danger.

It would be suicide to challenge the elements that were beginning to show their strength. He rode back to the house. Behind the house to the west of the chapel, a small shelter looked to be a stable. He dismounted and led Benj into the small barn and put him in a stall. The stable was well-swept and stocked. He hoped the owner wouldn't mind sharing a half-bale of hay. Mac found a well and pulled up a bucket of water for his horse. Benj would be comfortable for the night.

With an eye on the glowering clouds, he shoved his hat further down on his head as the wind climbed the legs of his whipcord trousers, circling around his ears. The deep arroyo that cut through the dry land a few hundred yards to the west of the hacienda was a sure sign that waters had raged through this area before.

Mac walked around the hacienda but could see no sign that anyone was home. It was well-kept; and through the windows that weren't shuttered, he could see that the rooms were furnished and in order.

Mac decided to check the chapel doors. Maybe someone was there. The entrance door was unlocked and he went inside. Quiet met him along with the dusty odor of neglect. The padre must have ignored the chapel even while attending to the house and stable. He would spend the night in here. Gathering his gear from the truck, he started for the chapel.

Rain suddenly pelted his head and shoulders and pocked the dry ground. He made it to shelter before a cloud burst overhead. He stowed his cell phone in his backpack. His family knew that the signal in this area would be spotty at best, so they wouldn't be expecting a call. Brett's sisters had pushed hard to come with him, and he almost wished that he had company. This was a desolate spot, and with the cantina closed and the proprietor gone, he was truly alone. The noise of the rain on the metal roof of the chapel was so loud that he couldn't have heard anyone coming.

The storm brought early darkness. Mac found a box of candles in a small cabinet, and he lit enough to keep from stumbling over some of the broken chairs. Torrents of rain continued as sheet after sheet pummeled the chapel windows. *The windows would be clean in the morning, he thought.*

Mac settled in a corner wrapped in a blanket he had brought with him. He wondered what daybreak would bring. The rain droned on, deadening his thoughts, and lulling him to sleep.

Chapter 19

Mac stood at the chapel door watching it rain. He had slept fitfully during the night; and every time he awoke, he could hear the rain pounding the chapel's roof. Thunder rattled the windows and lightning streaked from heaven to earth. Winds had been strong, and he could see limbs littering the yard, and a huge tree blocked the drive. The water rushed fiercely through the arroyo and overflowed until he and the house, stable and chapel were on an island. He thought of the cantina owner safe in his home with his children.

Mac was safe, but he had a child somewhere in the wilderness. It didn't matter that his son was a grown man. He was still his son, and Mac knew that he couldn't rest without searching. He had found the note that Brett had left, and Mac searched the tunnel through to the other side. He saw the converging trails. He would ride Benj around the back of the chapel and up the slope until he found the beginning of that trail.

Mac built a small fire at the entrance of the tunnel with some of the broken chairs from the chapel. There would be no wood dry enough outside. It might be a long time before he ate anything hot again, so he fixed his breakfast, ate, and scattered the ashes. There was still evidence of where Brett had built his own campfire.

The wind had calmed, and the rain now fell straight in a steady downpour. He shrugged into his rain gear and started in the direction of the stable. His mountain pony was surefooted and would find purchase on the slippery slope behind the chapel. But even so, it would be slow going.

The trail behind the chapel rose gently, so the mountain pony could keep a steady pace. They'd traveled only about a quarter of a mile when the shelter came into view. Upon inspection, Mac saw it was another stable. No spider webs covered the swinging doors, so it was plain that it had been used recently. The rain hadn't obliterated all the tracks yet; some tracks sank deep, holding puddles of water. The tracks included the wheels of a buckboard and would be easily followed until the rain washing down the mountain took the evidence with it.

He walked Benj back down the trail until they came to the mouth of the tunnel that led from the chapel. Maybe it had taken time he couldn't afford, but he felt it necessary that he get the lay of the land. Now he knew this circuitous trail held some mystery.

Back where he had started, he searched to find the trail that Brett had taken. The knife marks left in the trees were the signs he had been looking for. Where the bark had been stripped away, the light-colored wood gleamed its message to him.

Mac followed the trail slowly; his vision obstructed by the rain. It was slow going but he continued. As long as he could spy the notches in the trees, he knew he was on the right trail. Summer rains usually didn't last this long, but this storm was holding its own. Streams ran along his path as they washed down the mountain, bringing twigs, small rocks, and mud. Occasionally, a mud slide would slip in front of them on its way to the unknown below.

Through the rain, Mac could see the outline of a building. It was back in a clearing away from the trail. As he drew near, he could see wide doors that could accommodate a wagon. Upon inspection he could see the tracks of the wagon disappearing into the building. He had seen these tracks all the way from the back of the chapel. It had been a rough ride, indeed, to bring this wagon all the way here.

Warily, Mac dismounted and led Benj into the building. It was another stable and the wagon was parked in the large runway. Wherever the driver and his load were going, it would now have to be on horseback or on foot. The wagon was dry, so it had been here before the rains came. *Was Brett with this party? Or was he alone?*

He unsaddled Benj and rubbed him dry with a burlap sack he found hanging over the stall door. Again, this stable was stocked, so he threw a few flakes of hay into the feeding trough. From a rain barrel outside the door, he brought in a bucket of water for the horse.

He didn't want to build a fire inside the building, so he ate a cold supper and drank water, wishing for a cup of hot coffee.

The rain had stopped, but he wasn't going to travel any further with night coming on so fast. He would be no good to Brett if he or his horse were injured. He hoped that he could pick up the trail again in the morning.

He knew he had a trail marked well enough to find his way back down the mountain to the chapel, but he knew that he was in an unmarked, primitive wilderness that he had known existed in their territory but he had never known anyone who had explored it.

He did have a strategy if he failed to find any further trail markings. He would use this barn as his headquarters. Each day he would travel as far as the light would allow and return before darkness. He could pass the night in the safety of the building. Hopefully, on one of these explorations into this unfamiliar wilderness, he would pick up the trail again. It would be a long shot with all the rain and wind that had swept away any sign of human intrusion. But Brett was out there somewhere, and he would seek until he found him.

If he were careful with his provisions, he had enough food for a few days. The rain barrel was full, and the nearby stream would provide water when his canteens were empty. To stretch his food supply, he would set a rabbit trap.

Scouring the nearby forest floor, Mac found a forked stake to drive into the ground to act as his spring pole. His toggle stick would be no larger in diameter than a pencil. To finish out his snare, he would use the fine twine he had in his backpack as a snare line with an attached trigger line. It was a primitive apparatus that he had taught his scout troops to make many times. But it was never that they would depend on what they caught for survival. He might need what he could trap to keep up his strength. He had to plan for the long haul. Earlier, someone had stored hay pellets for a horse in a tin. No mold clung to them so they could be used as bait.

His plans in place, he settled down on some burlap sacks with the saddle for his head. It would get cold in these mountains, but the little barn had seemed tight. His saddle blanket tucked up under his chin, he drifted to the edge of sleep amidst the sounds of owls in nearby trees. Before succumbing to deep sleep, he thought he heard a panther scream in the distance.

The sun burned through the mountain fog, warming up the barn in which Mac slept. He awoke, threw back his saddle blanket and sat up anxious to begin his search. He built a fire just large enough to make his coffee. He chewed a couple of granola bars and sipped his coffee. As soon as the coffee cooled enough, he gulped it down ready to get started. The rabbit snare only waited to be baited.

Mac hiked until the sun was high in the sky, rested under a pine tree while he ate some trail mix and washed it down with water from his canteen. There didn't seem to be any significant change in his surroundings. Without distinctive rock outcroppings or unusual tree growths, a person could wander forever without finding a way out.

When Mac felt rested and had finished his lunch, he followed the trail he had left leading him back to the small shed. Darkness was falling when he reached camp, and his rabbit snare was empty. Supper consisted of beef jerky, an apple, and the cold coffee left from this morning. He would have to eat better than this to keep up his strength. He'd fry bacon and heat the canned beans tomorrow night.

The next three days followed the pattern of Mac's first day. Baiting the rabbit snare with one of his apples did furnish him a hearty meal the third day, but it was a cold meal with hot coffee tonight.

The fifth day followed like the other four, except as he approached the clearing, he smelled smoke from a campfire. A strange man sat before the fire where several pieces of meat were roasting on a spit. The aroma was tantalizing.

The man stood becoming a stalwart figure of an Indian like Mac had only seen in pictures. He came toward Mac and extended his hand.

"Father of Brett McAllister? Greetings in the name of Jesus Christ, our Lord."

Mac clasped the extended hand.

Chapter 20

Veins of lightning sliced through the black skin of the night sky, followed by thunder rolling like a landslide down the surrounding mountains. No longer were the mountains their protectors, but they became a trap. The valley was an arena where elements raged their fury. The wind continued howling, threatening devastation as it tried to sweep out everything before it. Perhaps these storms had to exact payment for the otherwise perfect weather.

Tohopka quickened his pace, and Brett drew his hood over his head to protect himself from the stinging fragments that the wind blew into his face. He walked closely beside the burro on the unfamiliar path because he'd seen how the path cut down steeply in the narrow places. It hadn't started to rain yet, but the lowering clouds choked out the remaining daylight.

The lamp lights from the windows of the Matriarch's hacienda glowed closer now, and by the flash of lightning Brett could make out the outline of a small building where Tohopka was leading them.

Another bolt of lightning struck a tall pine that fell across the trail, blocking their way back down the mountain. A burning smell arose with a wisp of smoke from the fallen tree, caught up becoming a small whirlwind. The next strike of lightning tore apart another tree that crashed onto the hacienda. Thunder rolled to accompany the crackling sound as the fire caught and blazed through the back entrance of the hacienda. Thunder chased the lightning as the storm began to move on. It was a hit-and-run attack targeting the highest structure with a damaging blow before roaring off to the next mountain.

Brett's first thought was Linda. She was in that house.

Brett followed Tohopka as they quickly ran to the fire. Tohopka had taken the blankets off of the burro and handed one to Brett. Two rain barrels stood at the back entrance of the house, and they quickly soaked the blankets and started beating the flames. A large man had come out, accompanied by four smaller figures, to join the battle. They fought to the sound of the fire splintering the wooden structure attached to the main adobe construction. Then rain began to come in blinding sheets, taking over for their feeble efforts.

A figure collapsed on the ground away from the burnt timbers. Brett had recognized Linda as they worked, and he knew she was the one who had fallen. Running to her side, he brushed back her hair and wet her face with a dripping cloth. He knelt down, slipped his arm under her shoulders, and gently raised her head.

She opened her eyes briefly. "Brett?"

"Yes, it's me. I've come for you."

Coughing, she choked on the inhaled smoke and lost consciousness. Brett picked her up and shouldered his way to the front of the hacienda. He followed Sam in as the man supported Elena. They stepped onto the wide veranda fronting the house and went through wide carved doors. Acrid air floated thinly into the house proper; it was obvious that they had stopped the fire from jumping into the main living quarters. However, rain had blown through the gaping hole, washing through the kitchen area stopping just short of the dining room.

Sam helped Elena into a large, soft chair near to the fireplace where a flame was sending out welcome heat to dry her clothes.

He turned his attention to Brett and nodded to the girl in his arms. "Put her on the sofa."

Carefully, Brett lay Linda on the sofa and covered her with the woven blanket that hung along the back. He stepped away and stood behind the sofa. He found himself in an open dining room where he could see beams, pine paneling and woven tapestries on the floor and walls. He couldn't show too much curiosity. He kept his head down, looking at the floor. He became aware of Linda's eyes upon him. He smiled at her and thought he saw a ghost of a smile in return.

Linda was forgotten by Sam as he stood, allowing the two maids to attend Elena. Elena roused, stiffened her spine, and looked straight at Brett whose face and hair were blackened with soot from the fire.

"Who is that?"

"Just a young man who helped Tohopka with the supplies. They reached the fire first, and without them we couldn't have saved our hacienda. He helped put out the fire and carried our granddaughter in," said Sam.

"We don't need you now." She looked directly at Brett. "Get out. Go help Tohopka."

"The storm is abating," Sam said to Brett. "You and Tohopka will be safe in the stable. Thank you for your help. We'll sort out the supplies in the morning. You can go to the pool and wash up."

As Brett turned to go, he could hear Linda stirring on the sofa. She asked for water, and a maid hurried to her. Over his shoulder he watched the maid support Linda and lift a cup to her lips. His heart hurt.

How could he abandon her once he'd found her again? But now he was sure where she was. Spirit Warrior had better come up with a plan soon. Even if he could attempt to get Linda away from this house, where could they go? He didn't even know where he was, and he certainly wouldn't be able to find his way home. This self-sufficient paradise was surrounded by dangers. Animals roamed at night, blocking safe escape even if he knew where to go.

As Brett left the hacienda, he found Tohopka waiting for him on the verandah.

"Spirit Warrior left you in my care. I've failed to keep you safe. No one except Spirit Warrior is allowed in the Matriarch's house."

"I'm not afraid, Tohopka, and I'm unharmed. The storm caused an accident; it was out of your control," said Brett. "Did I hear of a place where we could wash up?"

Tohopka led the way into the small stable that had been mercifully spared from the flying sparks. The hay inside would have ignited and destroyed the wooden portions of the building. As it was, the adobe walls were strong and the roof without damage. Strong doors kept the building secure from night predators, and shutters could be closed on the two opposing window openings.

"Let's go to the pool before sleep," said Tohopka. He handed Brett a piece of soap and a clean thick cloth from his burro's pack.

Brett followed Tohopka who held the blazing torch high to light the walk. It was a well-used path paved with flat stones. A small pool was dammed up and sheltered with walls and a wooden roof. As Brett stepped into the pool, he realized it was fed by an incoming stream, rushing in under a wall. To his surprise, the water was warm. He lathered his head and body, and he ducked below the water's surface to rinse. The warmth of the water relaxed the tension that had built upon seeing Linda and knowing he had no plan to rescue her.

"Tohopka, I like this pool!" said Brett. He stood where the water was entering the pool and let the fresh stream run over him.

"Yes, but something not right. Water come too fast. Water too hot, and a hissing sound come from ground," said Tohopka. "Maybe storm cause another opening. Many pools built around this warm stream."

The adrenaline was spent, and the men were silent as they made their weary way back to the stable. They spread their bedrolls in the safety of a boxed stall filled with cushioning straw. Brett drifted off to sleep with the sound of the burro snuffling in the next stall.

The thoughts that had been in the forefront of Brett's mind submerged with the weariness of his body. Maybe tomorrow he could think clearly. Maybe tomorrow Spirit Warrior would have returned. He sighed and sank deeper into his bedroll; instantly, exhaustion and disillusionment overtook his consciousness. The slight trembling of the ground beneath him couldn't awake him from his slumber.

Chapter 21

By morning light, the damage to the hacienda was an ugly scene. The entire back wooden addition was gone, and the intense heat had caused the adobe of the main back wall to begin crumbling. Although the rain had stopped, the damage had to be repaired at once to prevent further damage from creeping into the main structure. Brett knew that Sam must be aware of the earth's trembling. It had subsided for now, but there were no guarantees that it wasn't a precursor to something more.

Brett woke to see Tohopka standing outside the ruins talking to Sam. No one else was in sight. Their voices were loud enough that Brett could tell that Sam was instructing Tohopka on what needed to be done. A huge tarp had been hung to cover the back entrance and when the conversation ended, Sam disappeared back into the hacienda. Tohopka came back to the stable where they had slept.

"Sam say to go to villages and return with materials and workers to rebuild. He urges it to happen quickly so the Matriarch will be comfortable. The cook and I unpacked the food from the burro's pack this morning, but I've left some bread and cheese for you in the stable. There is a jug of coffee."

"Am I not to go?" said Brett.

"No. I can travel faster alone. Sam knows you are to stay here but stay out of sight of the Matriarch. She dislikes strangers."

Brett smiled. "Maybe if the stranger starts to rake up the debris into piles, she won't be too distrustful."

"Spirit Warrior doesn't expect visitors to work, but he will be pleased that you want to. There are tools at the back of the stable."

Brett watched Tohopka pull the baskets from the burro and mount the animal. His saddle was a thick woolen pad. It was of museum quality and colorfully dyed. When he left this valley, he would miss the artisanal cheeses and the luxurious, woven items. The clothing he now wore was soft and comfortable. He had only seen garments like them in the pages of history books. He thought of all the pictures that he'd amassed on his phone and all the notes he'd written in his journal. Ah, yes, never leave home without paper and pen; they were as important as foodstuffs. Nature might provide something to eat but not something for note taking.

It would be tricky. The valley and its secrets must be protected, but he hoped that he could find a way to weave what he'd learned into his teaching for his students. Maybe he could bring to life the people on the pages a from long-forgotten past. So little was known of their day-to-day existence.

The situation couldn't be more to his advantage. Spirit Warrior would understand his presence at the Matriarch's hacienda, and it would give him a chance to let Linda know that he was here. He wasn't sure if she had been conscious enough to know that he had spoken to her when he carried her out of the smoky atmosphere into the hacienda. She had looked at him but could she see past his disguise? He could pick her face out of any crowd, but he'd had the advantage of the many pictures that her father had shared with him in addition to the golden days that he'd spent with her after her father's funeral. She was in his heart to stay. He prayed that they had made a strong connection although their time spent together was short. Maybe the things they had experienced while together had created the beginning of deep feelings on her part. He was already in deeply over his head.

After eating the breakfast that Tohopka had left for him, Brett gathered the handmade tools from the back of the stable. He chose the one that would function best as a rake and started close to the house, pulling the debris into piles away from the foundation. He stacked some of the large hunks of adobe tile off by themselves. Perhaps they could be repurposed. He continued to rake the piles further away from the building, allowing him to get acquainted with the surrounding layout. The hacienda was built in the center of the flat mesa amidst flowers and a small garden waterfall. A large stable was constructed several hundred feet away. Brett could count at least five horses in a grassy paddock abutting the stable's back entrance. Even from this distance, he could tell that these were mountain ponies bred for picking their way over rough terrain.

By the time the sun sent splinters of light through the clouds in the west, Brett had most of the debris cleared from around the back of the hacienda. He hadn't seen anyone the entire day after Tohopka left, but Sam had to know that he was here. Brett's back was tired and his hands blistered from the friction of the tools. He wished for the leather gloves in his backpack. On the ranch he was never without them.

He thought longingly of the warm pool. Tonight, he would have his own personal spa. He gathered the dried towel from the night before along with the soap and a clean shirt and headed down the path. Tohopka had left the light, but there was no weapon. Maybe it was a little too early for the predators to start prowling.

The water seemed hotter than it had the night before, and the stream flowed with more strength. Although it felt relaxing on his sore muscles, it wasn't a good omen. The earthquake's trembling had caused a change somewhere. Hurriedly, he bathed, dried, and put on his clean shirt. He wanted to get back to the stable before darkness became real. Aloneness smothered him.

The light from his lantern showed that someone had been in the stable. Bread, cheese, fruit, and a jug of cool water rested on a small table. A small folded piece of paper was tucked under the bread. He held it close to the light. He breathed a sigh of relief as he read the note. She did know he was here.

> *Dear Brett, I knew you'd come for me. I'm being watched, but I will come to you when everyone is asleep. Thank you. Love, Linda*

He tucked the note into his pocket and stretched out on his pallet. The labor from the day's work and the relief from knowing that Linda knew he was nearby brought relaxation. Sleep overtook him.

Chapter 22

They came as a whisper through the dark; words accompanying Brett's dream of Linda. Soft words and a light touch on his shoulder caused him to open his eyes.

"Brett?"

He sat up and wrapped his arms around her. "Linda? Are you ok?" He searched her face.

"Yes. I was afraid it was a dream when you carried me in from the fire. But when I opened my eyes later, I knew." She made no move to leave the comfort of his arms. "They watch me constantly, but I waited until the house was quiet."

"But how did you get out?"

"My sister showed me a passage from her room to the outside. She's banned and not allowed in the house because she angered our grandmother. I guess it's like being disinherited or shunned."

"So, you've met your twin."

"Yes. Her name is Camila. She married a man grandmother disapproved of, but he was killed and Camila blames grandmother. She has a small boy."

Brett chuckled. "I've seen the boy, and now that boy has a puppy."

"My dog? I wondered what happened to him."

"You can't separate a boy from his dog, so I guess you've lost it." Their laughter was a release.

"I heard Sam and grandmother say they were leaving this morning and wouldn't return until the repairs to the hacienda are done. Camila said they often left together, but she never knew where they went. She said she was never curious enough to follow them."

"Well, I am curious, so I will follow them. I'm looking for a way out of this valley—maybe there's a back way out," Brett said.

"Oh, be careful, Brett. Elena is ruthless. She has me tapped for the next matriarch. Sam protects Camila from Elena's anger, but he has no reason to protect you."

"Linda, you know I won't leave without you, but this isn't a safe place to be at this time. There have been small earthquakes, and I've felt many aftershocks."

"Yes," Linda said. "I heard Sam tell Elena that the entrance to the valley has been sealed off by a rockslide. She didn't seem to panic, so there must be another way out. I know Sam comes and goes because he brought me here."

"Spirit Warrior has promised to help us, and I promised to wait."

"I heard them talking of Spirit Warrior. He seems to be the only one that Elena is fearful of."

"Tohopka should be back by dawn with the workers and materials to repair this hacienda. With all the activity, I shouldn't be missed. I'll just tell Tohopka that I'm exploring," Brett said.

"Tohopka? I haven't heard his name before."

"Spirit Warrior appointed Tohopka as my guide while I'm here," Brett said. "Or maybe, he's my keeper."

"Keeper?"

"Well, I really think that Spirit Warrior just wants to keep me safe while allowing me as much freedom as possible. Spirit Warrior is a Christian man."

"How can that be?" she asked.

"It seems your father took on the role as missionary while he was here for a year. Spirit Warrior was his first convert, and there were many more. Spirit Warrior continues teaching his people about the one he calls the True God from the True Book. Your father taught Spirit Warrior and others to speak English and to read. He left his Bible with Spirit Warrior."

It was quiet for a few minutes as they each were lost in their thoughts.

"Brett, I'd better get back. It gets light quickly when the sun rises over that mountain."

"Linda, we will get back home." He lifted her hand to his lips. "Be safe." He watched her until she disappeared into the darkness surrounding the hacienda.

It was now light enough for safe travel up the path from the valley to the hacienda. The sound of burro's feet and low-pitched voices reached Brett. Tohopka was heading a crew of workers who were leading burros loaded with the materials to repair the hacienda. The burros labored under the weight of the adobe blocks. The framing timber needed would be cut from the surrounding trees.

Brett saw Sam come out to meet Tohopka and his crew. They talked for a few minutes, and then Sam walked toward the stable. So, Linda was right, he and Elena were planning to leave soon. He had to be ready to follow.

Brett found Tohopka and explained that he wanted to explore the mountain, assuring him that he would mark his path and not become lost. Brett's hair dye was still holding and his camouflage consisting of the local dress would keep him from being noticed. Tohopka warned him to be back before sunset. Tohopka expected to have to descend the mountain again to obtain another load of adobe brick before nightfall.

Brett positioned himself in a copse of scrubby oaks near the corral fence. Sam had saddled two horses, and now he and Elena prepared to mount. They looked once toward the workers at the house before turning their horses toward the corral gate and out away from the house. They never looked toward his hiding place.

Brett looked longingly at the remaining horse in the corral but riding on an unfamiliar mount over unknown terrain was too risky. He didn't have to overtake them; he just wanted to keep them in sight enough to know where they were going. It would be rough, but he wasn't unfamiliar with hiking in the mountains.

Their horses' hooves made enough noise to cover the sliding rocks as his feet stumbled on the uneven path. Recent tremors had shattered more rock, causing a layer of unsettled gravel. The horses couldn't make very good time over the newly-formed path cover either, so Brett was able to keep the riders in sight. The path went upward and then reached a mesa. Traveling over the mesa was trickier keeping out of sight, but the distance across wasn't very far. The edge of the mesa on the far side dipped down to a path. The sound of a near waterfall now blanketed any sound that Brett might make, so he hurried to get closer behind the trees that edged the path.

The path led up to a waterfall. Brett watched as Sam led the way holding onto the bridle of Elena's horse. The passageway was narrow, bordered on one side by the solid mountain wall and the other by the cascade of water. The riders were visible; then they were gone.

Brett hurried through the passageway. He saw the couple enter a cabin reminiscent of a small chapel situated in the middle of a well-kept clearing. The leafy dell was marked with large overhanging oaks. Brett knew that oaks could be found growing at elevations as high as 5,500 feet in the Appalachian Mountains, but this was the first time he'd seen such giant oaks growing in these mountains. This plot of land must be made up of well-drained loamy soil, as well as, lighter sandier soil, allowing the oaks in this cove to become giants extending protective shade over the entire area. This entire valley was an anomaly.

Beside the chapel-like building was a small space of ground alive with flowers surrounding several large boulders. With Sam and Elena safely inside the building, Brett edged close enough so that he could see that this was, in fact, a burial plot with gravestones. Stealthily, he crept close enough where the carvings became names and dates. The oldest must have dated back to the time of the death of the first Matriarch. It simply read: First Matriarch Isabella. The dates had been worn away with time, leaving only a barely legible date of death in the 1880's. There had been five others before the present Matriarch Elena. One stone bore no carvings which Brett concluded would be for Elena. Brett had precious little battery life left on his phone to take a picture, but it was information that he couldn't find anywhere else. At the very back of the plot were lesser stones. One had the title of doctor before the name, dated nearly twenty years ago. A coral stone streaked with veins that looked like gold bore the name of Inez with the same date. Linda's mother died the same day as the doctor who was called to attend her.

Brett heard footsteps and saw them come back out onto the porch. They carried a pan-like utensil and a bag. They left their horses in a makeshift corral and started down the slope of a ravine to the far side of the clearing. When they disappeared from sight, Brett followed and watched them enter the mouth of a cave. A stream ran down one side of the cave below an elevated rock ledge. He followed the downward path. Their feet were noisy as they made their way on the rocky path. Their voices carried back to him from the cave walls.

"Elena, the earthquake and tremors that we've had are changing the valley. This stream is running slowly; it must be blocked. The large entrance to the valley is completely locked off by a landslide of earth and rock. Out beyond our cave is the only exit now.

"This was a sentimental visit; we won't need to come to this cave again. We have plenty. When we're safely away, I hope this exit does become blocked. We'll be free and no one can follow us. Let's just pan a while and see if we can find one last nugget just for fun." She stooped and began to pan the stream.

"What about your plans for Linda?" asked Sam.

"Since she has no way to leave, she will have no choice but to stay and take responsibility. Sam, I must get away. I've fulfilled my destiny. I want our life away from here. We had it once."

"Yes, my dear, we did. And we will again, but what about Camila? She was groomed to follow you. She wants to be the next Matriarch. Linda doesn't. I was wrong to bring her here against her will," Sam said.

"No, you were right! Camila made her choice. She defied me. Linda will wake up with the deed done. It's now her destiny. Camila can't be forgiven."

Even from this distance, Brett could see the determination on her face.

"Spirit Warrior has to agree."

She didn't respond to his last remarks.

Brett followed and watched them as they stooped to work the stream. He heard Elena's laughter as she picked up a nugget and held it in front of Sam. "Let's make this our last," said Elena. "We can stay in the cabin here tonight. The hacienda repairs should be finished by tomorrow evening. But, Sam, let's leave the valley soon. I won't pack, I have nothing here that I want to take to our new home, and the jewels of the Matriarch have been passed from generation to generation. I want to take only the wedding ring that you gave me long ago in San Francisco."

Brett watched them embrace, and then he hurried through the mouth of the cave and back down the way he had come. His mind reeled with all the he had learned. It was no longer a mystery as to where the wealth had come from. Elena's ancestors had been taking gold from these streams for generations.

It was obvious that for years Sam had continued to sell the gold. No doubt he had traveled many different places to sell it. He had the savvy of being a lawyer hidden under the garb of a priest. There would be plenty for any lifestyle that he and Elena now wanted. He knew Sam had come here with Elena many years ago. With the exit from the valley so close to the hacienda, he could come and go without anyone being the wiser, bringing anything he wanted to make life more bearable for the one he loved so very much.

Brett knew he must find Spirit Warrior. Spirit Warrior had promised him a plan to get Linda away. He had found a way out himself, but it was quite another thing to find his way back to familiar territory that would lead home. They had to act soon. Nature was signaling that a catastrophic change could follow with further quakes and tremors.

Chapter 23

Spirit Warrior left Mac, Brett's father, with the promise that he would return his son to him. Now he had to plan, and he hoped that it would be possible. The rumblings and tremors in the ground had become closer together. Perhaps, the earth was bringing forth something evil. Spirit Warrior felt the danger was becoming imminent. And, Mac had come looking for his son because of warnings he had learned in the outside world.

Spirit Warrior listened carefully as Mac explained his fears. The moving of the earth could cause openings called faults. He explained that a fault is a break in the earth's crust. Valleys can appear where the crust has been stretched to the point that it becomes faulted or broken apart. Mac didn't understand the crustal structure of the land where he lived, but he knew of an unnamed fault that ran through it. If the trembling of the earth becomes extreme, abysses can open, swallowing whatever lies on top. Entire landscapes with men and animals can disappear if the hole is deep enough. At the very least, people would be in danger from flying rocks and falling trees.

Spirit Warrior told Mac of a time when their valley shook. The elder Spirit Warriors had passed down these stories. The directions of many streams had changed, and a few streams became warmed. High in the mountains surrounding the villages of their clans, deep basins existed. These areas were home to the many wild predators which sometimes roamed far down the mountain, requiring herdsmen to post guards around their flocks at night.

Spirit Warrior knew he could travel faster alone, and he felt the urgency to be with his people. The trail had become dangerous with rocks loosening and rolling down the mountain when a particularly strong vibration came. Spirit Warrior prayed to the True God as he hurried back as fast as the trail would allow. *Help me. Help me get back to my people.*

Upon arriving at the ingress to their valley, Spirit Warrior encountered large boulders blocking the path, nearly causing the entrance to be impassable. Spirit Warrior lay flat and bellied his way through the opening. As he cleared his way and stood, a tremor rolled more rocks into the entrance, shutting off Spirit Warrior's world to the outside. Quickly, Spirit Warrior lay down and waited until the tremor stilled.

He picked his way carefully over the broken trail to his village. He must find Tohopka. Tohopka traveled from village to village and could give him an update of any damage. And Brett was with Tohopka. Only one other exit of their valley existed, and he must see if it remained open. He had promised Mac to return his son, and Brett wouldn't leave without Linda. He prayed again to the True God for guidance in directing the future for these under his protection and care.

Spirit Warrior met the band of workers coming down from the hacienda to get more adobe bricks. Tohopka explained that Brett had to travel with him when the order came from the hacienda for more food supplies, and they had been caught in the darkness and were forced to spend the night on the mesa. Tohopka told him that they were able to help when the lightning ignited the tree and sent it crashing into the hacienda.

"Was anyone hurt?" asked Spirit Warrior.

"No," said Tohopka.

"Praise be to the True God," said Spirit Warrior.

Tohopka nodded his agreement.

"Now, go back to the hacienda and make repairs as quickly as possible. There are changes that need to be made that may be as shocking as the earth tremors we have been feeling," said Spirit Warrior. "I will be up in the morning. I must talk to the Matriarch."

Brett had made it back to the shed safely. The ground was more uneven than before, but now the tremors had stopped. Clouds covered the sun, and it was nearly dark inside the shed.

"Brett?" Linda said, as she stepped from the back stall in the shed.

"Linda," said Brett. "Is it safe for you to be here now?"

"Yes. The maid locks my door, so I know she plans on doing something that doesn't require watching me." They laughed together.

"Well, I have found out some things. I followed Sam and Elena to a small cabin beside some well-tended graves. Your ancestors on your mother's side, I presume. There is another gravestone with a doctor's name chiseled on it dated about twenty years ago. There are many mysteries here."

"Well, I don't want to stay and be buried in the family plot," Linda said. "Tell me you found a way out."

"Yes, I did. But I can tell you that you are a member of a very wealthy family. I came upon them in a cave, panning for gold nuggets in a stream that flowed from the mountain through the cave. Sam said they had plenty. They plan to get away and live in our world."

"So, she expects me to stay and take her place?"

"That's her plan."

"But a way out. You found it?

"Yes, it's tricky and narrow with a rock wall on one side and a waterfall on the other. But as Sam uses it for his trips in and out of the valley, I'm sure we can, too," said Brett.

"Can we go tonight?"

"Linda, we can't. I must see Spirit Warrior first. I promised. And, once out, I don't know the way back down."

"As anxious as I am to get away, I would like to meet Spirit Warrior. You said my Dad did missionary work while he was here, and Spirit Warrior was his first convert?"

"Yes, there's a group of Christians here now. Your Dad was quite a busy man the year he was here."

"Wow, this is quite a legacy," Linda said.

"Of course, the old ways are strong, but no one challenges Spirit Warrior's leadership, not even Elena. And from what I've witnessed, he treats everyone with wisdom and kindness. A truly remarkable man."

"And think of all you've learned about this civilization. It will make your teaching all the more exciting."

"It will, but I would never reveal my sources or betray this valley. Your father denied himself the benefit of his findings. He didn't know that he had another daughter, but he kept you as safe as possible just in case they would learn of your existence."

"And they did learn in spite of all he could do."

"When we leave, I won't take anything with me from this valley except the pictures I've taken," said Brett.

"You could write a book updating my father's textbook as a tribute to him.," Linda said. Then she hesitated, "One thing you need to leave behind is your disguise."

"Don't you like my hair?"

They could laugh together, keeping their uncertain future at bay.

He took her hand. "Linda, we will get out. But we can't go wandering in these mountains. We must wait."

She quietly slipped out of the stable and into the garden toward the hidden entrance to her room. She had just moved out of sight when the clansmen appeared over the last rise and onto the mesa.

He went to meet Tohopka and help finish the work.

"Brett, Spirit Warrior back. Be here in morning. Say you stay in stable. Not with workers."

That meant he would have to be idle. Brett didn't know how long his disguise would hold, anyway. Bathing in the warm stream with the soap Tohopka gave him had begun to wash the dye from his hair. When the sun came back, he could be found out. Spirit Warrior had assured him that he was the only one in the valley with hair the color of a sunset.

Early afternoon the work was finished. The clansmen would make it safely back before nightfall. Food was brought out from the hacienda for Tohopka and Brett. They ate in silence. Tohopka was too weary for conversation, and Brett's mind was too full of thoughts that he couldn't share.

Chapter 24

Elena searched the sky as though for answers. Surely her life wouldn't fall apart now that her departure from this valley was so close. All she had sacrificed to bring about the kingdom's continuation might be coming to an end. She'd allowed her father to take her to Spain and barter her to the most suitable bidder. Allowed him? What choice had she had?

They'd been expected when they arrived in Spain. A whirlwind of parties had clouded her thinking. She was pampered, her every wish granted and dressed to attract the very elite. Her freshness had been a delight to the aristocracy. Her mode of speech, her beauty and her innocence drew the attention of the most eligible bachelors.

Now, in derision, she looked back and saw it for what it was. It was merely a livestock show. She'd been groomed, paraded, and partied. Her dowry was large enough that she could choose her buyer. Her father even took that choice from her. She was not unhappy with his choice. Paulo had been amusing, handsome and willing to enter her world. Paulo's impoverished family was more than willing to allow this second-born son to enrich their family and elevate their circumstances. They still had the firstborn.

Poor Paulo. His future with her may have been his best choice. They were married in an elaborate ceremony. She was a virgin caught up in the dazzle of her sequins and pearls. In the first year they produced a baby girl that they named Inez. Everything was working out as designed. Now plans were made to come home.

Sailing had to be postponed for a few weeks. Her father succumbed to the plague that was raging in the town. Shortly after his funeral, the little family of three, along with her maid, Adella, sailed toward home. Unknown to them, Paulo had been infected and his death came just after sailing, and he was buried at sea. She was left with a baby daughter and a maid younger than she was. There was no way to notify her mother. The place of contact was her hacienda in *Dos Tigres*. That would be her destination.

Elena remembered standing alone, holding Inez, at the dock in San Francisco. It was hot, the baby was quietly fussing and the crowd pushed in around them. She raised her head, and there he was, his eyes held hers and he never looked away. Sam.

He was hers immediately. He was hers to this day. He took Inez from her arms straight into his heart. She became his daughter. He loved her as she herself was never able to. Sam gave up his life and merged it into hers. He never complained, never looked back. Nothing would have been possible without Sam.

They were married in San Francisco; they spent honeymoon days at the hacienda in *Dos Tigres*. Then Consuelo found Elena and called her back to her destiny.

Her destiny, she had explained to Sam, was as the next Matriarch in line after Consuelo. Generations of the women in her family had provided for the care and well-being of the clan, or Indian tribe, in their mountain valley. She drew strength from Sam as she accepted her destiny. He accepted her secret along with her and her fate.

Maybe she'd become too domineering after Consuelo's death. Many years later when Alan Griffin stumbled into their valley and met Inez, Sam had stood between her anger and the couple. Inez and Alan were married in the Indian tradition. Her anger had cooled when Inez was expecting a child. If it were a girl-child, maybe the line could continue, even with tainted blood.

Elena had learned that they planned to secretly leave the valley before the baby was born. Even Sam couldn't cool her anger. She had them spied upon day and night. *The baby was hers. She couldn't be the matriarchal presence here forever. Before she died, she wanted to leave this valley. She wanted another sort of life for herself. And for Sam.*

Inez went into labor before the couple's plan to leave could be carried out. Inez was suffering greatly, her strength flowing out with her life's blood. Without consulting her, Sam brought a doctor to their valley. But it was too late. Inez died as the baby came, and Alan had fled into the night with the tiny infant. When they again joined the doctor, Alan was gone and Inez was dead. The doctor had handed her a scrap of humanity that he said might not live. He made no mention that there had been another baby in the womb.

But it was a girl-child. She would make it live! She handed it to Adella who left hurriedly for the big house. Her anger overcame her. Before Sam could stop her, she plunged a knife into the doctor's back. *He could not be allowed to leave the valley. He had learned too much. Besides, he'd deserved to die for deceiving her.*

The hurt she saw in Sam's eyes cooled her fury. She mourned her action. They buried Inez in the family plot. The doctor was buried in a grave at the edge of the family cemetery.

Now they had come full circle. Inez's daughter, Camila, had been a disappointment. But there was hope: the twin whose identity had been hidden from her until fate had intervened. It wasn't accidental; she was destined to learn the truth that paved her way out. Camila could never be forgiven.

Linda was here. She was alone, no family, no future but the one that she could offer her. Elena knew she herself must get out of this valley. Her life here had grown too dark.

But the gods seemed to fight her again. The lightning had caused fire to the hacienda, and the earth's trembling was causing changes to the landscapes. If it hadn't been for Tohopka and the stranger, there would have been more loss.

But there was something off about the stranger. He didn't seem to honor her as the other clansmen did. He dared to carry her granddaughter in and stood waiting. Waiting for what, she wondered.

Her spies had told of a stranger that Spirit Warrior was tending. It didn't happen often, but occasionally someone did stumble in from the outside. Of course, the tribes thought the stranger was sent from the sky gods for Spirit Warrior to heal. But this one was different. It was almost as though he had a purpose. Elena knew that he must be dealt with.

In the early morning before Adella could prepare breakfast, Elena went to the kitchen. Gathering the ingredients that she needed, she quickly prepared a fried pastry drizzled with honey and sprinkled with cinnamon. She arranged it on a platter with a jug of coffee.

"Elena, what are you doing?" Sam stood at the backdoor where he had come in from assessing the damage to their building.

"Something for Tohopka and his friend," she answered.

Gently, Sam took the platter of fried pastry and held it close to his face. "I think you have added too many flaxseeds; I detect the smell of bitter almonds." He emptied the contents of the platter. "No more, Elena. Let the cook prepare food for the men."

"Sam, I don't trust the man with Tohopka. He shows too much interest in Linda. He dares look at me."

"Tohopka is to be the next Spirit Warrior. Would you risk harming him? Our time here is almost over."

"You're right. I must wait," she said.

Chapter 25

Brett and Tohopka had just finished breakfast when they heard the clip-clop of the burros coming up the rocky path. Then the footfalls became muffled as the animals reached the smooth, grassy mesa. His heart beat faster with the anticipation of getting Linda safely away from the Matriarch and back into his world.

As the burros got closer, he recognized the riders. Spirit Warrior was on one burro, leading another one with baskets hanging on each side. Brett was surprised to see Camila mounted on the third one. Her son was strapped to a carrier on her back, his head nodding gently as he slept. Brett and Tohopka went to meet them.

"Greetings, Brett," said Spirit Warrior as he dismounted.

"Spirit Warrior," responded Brett, shaking the leader's outstretched hand.

"The time has come for your departure," said Spirit Warrior. "The earth is restless and the doors may close. Have you seen Linda?"

"Yes, she's in the hacienda. Sam and the Matriarch left yesterday when the repair work started. They have gone to a cave which leads to a way out of the valley," Brett said.

"Yes, I know the way they go. It's a way unknown to any of the villagers. The knowledge of this valley doorway has been passed down only to matriarchs and spirit warriors. We must wait for the Matriarch and Sam to return.

The atmosphere in the hacienda was uncomfortable. It seemed to be a triangle: Sam and Elena on one side, Spirit Warrior, Tohopka, and Camila on one side, and Brett and Linda made up the third side. Camila's son sat on her lap, his eyes alert to those around him.

Spirit Warrior spoke gently to Elena, "so, you decree that this is the time for a new Matriarch?"

"Yes, I so decree. I name Linda as the new Matriarch," she said.

"No," said Camila. "It's my right."

"You disobeyed me," said Elena.

Spirit Warrior held up his hand, and it became quiet. "Linda knows nothing of what's required of a matriarch; she doesn't love the people. Nor does she want to stay. She wants to go back to her life."

"She has no one," shouted Elena.

"She has me," said Brett, moving closer to Linda's side.

"You are no one," countered Elena.

Spirit Warrior again held up his hand and stilled the voices.

"I have prayed to the true God, and this is how it will be," said Spirit Warrior.

A small quake caused the ground to tremble as if to underscore Spirit Warrior's authority.

"Elena," said Spirit Warrior, "you will bestow the title and responsibilities of matriarch upon Camila. Only then will you be allowed to leave." He held up his hand as Elena started to protest. "Camila is a woman of the valley and loves her people. Camila, you will marry Tohopka to provide a father for your son and a companion for yourself."

Brett saw Camila lower her head, but she couldn't hide her smile or the blush on her cheeks. It seems that Spirit Warrior was acutely aware of human nature.

"We will go now, and the ceremony will happen at the place of departure," said Spirit Warrior. "Brett, I've brought your belongings to you on the burro. Elena, you must leave all that belongs to you and that has been passed down from other matriarchs to bless Camila as she assumes the role of new matriarch. Sam, you must lead the way back and never return. Brett's father awaits his son at the half-way camp."

Brett was impressed with the wisdom of Spirit Warrior. All seemed to accept his words. He watched Elena lean back on Sam as she gave way to Spirit Warrior's authority and released her role.

Spirit Warrior, Elena, Sam, Tohopka, Camila, Brett and Linda made up the small band that rode single-file up the path leading back to the cave and the valley exit. The tremors in the earth came closer together, causing rocks to slide into their path. The walking for the horses became more difficult.

As they reached the cave, Spirit Warrior motioned for Elena and Camila to follow him away from the rest. Elena wore the white ermine cape that Spirit Warrior had brought signifying her position. Brett was too far away to hear their words, but he knew Elena was relinquishing her matriarchal reign as she removed the ermine cape from her shoulders and the golden band from her head.

Suddenly, an earth tremor loosened a rock ledge. Too late, Elena saw it falling toward her. Sam and Spirit Warrior rushed to her side. Sam tried to take the weight of the stone from off of her chest. Her countenance became pained, color drained from her face.

"Spirit Warrior," Elena whispered, "talk to the True God for me. Tell Him I'm sorry for the evil I have done."

Spirit Warrior leaned closer. "Matriarch, just ask for your sins to be forgiven. The True God loves you, and He will forgive."

Elena whispered her prayer and the stress left her face. "I did ask. He did forgive."

Elena smiled at Sam. "Please tell Camila that I didn't cause the death of her husband. Tell Linda that I'm sorry. I love you." The words came out on a labored breath. Then she was gone.

Brett helped Sam dig the grave. Elena was laid to rest in the small family plot surrounding the cabin that had been her and Sam's hideaway for their life on the mountain. Spirit Warrior and Tohopka turned from them, going back to the hacienda where Camila would take up her destiny. The cape draped over her shoulders signified her new role as the next matriarch. They would make their way down the mountain and the ceremony would take place in the presence of all the villagers.

The ground continued to tremble, and hurriedly, Sam led Brett and Linda through the cave and outside the land of the hidden valley. Behind them, they witnessed the rockslide that obstructed the exit, forever blocking a way back in.

"She was never really mine," Sam said softly. He was lost in his grief.

They traveled silently all day to where Brett's father waited. The last earthquake had subsided and all was quiet. Brett had left his belongings with Spirit Warrior, bringing only his phone and camera. He hoped the books he'd left in his backpack, especially his Bible, would be some small compensation for all he'd learned from Spirit Warrior.

Linda had lost her sister and grandmother. Their worlds could never be joined. They would remain a bittersweet memory of what could have been.

Chapter 26

Late twilight offered little light when they stumbled into the area surrounding the small cabin and stable. A glow came through the window from the fire burning in the fireplace. Mac came out to meet them. He greeted his son and helped them stable their horses while Linda went on inside. As the sun dipped behind the last peak of the mountain, all light fled. The forest was now an encroaching enemy.

Introductions were made and Mac dipped up the rabbit stew that simmered in a pot hanging from a hook in the fireplace. They ate in silence, fighting the fatigue that drained their souls as well as their bodies. Sam sat hunched away from the others. His loss sat heavily on his shoulders and he seemed to crumble beneath it. The lines in his face had become deeper.

When Mac and Brett went out to the stable to retrieve the saddle blanket to sleep on, Linda went over and touched Sam's arm gently.

"Sam, I'm so sorry," she said.

"Thank you. But how can you feel sorrow for me when I kidnapped you away from your life?"

Linda shrugged. "I don't know, Sam, but I feel forgiveness. I met my sister who had been standing in my shadow all my life. I saw my tiny nephew. I saw a grandmother that I didn't know I had. Most of all, I learned how much my father really did love me. He was only trying to keep me safe."

"Your grandmother was desperate to get away, but there is no real excuse. And, you will never see your sister or nephew again. There's no way back."

"There are still the shadows," Linda said.

"Perhaps. Perhaps not," said Sam.

"I'm glad you gave the puppy to Ahanhu. Maybe Camila will tell him it had belonged to me."

"Linda, I don't feel bad about the puppy. It made the little boy happy. Can we trade the dog for your horse?"

"Sam," asked Linda, "what do you mean?"

"I'm the one who bought your horse and had it shipped to a stable not too far from the house down the mountain. I was going to bring him to you when you were settled," Sam said.

"Oh, Sam, I don't know what to say. That horse was so important to me. He was my friend really."

"I'm glad I've given him back to you. The house in *Dos Tigres* is yours, too."

"Mine?" asked Linda.

"I was telling the truth when I said your mother's house was yours. Inez never lived there, but it was part of the ruse that we made up to lure you here. So, the house is yours and there is a great deal of money that goes with it," said Sam.

"No, Sam. It's all yours," Linda said.

"I don't want it, Linda. The people know me as the Padre because that's what I've been for many years. I will slip back across the border and remain with the people that I've been serving. I have a small school for native children, but I will no longer be able to provide homes for the babies abandoned on the streets. They did have a better life where I took them. But I've confessed my sins to Spirit Warrior's True God. I can now start over with clean heart and hands," said Sam.

"Sam, take the money and build an orphanage. Don't leave the little ones without care," Linda said.

"Thank you, Linda. I'll try to do that. But there will be much money left. Use it for your life. The house in *Dos Tigres* is your legacy, your destiny," said Sam.

"I think Brett will be my future," Linda said.

"Yes. He fought against the odds to find you and to bring you home," said Sam.

Brett and Mac returned to the cabin with the blankets, and they all settled to sleep. Each was buried in his own thoughts. The morning would find them up early and on their way back home.

Epilogue

One year later

The church was decorated beautifully: white satin bows marked the seats for the family members. Huge palms canopied the white arch woven with yellow daisies and purple sweet peas. The candelabra held six tall white tapers. The aisle was covered in white cloth from the back all the way to the altar.

The music began and Linda started down the aisle toward her future, toward Brett. She stopped and looked at those already lined at the front. Her new family. Five bridesmaids! Five new sisters, and she loved them all. From lonely to blessed. She wanted to think that her own father was smiling down on her, giving them his blessing. He had done what was best for her.

She thought of the Psalm that Brett had read to her, *"And the Lord puts the lonely in families;"*. She had become surrounded by the warmth extended to her from Brett's family.

And Sam. She squeezed his arm as they began to walk down the aisle. He had returned for her wedding and was giving her away. Perhaps, he had loved Elena too well, but he had held the family together. It was the closest she would ever come to having a grandfather. In her abundant love for Brett, she could allow Sam this role.

At the altar she stood basking in the love that she felt coming from the man beside her. Brett was solid, he was real. And he loved her.

The minister was drawing the ceremony to a close. "What therefore God hath joined together, let not man put asunder."

Outside the church, Sam slipped away. He had said his good-byes, and his future lay across the border with his parish. He would not return.

www.ingramcontent.com/pod-product-compliance
Lightning Source LLC
LaVergne TN
LVHW011933070526
838202LV00054B/4613